# THE CASE OF THE CHRISTIE CONSPIRACY

## A DETECTION CLUB MYSTERY

## KELLY OLIVER

Boldwood

First published in Great Britain in 2025 by Boldwood Books Ltd.

Cover Design by Alexandra Allden

Cover Images: Shutterstock and iStock

A CIP catalogue record for this book is available from the British Library.

Paperback ISBN 978-1-83617-546-9

Large Print ISBN 978-1-83617-545-2

Hardback ISBN 978-1-83617-544-5

Ebook ISBN 978-1-83617-547-6

Kindle ISBN 978-1-83617-548-3

Audio CD ISBN 978-1-83617-539-1

MP3 CD ISBN 978-1-83617-540-7

Digital audio download ISBN 978-1-83617-542-1

This book is printed on certified sustainable paper. Boldwood Books is dedicated to putting sustainability at the heart of our business. For more information please visit https://www.boldwoodbooks.com/about-us/sustainability/

Boldwood Books Ltd, 23 Bowerdean Street, London, SW6 3TN

www.boldwoodbooks.com

*Dedicated to my dearly departed feline familiar, Lord Peter Mischief Wimsey*

# 1

## THE INTERVIEW

Eliza Baker tossed the book into the bin. She was no expert on detective fiction, but she knew the author was expected to "play fair" with the reader. And Mrs. Agatha Christie was not playing fair.

Standing at the stove, she tapped the side of the coffee pot with one finger. Still warm. She lifted it and gave it a swirl. Not much left. She poured herself half a cup and saved the rest for her sister. After all, Jane had made the coffee, not to mention, it was Jane's percolator on Jane's stove in Jane's flat. And although her sister insisted it was a "pleasure" to have Eliza living with her, Eliza couldn't help but feel like a burden. She was the older sister, after all. *She* should be providing for Jane and not the other way around. Hustling chess at the Gambit was not exactly a steady income. She absolutely had to get this job with the Detection Club, even if it meant complimenting Mrs. Christie on her unreliable narrator.

Queenie stared up at her, waiting for a treat. Like her, the dog had been rescued from the streets of London as a pup. She gave Queenie a scrap of meat from last night's dinner. The beagle wolfed it down and then wagged her tail in appreciation. Even the leftovers she fed Queenie were paid for by Jane, along with everything else in the flat.

Long and narrow like an airstrip, Jane's flat was nice enough. And the Victorian black marble fireplace in the reception was stunning, not to mention warm on a cold December day. But sharing a bedroom was not ideal for two single women in their late twenties. Someday, *maybe*, they would have a bigger flat. Since she was a kid surviving hustling chess on the streets of London, it was always, *someday, maybe*.

Careful not to spill her coffee, Eliza navigated the hallway to the sitting room and then turned on the radio, hoping to hear the news. Queenie trotted at her heels. It was 1926, for heaven's sake. The Great War had ended eight years ago and, in three years, she would be thirty and able to vote. She had an obligation to keep informed, not bury her head in some made-up story. There was enough murder and mayhem in the world. Why did those mystery authors have to go inventing more?

She needed real news with real crimes. Not Mrs. Christie's far-fetched, made-up misdeeds. Of course, she didn't enjoy hearing about embezzling bankers or the latest natural disasters or starving orphans begging for bread; not so long ago, she'd been one of those starving children. But that was the past.

She sat in an upholstered chair near the fireplace. Queenie curled up at her feet. The sitting room was cozy with a sofa and two easy chairs positioned in a semi-circle on a braided rug. Her sister's taste in décor was understated, with colors so bland and pale, they faded into the beige wallpaper.

A man's voice announced, "I'm broadcasting from outside the barricades of a riot at Trafalgar Square." She listened with rapt attention, wondering if she should inform Jane. It sounded like serious business. A riot?

She pulled her jumper tighter and hugged herself. A chilly draft blew in through the cracked windowsill. A casualty of the war. Her sister's flat was on the third floor of a brownstone building on Liverpool Street where the Germans had concentrated their last desperate blitz before the end of the war.

Holding her cup in both hands, she stepped closer to the radiator and listened to the report. Queenie perked up her ears as if she were listening too.

"Do you hear that crowd?" The announcer's voice was gleeful. He was taking way too much pleasure in the unrest. A loud crash from the radio made her start. *What in the world?* Queenie barked.

The newscaster gasped. "Seems there's been an explosion at the Savoy Hotel." There was a commotion in the background.

She gulped. *An explosion.* She sat her cup on the mantel and went to find Jane. In her hurry, she nearly tripped over Queenie.

Wearing a tan tweed jacket over a cream silk blouse, her sister came dashing down the stairs. She gathered up her gloves and a valise from the side table. "I'm off." Jane smiled. "Be good." When she winked, her green eyes danced. "And if you can't be good, be careful."

Looking at Jane was like looking in a mirror, they were so much alike. Everyone thought they were twins. The same straw-colored hair, grass-colored eyes, and high foreheads.

"Have you heard about the riot at Trafalgar Square?" Eliza stood between her sister and the front door, blocking the path.

Jane squinted. "No. Should I have?"

"Since you know the identities of local agitators..." Eliza smirked. "Yes. Yes, you should." Jane worked for British Intelligence after all.

"Local agitators, are they?" Jane tugged on a glove.

"Listen." She cocked her head toward the sound of the radio.

"I can't be late for work." Jane tapped her hat onto her head.

"Rioters blew up the Savoy." Eliza took her sister by the elbow. With Queenie's help, she herded Jane into the sitting room.

"What?" Jane's mouth fell open. She let Eliza lead her to the sofa.

The radio announcer was giving the latest cricket scores.

"Who cares about cricket?" Jane glanced around the room as if she expected rioters to rush through the walls.

"You'd be surprised." Eliza sighed.

"Should we go down there and see what's happening?" Jane's pretty cheeks turned pink with indignation. "My boss might want some information on these rioters." Her boss was none other than Sir Vernon Kell, Director General of MI5.

"I have that interview today with the detective writer lady." Eliza paced the length of the room and then stopped. "Look, I'll skip it if you think we should go down and see what's happening." What a waste. For the last week—since Theo had insisted she apply for the job with the "prickly" author—she'd been reading detective fiction to prepare. "This riot is more important than those silly writers."

More crashing and banging. "I'm going to have to sign off now." The announcer sounded breathless. "I hope you've enjoyed *Broadcasting from the Barricades*," he said triumphantly. "My latest short-story." He chuckled. "As read by yours truly, mystery writer extraordinaire, Neville Lively."

"Good grief." Eliza looked at her sister, who was staring back at her with wide eyes. "Damn writers." So, it was all a hoax. There was no riot. Only a mystery writer with a perverse sense of humor reading his stupid story on the radio.

"Neville Lively should know better," Jane said, shaking her head. "I'm going to tell Dillwyn to put his friend on a leash." Oxford classics professor and former codebreaker, Dilly Knox traveled in literary circles. He was good friends with Agatha Christie, no less.

"Dilly Knox is no better." Eliza had worked with Dilly during the war. At the time, she was a Girl Guide at the War Office doing whatever the captain or the men asked of her, except for what Dilly asked because he was a rake. Now, Dilly was back at Oxford teaching classics and no doubt flirting with all the Bright Young Things. If Eliza didn't know better, she'd think he wrote her a reference letter because he liked her *pretty smile*. He'd told her often enough.

"I saved you some coffee." With Jane in tow, Eliza padded back to the kitchen and poured the dregs into a cup for her sister.

"Thanks." Jane took a sip and then made a sour face.

Eliza plopped into a chair at the kitchen table. Queenie sat next to her looking up with those irresistible, chocolate-brown eyes. She patted the dog on the head.

"Eliza..." Raising her eyebrows, Jane pointed at rubbish bin where the duplicitous Doctor James Sheppard stared out from the cover of *The Murder of Roger Ackroyd*. "What is this library book doing in the rubbish?" She marched over and plucked it out. "Agatha Christie. You tossed out an Agatha Christie! Have some respect. We don't throw books away in this house. Especially not by the Queen of Mystery." She examined the book. "This belongs to the library, for goodness' sake." She sat down and slid the book across the table. "Did you at least finish your homework for the interview?"

Eliza gave a brisk nod. *Queen of Mystery*. More like Queen of Misdirection and Cheating. Anyway, Mrs. Christie had only published four books, all with that queer little detective Hercule Poirot, so she could hardly be called the Queen.

"I was going to wait until you got the job to tell you." Jane paused as if having second thoughts. She reached out and fingered the book cover.

"Tell me what?" She knew that look. The one Jane got when making an important decision. "Tell me what?" she repeated.

"There have been rumors."

"Rumors?" Eliza scratched Queenie's ears. "About me?"

"No." With determination, Jane placed her cup on the table. "We have reason to believe your lady detective writer and her friends know state secrets." She lowered her voice. "It's imperative we find out what they know and how they know it. And your employment with the Detection Club presents the perfect opportunity."

"I'm done with police work." Eliza clenched her jaw. "Anyway, I haven't got the job yet." She stared down at her cup. "I can't... Not after what happened."

"You can't keep moping around here or loitering at that stupid chess club." Jane let out a loud exhale. "It wasn't your fault." She softened her tone and reached across the table and took Eliza's hand. "Please, Lizzy, you're one of the best—"

"*Was*, past tense." Eliza withdrew her hand. "I can't. Not after what happened to—" She couldn't bring herself to say his name. Her *partner* during her one failed month at Scotland Yard. She couldn't bear to think of him as anything more— certainly not the person she'd hoped to marry. And it was her fault he died. If only she hadn't slipped on the dock chasing that bloody woman. She sucked in air.

"Yes, you can." Jane buttoned her jacket and let out a loud breath. "I didn't want to tell you until after you got the job, but I may be reassigned to Paris." Her lips stretched into a thin, pink line. "So, if you want to keep this flat, you have to get that job."

"What?" Jane's words sunk in her stomach like a rock. "You're throwing me out?" She'd lived on the streets as a girl. She didn't want to do it again.

"It's for your own good." Jane stood up. "You can't go on wallowing in guilt. You've got to get your life together and get on with it." She tugged on the hem of her jacket. "You're going to go to that interview. You're going to get that job." She wagged her finger. "You can do it." She leveled her gaze. "Right?"

Eliza sat blinking at her sister.

"Right?" Jane had that glint in her eyes, the one where she wouldn't take no for an answer. "Please, Lizzy. Do it for me? I need your help on this one. With your innocent face and those blonde curls, you'll be our perfect undercover operative." She smiled. "Please," she said again softly.

"Oh, alright." Eliza took a deep breath.

"Alright what?" Jane stood with her hands on her hips.

"I'll try." Eliza exhaled in resignation. "Agreed." How could she refuse helping her sister?

Queenie barked her approval.

"Agreed what?" Jane tapped her foot. For a younger sister, she sure was bossy.

"Alright. I'll do it." A smile tickled the edges of Eliza's mouth. "From now on, I'm an aspiring author of impossible mysteries." She doffed an imaginary hat. "And, with any luck, future assistant, undercover, to the secretary of the London Detection Club." She crossed her fingers behind her back, both for luck and because she was fibbing her head off.

\* \* \*

To delay the agony of presenting herself to the "prickly" author, Eliza stopped off at Budge Row. She could play a game or two at Gambit, make a few quid, and still get to the interview in time.

Gambit Chess Rooms was a no-frills flat set up with two long tables sporting rows of chess boards. Along with a lavatory, there was a small kitchenette in the back where, in between rounds, she could make a cup of tea. It had a bachelor's burner and a stained sink and a few mismatched cups and plates. Owned by Edith Price, a chess champion in her own right, Gambit was one of the only places in town that allowed women to play. Even so, almost all the players were men.

As she hung her coat on a peg near the door, a few familiar faces looked up from their boards and gave her welcoming smiles, most of them genuine. She'd been coming to Gambit since she was twelve after Captain Hall plucked her off the streets. Before that, she picked up games in St. James Park. Even as a child, she'd had a knack for chess. Good thing, too. Otherwise, she and Jane might have starved.

Eliza glanced around the club. Two regulars, Michael and Herb, were playing practice games by themselves. Eliza had an idea. She challenged them both to a game of speed chess. She'd play them both at once. A quid a game.

"You're on," Michael said.

"You're mad," Herb said, laughing. "You can't play two games at once."

"Watch me." She removed her hat and then pushed up the sleeves of her blouse. "Set up your boards."

Standing on the opposite side of the table from where the two men sat, moving from one board to the other, she forced her mind into overdrive. The adrenaline coursing through her veins was exhilarating. Her palms were sweating, but she kept her stride, outpacing the clock every time. Even if she hadn't had the interview looming, she would have moved as fast as she could. The discipline it took to concentrate all her mental energy on nearly limitless possibilities was thrilling.

Herb, the lad who'd doubted her abilities, lost first. She pinned his rook with hers and checkmated him. The other chap, Michael, took a few minutes longer to defeat, but after she skewered one of his bishops, it didn't take long to mate him too.

"That will be a quid each." She opened her palm. "Thank you, gentlemen," she said with a smile. It felt good to win.

Pocketing her winnings, she approached the end of the table where Theo was playing against another club regular. She hung back and watched. Theo Sharp had wavy, chestnut hair which was just a bit too long and unruly to be stylish. And his full lips gave him a perpetual pout. "Did you have your interview yet?" he asked without taking his eyes off the board.

She moved closer to the table. "Not yet." Squinting at the board, she visualized Theo's options. "But I'm on my way now."

"Good." A lock of chestnut hair fell over his forehead; a dab of Brilliantine wouldn't have gone amiss. He took his opponent's bishop with his knight. When his opponent toppled his queen, Theo's lips turned up slightly.

She held her breath, waiting for the next move. Funny— when she played, she was as calm as a purring cat. But watching Theo play was nerve-wracking. She wanted to reach down and move his pieces for him.

Finally, Theo looked up at her and smiled, a misaligned front tooth leading the way. Why was he smiling? He couldn't move his rook or he'd put his king in check.

Three moves later, she saw why. He'd managed to leave his opponent with only a couple of blocked pawns and promote one of his own pawns to checkmate. His sacrifice had paid off. Too bad life wasn't more like chess. She thought of her mother.

And then Jamie, the gnarled dockhand who'd taught her chess in Devil's Acre after her mum died. And later, her more-than-partner, Billy. She'd only known him a month, but the connection was immediate. Then he'd died on the docks during her first, and last, official case. So much death. Everyone she'd ever loved had died. Except Jane. Thank goodness for Jane.

Grumbling, Theo's opponent ponied up a gold sovereign and left shaking his head.

"Well done, you." She punched his shoulder. "Now, let me try." She started picking up the pieces to set up the board.

"Not until you have a steady income." He snatched a rook out of her hand. "I don't want to be responsible for ruining you."

"What makes you think you'll win?" She tilted her head and picked up a pawn.

"I always win." His amber eyes sparked like a flint.

"So do I." She placed the king and queen side by side on the board.

"We can't both win." He counted the stack of coins in front of him and then with a jingle dropped them into his jacket pocket. His worn tweed jacket had seen better days. So had the raggedy jumper he wore under it. He could use some of his winnings to buy a new one. But she knew he never would.

"You're just afraid I'll break your winning streak." She flashed a sly smile. She'd finished setting up black, so she reached across the table and started on white. "Come on. Just one game."

"No." He stood up. "I can't play you."

"Why not?" He took on all comers. Why not her?

"I told you." He clapped a newsboy hat onto his head. "We can't both win."

She tightened her lips and pointed a bishop at him. "That's not a good reason."

He clasped his hand around hers and guided the bishop to the board. His hand was warm and soft but strong. "Well, it's my reason." He let go and stuffed his hands in his pockets.

She huffed. "You're a stubborn ass," she said, jamming her elbows onto the table and then putting her chin in her hands.

"Look." His tone softened. "You get that job and then maybe, *maybe*, we'll play." He pulled a toothpick from his pocket and clamped it between his teeth.

"Why are you so concerned about me getting that job?" First her sister, and now Theo. Everyone had a job for her.

"Maybe I just want you around." He doffed his hat. "That and the fireworks."

"Fireworks?"

"Metaphorical fireworks." He chuckled. "When you meet Madame Secretary." He laid his hand on her shoulder and then quickly retracted it as if he'd got burned.

"Madame Secretary." She glanced around. "Is that what you call her?" She'd love to pick up another game. Then she remembered her sister's ultimatum. Would Jane really leave her on the streets? "The prickly author?"

"Get going, already." Theo shooed her away with the back of his hand. "Tell me about it later."

Geez. Theo and Jane were ganging up on her.

"Alright." She stood up. "I'll go." She glanced at her watch. Plenty of time to get to Kingsway Hall.

"Good." He nodded and then headed for the door. He turned back at the threshold. "See you later, mate."

"Cheerio." She followed him out. After another wave and goodbye, she went to the Tube station and boarded the line toward Holborn. On the train, she reread the advert for the position:

> Assistant wanted to help with organizing monthly meetings of the Detection Club, a new supper club for mystery writers. Send inquiries to the club secretary, Miss Dorothy L. Sayers.

Eliza had done her homework. Dorothy L. Sayers, AKA Madame Secretary, was the "prickly" author of two mystery novels featuring an aristocrat amateur sleuth called Lord Peter Wimsey and his faithful manservant, Bunter. They'd received mixed reviews but were selling well. When she wasn't writing mystery yarns, Miss Sayer worked at S. H. Benson Advertising Agency, which was where Eliza was to meet her in twenty minutes.

She practiced smiling and introducing herself... until she noticed other passengers staring. Until the train stopped at Holborn Tube Station, she sat looking forward, avoiding eye contact. As soon as the train stopped, she dashed off and headed to the street.

The S. H. Benson Advertising Agency was in the new Kingsway Hall. The imposing, white-stone building was in the modern style: a boxy, no-nonsense structure with heavy columns and not one superfluous decorative flourish. Eliza took the lift to the second floor and strode halfway up the hall to a door marked *Dorothy L. Sayers*. Standing in front of the door, she cleared her throat. "I'm Eliza Baker," she repeated to herself, her hand on the doorknob. "Here to apply for the position as your assistant." She smoothed her skirt, adjusted her hat, and then turned the knob.

The woman behind the desk was not what she expected. She didn't know what she expected, but not her. In her early thirties and stout, Dorothy Leigh Sayers looked like a mama bear. Not a nice cuddly teddy bear, but a scary grizzly masquerading as a mild-mannered advertising agent. "Can I help you?" she asked without looking up from her notepad.

"I'm Eliza Baker." She recited the lines she'd rehearsed. "I'm here about the position as assistant to the secretary," she lowered her voice, "of the London Detection Club."

The mama grizzly bared her teeth. "You know about the Detection Club?"

"From the advert in the *Daily Chronicle*?" It came out as a question.

"Oh, right." The grizzly glanced at her watch.

"I guess even detectives must advertise," Eliza said with a forced smile.

"I like it." She jotted a note. "Death must advertise," she said more to herself than to Eliza.

"Detectives," Eliza corrected.

"Murder." The bear cocked her head. "Murder must advertise. Yes, murder is better." Paying no attention to Eliza, she continued making notes. Suddenly, she looked up with soul-piercing, icy blue eyes. "We're writers, not detectives. Don't make the silly mistake of confusing the writer with her characters."

"No, ma'am." *Writers who want to be detectives and live vicariously through their characters because their real lives are boring as sin.* "Working as your assistant would be invaluable experience for me." Eliza forced another smile as she lied through her teeth. "Someday, I hope to be a published author too."

"Why?" Dorothy Sayers let out a guffaw. "Do you like working like a dog to make less money than a scullery maid while getting hate-mail from readers who think they know more than you do, and being raked over the coals by jealous critics who don't have the talent to write their own novels?"

Eliza's cheeks warmed. "I just want to learn from the best." More lies.

"Don't try to butter me up. It won't work. I'm immune to flattery." Dorothy Sayers scowled. "What experience do you have?" She tapped her pencil. "Do you have references? And most importantly, can you keep secrets?"

*Can I keep secrets?* She smiled to herself. During the war, her work was top-secret. "Yes, I can keep secrets." Of course, her experience keeping secrets during the war was itself a secret, so she couldn't mention it. And she'd spent the last year trying to forget her experience at Scotland Yard, so she wasn't about to mention that either. "May I?" She pointed at a chair across from the desk.

Dorothy Sayers nodded.

"I can take dictation, and type, and file papers, and run errands." She waved a hand. "Whatever you need. No job is too big or too small." More lies.

"Tell me about yourself. Your upbringing. Where you're from. What you're made of." The intensity of Dorothy Sayers's bright eyes could have lit the entire building.

"Actually..." Eliza paused.

Maybe it was the woman's long, dangling earrings or the way she wore her hair pulled around her ears like a scarf or those silly little pince-nez atop her pug nose... Something about Dorothy L. Sayers told Eliza that an unconventional childhood—and even her questionable birth—may not count against her. She decided to tell the truth, for a change. "My mum died when I was young. I never knew my father. I was an orphan..." She took a breath. Saying it aloud made her shiver. "Saved from the streets by a kindly military man and his wife."

"An orphan," Dorothy Sayers said softly, a blush blooming on each round cheek. Was that a tear forming in her eye? Was her reddening face a sign of anger? Maybe Eliza shouldn't have told the truth. The change in Miss Sayers's countenance was so dramatic, Eliza wondered if she'd misjudged the woman. Was the new gentleness in her voice a clearing after a torrent or the calm before the storm? She was about to find out.

"That's right." Eliza squirmed in her chair. "An orphan." To the Devil with her if she couldn't abide a girl of low birth. It wasn't Eliza's fault she was born poor and ended up alone and abandoned— except for Jane, of course. She'd learned some valuable skills living by her wits on the street. Not the least of which was how to read people. Real people, not made-up characters in books. She'd also learned the more practical, if questionable, arts of picking pockets, breaking bolts, roasting rodents, and hustling chess. In other words, how to survive in the real world without resorting to fantasies. She fished in her briefcase for the reference from Dilly Knox. "My reference." She thrust it at the writer.

"Neville's friend." Dorothy Sayers laughed. "Did you hear Neville's bang-up performance on the BBC this morning?" She smiled. "The BBC has asked several members of the Detection Club to read their work on air. And Neville is one of the best at performing his work."

*Performance? Hoax, more like.* "It sounded like quite a scene."

"Good old Neville." Dorothy Sayers shook her head and scribbled something on a notepad. "A good Catholic with a sense of humor." She stood up from her desk. "Then again, God himself has a sense of humor. And appreciates a good shake up now and then. What a hoot. Spicing up the BBC." She chuckled.

"Yes, a hoot." Eliza tried not to scowl. *A public nuisance, more like. Such a hoax should be criminal. Damn writers.*

"Alright, then." Again, Dorothy Sayers's countenance changed as fast as an August sky. "Be here at seven sharp." She held out a slip of paper.

"I got the job?" Eliza stood gaping. She'd better accept before the impulsive writer changed her mind.

"Isn't that why you came?" She waved a hand. "Now, off with you. I must get back to work." Obviously, the interview was over. "Before one of the men comes in and finds out I'm conducting personal business at the office."

"Seven sharp. Yes, ma'am." Eliza slipped the address into the pocket of her jacket. She should feel happy. Instead, she was terrified. What if she couldn't do it? Or worse, what if she got someone killed again? *Come on, Eliza. Pull yourself together. Being an assistant to a secretary is hardly dangerous work.* Not like being a Special Constable for Scotland Yard. Then again, the Met tried to keep the few women policing relegated to domestic cases involving women and children. As usual, the men in charge underestimated women's abilities, including the armed female fugitive Eliza and Billy were pursuing at the docks that terrible night.

At least her sister and Theo would be happy. Although he'd be disappointed there had been no fireworks.

"Don't call me ma'am!" Behind her wire-rims, Dorothy Sayers narrowed her eyes. "Makes me feel old. Dorothy will do."

*Alright. Maybe a tiny popper.* "Thank you, Dorothy." She pocketed the address. "I'll let you get back to work."

"If your digestion's at fault." Dorothy brandished her pencil like a baton. "Try Andrews Liver Salts." She stabbed the air.

"Drink Lipton's tea." A broad smile cracked her face. "It makes you wee."

Dorothy L. Sayers was full of surprises. She was not at all the snobby, Oxford-educated author Eliza expected. Not a teddy bear, certainly. But not quite a grizzly either. More like an outlandish circus bear performing for her audience.

*　*　*

A pile of magazines at his elbow, Theo Sharp sat at this makeshift desk in his tiny flat above Bookworm Bookshop on the Thames. The owner gave him a break on rent to help in the shop. Theo didn't mind. He loved being surrounded by books. Every time he walked by the rare books section, he got a rush of adrenaline. His favorite section was true crime. Reading Sherlock Holmes stories in *The Strand* was always brilliant, of course. But, really, how many times did an orangutang or a poisonous snake commit a crime? Theo preferred to base his stories on real events. Cold cases. Unsolved crimes. It was easier that way, too. The newspapers provided the characters and plot for his stories. All he had to do was bring them to life through words.

*All he had to do.* Like it was easy.

He sighed and went back to writing. Or, trying to write. Or, more accurately, staring down at the blank page. The whiteness of it taunted him with its purity, as yet undefiled by his black ink: the void into which he spun tales of justice out of the everyday poetry of ordinary words. God, writing seemed pompous. He closed his eyes and thought of Eliza.

*See you later, mate.*

Was he daft?

*Maybe I just want you around.*

God, what an idiot he was.

Eliza once asked him, "Why write when you can live?" What she didn't understand was he wrote *in order to* live. For him, writing was a way to survive living. Otherwise, what was the point? Without meaning, so-called experiences were nothing more than sensory perceptions, unfiltered stimuli, random bits of jetsam floating downstream. Before he discovered writing, he felt hollow, his own emptiness gnawing at his guts, his insignificance eating away at him. But when he wrote, he channeled a transcendent power. He completely forgot himself, and the world disappeared. And yet, paradoxically, only by losing himself in words did he find himself. As if something or someone else spoke through his pen, the ink of generations. Words that belonged to others, now in his hands. Holding them. Holding him.

Without writing, he was nothing, no one.

Without writing, life was mere survival. Hanging on by a breath.

He closed his eyes and enjoyed the weight of the fountain pen between his fingers. His mother had given him the Spot Deluxe for his last birthday. After twenty-nine years, she'd finally resigned herself to the fact that he was not going to follow in his father's footsteps and live a life of leisure as part of the landed gentry. Not to mention the title his mother was always throwing at him. To be the Earl of Fife was the last thing Theo wanted. Instead, he was determined to make it as a writer.

"But, darling, you could have anything," she'd said, "and anyone, you want."

What did he want? At this moment, he wanted to describe this blasted pen. How could he describe this sensation in words? The cool metal against his skin. He thought of Eliza's hand, cool against his. The way she allowed him to guide the bishop back to the board with the grace of a dance partner, her fingers folded into a fist small enough to fit into his palm. Her slim wrist peeking out from the sleeve of her blouse, the blue veins running like rivers under her nearly translucent skin, almost invisible, tiny, blonde hairs... He stopped himself.

The pen. He was supposed to be describing it, not her. Alright. He rolled it between his fingers, concentrating on the alternating roughness and smoothness of its surface, rough where it was engraved with his name, a scar marring its perfection. Marked for ownership like a branded calf. This pen belongs to Theodore Torrent Sharp.

Could *she* belong to him? Fourteen years ago, his roommate at Eton introduced her as his "adopted little sister." She was just a girl, so small and sad, immediately Theo had wanted to protect her. Now, she was a lovely young woman and he wanted more. So much more. He shivered. He wanted to keep her all for himself.

Good God. What a thought. Why couldn't he get her out of his head? That little scar on her wrist. And another matching scar on her jaw. What did they mean? Time's alphabet writing on her body. What had she suffered? She never talked about her childhood. All he knew was she was adopted by his roommate's father, Captain Hall, when she was eleven years old. He would love to learn to decipher the poetry of those marks. Who was she?

Did it matter? After his roommate was killed on the Western Front, Theo had vowed to watch out for Eliza. He shook his head. Watch out for? Or seduce? What was he thinking?

He opened his eyes and gazed at the gold pen. Cold and hard and lifeless. His mother's voice: "You could have anything, and anyone, you want." He dropped the pen on the desk.

All he wanted was to write. And play chess, of course. Getting published and selling books would be nice, too. Not for the money. But for the recognition, connection even. Knowing his words had spoken to someone else would make it all worthwhile. He tapped his pen on the paper. *Anything and anyone.* He didn't *want* to *have* anyone. He wanted to travel the world of the heart and the mind and the soul with a companion who shared his passion for making sense of it all. Someone who would give his life a greater purpose. Someone who would support him in his quest for justice, even if only on the page. Someone who appreciated his life's work.

He wrote *Life's Work* at the top of the blank page and then laughed at himself. Life's work. At age twenty-nine. With only one book to his name, a true-crime fiction yarn that had sold twenty-seven copies so far. What a joke.

If it weren't for the vexing Eliza Baker haunting his dreams night and day, maybe he could concentrate long enough to finish this second blasted book.

# 2

## THE DINNER PARTY

The address Dorothy Sayers had given Eliza turned out to be the home of Mr. Anthony Berkeley Cox. He lived on the top-floor flat in a northern district of London called St. John's Wood. The flat was comfortably furnished with plush upholstery and flowery wallpaper. Like an apparition appearing out of a cloud of pipe smoke, their host rose from an easy chair in the foyer where he'd obviously been waiting to greet his guests. Clad in a pinstriped three-piece suit and tie, with his hair neatly parted down the middle and slicked back, Mr. Cox looked more like a banker than a mystery writer.

"This is Miss Eliza Baker, my new assistant," Dorothy said with a backwards glance. "She will be helping us turn our little soirees into a formal supper club for mystery writers."

"The Detection Club," Mr. Cox said with a wheeze. "Only for the very best mystery writers." The well-turned-out man flashed a jovial smile. "The crème de la crème." He held out a hand "Your coats?" Instead of hanging them up in the nearby closet, he flung them over the back of a chair. "Shall we?" He led them into the living room where the other guests were already seated enjoying cocktails and canapés. "The club expects the highest standards of detective fiction. Tonight, we'll decide on our charter. Murder is a serious business, you see. And we need to get it right." He chuckled. "Which assuredly means we will in fact get it wrong." Although with his tall physique and sturdy build he looked the picture of health, there was a breathless quality to his speech.

Dorothy plucked a canapé from a tray on her way to the sofa. Eliza followed on her heels. A rather portly man already occupied three-quarters of the couch not taken by her boss, so she awkwardly glanced around the room looking for an out-of-the-way place to perch and get a bead on the group. As an afterthought, Dorothy introduced her around.

"An aspiring mystery writer and our new club assistant." Dorothy waved a biscuit at Eliza. "Miss Eliza Baker."

Eliza nodded. "At your service."

In addition to Anthony Berkeley Cox and Dorothy Leigh Sayers, the guests included Anthony's wife, whom he introduced as his "almost ex-wife," and his fiancée, "the new and improved Mrs. ABC." It took all Eliza's self-control not to raise her eyebrows. Reclining in an easy chair sat a gaunt, middle-aged man with thinning hair and a gray complexion. Anthony introduced him as Neville Lively. Aha! The radio trickster with poor taste in jokes. With his thick legs and spindly arms, he resembled a tree whose branches had withered. Sitting next to him wearing a plain wool skirt and a determined look was a petite young woman introduced as his daughter, Alice Lively.

The large man installed next to Dorothy on the sofa was Gilbert Chesterton. The paradox of chestnut curls cascading off his crown and tiny oval pince-nez perched atop his strong nose juxtaposed with an unruly mustache and proper double-chin that gave him the appearance of an overgrown schoolboy. Across from him was Fergus Briggs, a balding man in his forties; he folded in on himself like a bundle of ragged clothes. Unlike the rest, he called himself a publisher who only "dabbled in mystery writing." Next was Maud Wilkerson, whose thick make-up looked like a mask. Her dress, a flowing orange flowered number, made her red hair look aflame. She was engaged in a lively conversation with whoever would listen.

Finally, sitting in an easy chair near the fireplace, a lovely woman in her mid-thirties with kind, sage-green eyes and soft brown curls was introduced as Agatha Christie. Wearing an understated but elegant lavender wool skirt set and a string of pearls, she looked a proper English lady. Not at all how Eliza imagined the maniacal mind behind the tricky narrator of *The Murder of Roger Ackroyd*. In fact, her quiet presence had a calming effect. When she said softly, "Pleased to meet you, Miss Baker," a hush fell over the room. Even the excitable Maud Wilkerson went still.

Wondering how she would remember all their names, Eliza took a seat on a small divan next to the fireplace. It was just outside the circle of writers where she could get a good view and take it all in. She pulled a scrap of paper from the chatelaine bag attached to her belt in case she was expected to take notes. What exactly were her duties as assistant to the secretary of the Detection Club? No one had bothered to tell her. The dinner party seemed an inappropriate place to ask. If only Theo were here, she could ask him.

Where was he? He'd wanted her to get this dumb job. He'd even teased it was because he wanted her around.

She quickly wrote down the guests' names along with a short descriptor:

*Anthony Berkeley Cox—smooth operator*
*Dorothy L. Sayers—circus bear*
*Gilbert Chesterton—overgrown schoolboy*
*Maud Wilkerson—fashion dish*
*Neville Lively—practical joker*
*Alice Lively—dormouse*
*Agatha Christie—elegant pearls*

If this were a game of chess, she could divide them into black and white knights, bishops, kings and queens. Unlike chess pieces, the moves of these writers were far from rule governed.

While the wife and the mistress passed around cream crackers dolloped with soft cheese and topped with a bit of gherkin along with boiled eggs stuffed with fish paste, the writers haggled over the rules for their new club.

Neville Lively pulled a sheet of folded paper from his breast pocket and snapped it open. "I've come up with what I call, 'The Ten Commandments of Detective Fiction.'" He slid a pair of eyeglasses up his nose. "First, the author must always play fair with the reader. No hocus pocus or deus ex machina."

"Hear, hear," Anthony Cox said. "Unless of course the plot calls for a bit of hocus pocus or deus ex machina." He winked.

"Second," Neville continued. "No more than one secret passageway allowed."

Eliza made a note listing Neville's rules.

"One." Agatha Christie laughed. "That's rather arbitrary."

"Third." Neville ignored her. "The criminal must be introduced early and the reader cannot be privy to his thoughts." He cleared his throat. "Otherwise, we veer into thriller territory."

"And what's wrong with thrillers?" Anthony asked.

"Don't get me started." Neville waved him away "Fourth—"

"Literature must be alive, Nev," Dorothy interrupted. "Your commandments, as you call them, kill all creativity and any possibility for ingenuity." She took a sip of her wine. "Isn't detective fiction all about inventing new possibilities?"

Eliza thought of chess. It had rules. Rules gave life order. And discipline. She played chess to discipline her mind and practiced ju-jitsu to train her body. It was all about control.

"Fourth," Neville repeated louder. "The detective himself cannot commit the crime." He coughed. Once he started, he couldn't seem to stop hacking. Anthony went to him and handed him a handkerchief while his wife fetched a glass of water. Neville nodded in appreciation.

"Come now, Nev," Dorothy said. "In real life, detectives can commit crimes. Why not in fiction?"

"What of Agatha's latest?" Fergus Briggs said with a smirk. "She's broken all your rules."

Eliza perked up her ears. This was going to be interesting. Of course, she agreed with Mr. Briggs. But to say it with the author present. That took gall.

"Yes." Maud Wilkerson sat up in her chair. "I read it in installments in the *London Evening News* and couldn't believe the narrator was the killer." Balanced on the edge of her seat, legs crossed, she smoked a cigarette with a long holder. "It seemed jolly unfair to me." She glanced at Agatha. "With all due respect, of course, dear Agatha."

"Of course." Agatha's cheeks flushed.

"I thought it was jolly clever," Dorothy piped up. "Bravo, Agatha."

"Clever!" Neville poked a finger at his sheet of paper. "Cheaters can be clever. That's not the point. Detective fiction must have rules. No cheating. Otherwise... Anyone can be clever—"

"Hear, hear." Maud waved an elegant hand.

"It's just not cricket." Neville coughed again.

"Writing is not a game," Dorothy said. "It's an art."

"I agree with Dorothy." Theo appeared at the threshold, cap in hand. "We're artists. Or in my case, I want to be." He smiled. "And if it's worth wanting, it's worth working for." He was still wearing the same shabby jacket and jumper he'd had on at the chess club. Compared to the assemble of posh writers, he looked like a poor relation come to ask for a handout. For that reason, Eliza was glad to see him. She wasn't the only one out of place. "Like chess is an art," he said, as he crossed the room toward her. "Taken in isolation, the pieces may seem as though they move according to principles, but taken together, and when well-played, they sing in a harmony of music and art."

*Science versus art.* She smiled and made room for him on the divan. She'd take science over art any day.

"I disagree," Neville said. "Like cricket, chess is most certainly a game. And so is detecting when it is in *fiction*. Fiction being the operative word."

"Chess is more than a game. It's about discipline and logic," Eliza said. "And visualizing the future." More like a science. Like forensics. It occurred to her that could be why Theo thought she should get this job. Thanks to her short-lived stint at Scotland Yard, she was trained in forensics. Perhaps the writers needed someone who could advise them on investigation techniques. Then again, Dorothy hadn't asked about her detection skills.

"I don't know about cricket," Dorothy said. "But good writing requires creativity. Like painting or music. Is it possible for artists to cheat? What would that even mean?"

Theo squeezed onto the divan next to Eliza. His warmth was reassuring. He smelled like cedarwood and lime and dust, good dust like the kind in a rare-books room. She'd liked him from that day she met in his dormitory at Oxford. Since then, he'd been like an older brother, always watching out for her. Not that she needed protection.

"To be a good artist, you must first learn the rules," Anthony said. "To be a great artist, you must learn the rules to break them to bits."

"Are you saying we're not great artists?" Neville pointed from himself to Maud. "Just because we believe in rules?"

"We were talking about Agatha's *Murder of Roger Ackroyd*," Maud said. "And—with all due respect, dear Agatha—how it cheats the reader." She flashed a coy smile. "Much like my ex-husband did with me."

"So, Neville, old boy." Anthony pursed his lips as if the whole discussion amused him to no end. "If we adopt your ten commandments, will we expel Agatha from the group?"

"Expel Agatha!" Alice Lively finally spoke. "With all due respect to my father, she's the most famous writer among you."

Neville Lively gave her a stern look and then dabbed at his watery eye with a handkerchief. "You sound like the BBC when they pay her more than the rest of us." He flung his remark in the direction of Fergus Briggs, who received it in the spirit in which it was delivered.

Squirming in his seat, Mr. Briggs sputtered and then blurted out, "I say, I'm not to blame for the whole beastly publishing game." His face reddened. "Anyway, authors who make more money for their publishers should get paid more."

"Same work deserves the same pay," Neville said matter-of-factly.

"What happened to meritocracy?" Dorothy asked. "Or are you a communist?"

"Do you think a man who digs a very pretty little ditch should be paid more than a man who gets the same job done, perhaps in half the time?" Neville huffed.

"How about you, young Theo?" Anthony held up his hand. "What's your latest mystery about?"

Theo's cheeks turned a lovely shade of mauve. "It's based on the Charles Bravo case." He troubled the edge of his jacket.

Eliza felt a low vibration emanate from his body like she was sitting next to a steam radiator. Theo was obsessed with cold cases. She'd heard of the Charles Bravo cold case, the young lawyer who was fatally poisoned in 1876. By whom, no one knew for sure.

"Ahhh, true crime," Dorothy said knowingly. "Poison at the Priory. So, who do you think did it?"

"I think the doctor did it," Agatha said. "He was having an affair with Bravo's wife." Her bright eyes sparkled. "There's some of the Bravo story in my latest novel, too."

"What about the wife?" Anthony asked. "She was a widow when he married her. A black widow in my opinion."

"Always suspect the wife," Anthony's wife said, giving him a look like she just might consider a similar manner of disposing of him. Both she and the mistress had donned aprons and were coming and going from the kitchen.

"I've heard it was the other way around." Dorothy made a whirling gesture with her finger. "Charles was slowly poisoning his wealthy new wife in order to get her money." She chuckled. "Overcome with a toothache, one night he accidently ingested the bottle of poison instead of laudanum."

"We haven't heard from young Theo." Anthony waved a manicured hand in Theo's direction.

Theo's body stiffened. Eliza was tempted to take his hand to reassure him. "You're *all* right about the suspects," he said in a low voice. "The wife, her lover, and Charles accidently poisoning himself." He raised his eyebrows. "But what of the housekeeper? *She* gave him the medicine bottle. *She* knew he was poisoning his wife." His voice grew stronger and more confident. "He'd threatened to sack her if she told anyone." He glanced at Agatha. "Taking a lesson from the master—or should I say Queen—of crime, the least likely suspect makes the best killer." He was picking up steam. "And hopefully a satisfying conclusion—"

Agatha smiled.

"In fiction maybe," Dorothy interrupted. "Life isn't always so obliging. In fact, rarely does life play fair with the reader, so to speak."

Eliza leaned into Theo. *Why won't these arrogant windbags let Theo finish a sentence? The next person to interrupt him gets a knife-hand across the kisser.*

"All the more reason fiction should!" Neville stabbed the air for emphasis. "People read detective fiction because they crave the order and justice lacking in our finite, mortal world."

"They crave eternal justice," Gilbert added. "Religion and detection fiction provide a counterbalance to the injustices of worldly things."

Agatha shrugged. "What about entertainment?"

"I agree," Maud said. "Readers just want to be entertained. To forget about their troubles for a while." She turned her gaze away from Agatha. "Which, with all due respect, is why we must play fair. There's enough unfairness in the world without repli-cating it in our stories."

"Dinner is ready," Anthony's wife announced. The mistress helped her herd the guests into the dining room.

The food was nothing fancy but hearty and delicious. Roast beef and mashed potatoes, which served as much as an excuse for drinking more wine as sustaining the body. At least the meal had distracted the writers enough to move on to less contentious topics than Agatha Christie's latest novel or unsolved murders. Instead, they complained about their publishers, their editors, their agents, and anyone else they could blame for their lack of sales.

During the pudding course, Dorothy proposed a game. "Let's play Perfect Murder." She smacked her hands together like a clap of thunder.

Eliza jumped in her seat and nearly spat out a bite of Victoria sponge.

"Who can devise the perfect murder?" Dorothy wiggled her eyebrows.

"I have a better idea." Anthony's face was flushed from the wine or maybe the excitement of his better idea. "Let's do it round-robin style. Dorothy, you start us off and then we'll each take a turn advancing the mystery and let Gilbert do the honors of wrapping it all up." He lifted his wineglass. "What do you say? Unless, Agatha, you'd like the final honors."

Agatha shook her head. "Gilbert deserves to go last."

Eliza wondered if that was a dig or a compliment.

"And mop up the mess made by the rest of you," Gilbert said. Laughter made his belly jiggle like a steamed pudding.

"Before we start." Dorothy tapped her knife on the edge of her glass. "I almost forgot. I have an announcement." She smiled. "I've secured a place for the Detection Club to meet." She chuckled. "Rooms in Soho, between a brothel and a pub," she said, obviously pleased with herself. "Isn't that perfect?"

"A group of mystery writers convening to drink and talk

murder in the seediest part of London." Anthony raised his glass again. "What could go wrong?"

Except for Neville, who was busy coughing into his napkin when he wasn't sulking, for the rest of the evening, the writers cackled over their Victoria sponge and bottles of wine like a murder of crows.

# 3

## THE SKULL

Eliza had been working for Dorothy Sayers and the Detection Club for two weeks now. Monday and Wednesday evenings and Saturday mornings, she made the trek to Dorothy's flat at 24 Great James Street in Bloomsbury to get her marching orders. The three white-paneled rooms were modest but cozy. Dorothy must have believed in a cat for every room because she had two black-and-gray tabby sisters named Dante and Dickens and one long-haired orange cat called Cat. They were entertaining on the rare occasions they woke up and chased each other through the flat, leaping and rolling and twirling as if they'd spent the day choreographing their evening routine.

The job was a ridiculous treasure hunt. So far, Dorothy had sent her out to find a long black cape, a red satin pillow, a toy cap gun, and a skull. "Make sure it's human," Dorothy said. "And mum's the word. Remember, you're sworn to secrecy." She wouldn't dare tell anyone of her acquaintance about these odd ducks who wrote mysteries for fun and profit. Any normal person would think them completely daft. Dressing up and acting out fake murders, for Pete's sake.

Although the next Detection Club dinner was still a month away, Dorothy was fizzing with ideas and plans. While the writer scribbled scripts for elaborate initiation rituals, Eliza, the dogsbody, ran all over town collecting the props. More than a writer's club, this was a theater production. Dorothy even had her rehearsing lines.

"Do you promise that your detectives shall well and truly detect the crimes presented to them, using those wits which it may please you to bestow upon them, and not placing reliance on, nor making use of, Divine Revelation, Feminine Intuition, Mumbo Jumbo, Jiggery-Pokery, Coincidence, or Act of God?" Dorothy read off her script. She looked to Eliza, awaiting her reply.

Eliza scanned the sheet of paper, looking for the next line. "I do."

"And do you solemnly swear not to purloin or disclose any plot nor secret communicated to you before publication by any fellow member while under the influence of drink, no matter how strong?"

"I swear."

"If you fail to keep your promise, may other writers anticipate your plots, and may your publishers do you down in your contracts..." Dorothy giggled. "And may total strangers sue you for libel, and your books be full of misprints, and your sales constantly diminish?" Now, she was outright laughing.

Eliza recited the initiates' last line: "Amen." She shook her head. Did these mystery writers have nothing better to do than engage in tomfoolery of the first order? Apparently not. She reminded herself she was getting paid to do this. It was a job. An extraordinarily silly job. But it would keep Queenie in Milk-Bones if nothing else. And it made Jane happy, although so far, Eliza hadn't seen anything to suggest the writers were ferreting out state secrets. And every time Jane asked, which was daily, she told her as much.

The doorbell rang. When Dorothy opened the door, with Agatha Christie in tow, Maud Wilkerson flitted across the foyer and into the sitting room.

"What a day!" Maud dropped into an easy chair with an exaggerated sigh. "I took Agatha shopping at Harrods. She needs a new wardrobe if she's to win Archie back."

Agatha blushed and her lips disappeared into a thin line.

"I wouldn't take him back if he crawled on hands and knees with a dozen roses between his teeth." Dorothy huffed. "Would you dearies like some tea? Or something stronger, perhaps?"

"I'd love a gin fizz." Maud tugged off her gloves. "On the rocks, like Agatha's marriage."

"Cream tea would be lovely." Agatha gave a weak smile. "And might we talk of something other than my marriage, please?" She took a seat on the divan.

"Of course, dear." Dorothy nodded. "Let's talk murder." She grinned. "That will take our minds off unfaithful lovers."

Eliza sat in the corner sewing a fur collar on one of Dorothy's capes, wondering what the grizzly bear knew of unfaithful lovers.

Dorothy had just returned with a tray of drinks when the telephone rang. Whoever was on the other end must have said something to upset Dorothy. The writer's round cheeks reddened and she paced back and forth the two short steps afforded by the telephone cord.

"Oh, dear. A fever," Dorothy said, putting her hand to her own forehead. "Will the little mite be alright?" She stopped in her tracks. "Nothing? Not even a thin porridge?" She bit her lip. "I see. I'll come down right away."

"Is everything alright?" Agatha took the teacup from the

tray and poured in a great deal of cream before stirring. "You look quite pale, Dot." She blinked at her friend. "Perhaps you should sit down."

Eliza tied off the stitch.

"I have to go to Cowley right away." Dorothy clutched at her sweater.

"Has something happened?" Maud sipped her gin fizz. "My driver can take you if you like."

"My... er... a relative..." Dorothy glanced wildly around the room. "He's ill." She gathered up her keys and purse. "I must go to him." She tugged on her coat and hat. "I'll take my motorcycle." She bit her lip. "Stay as long as you like." She glanced around again as if looking for something. "Can I ask you to lock up when you leave. My apologies..." Her voice trailed off and she rushed out the door.

"What was that all about?" Maud drained her cocktail glass.

"I don't know." Agatha had a perplexed look on her face. "What, or who, is in Cowley?" She turned to Eliza. "Do you know?"

"I'm afraid not." Eliza blinked. How odd. She'd never seen Dorothy so flustered.

"Well, we best be going." Maud slipped on her gloves. "Tell Dot thanks for the drinks." She gestured in Eliza's direction. "Come on, Agatha, I'll drive you home."

Agatha took a last sip of tea. "I hope she's alright."

"She's tough as nails." Maud held out a hand to Agatha. "She'll be fine. Now let's attend to you."

Agatha stood up and brushed the wrinkles from her skirt. "I'm tougher than I look."

"I'm sure you are, my dear." Maud's laughter sounded like the tinkling of a spoon in a glass. "You'll lock up then?" she said to Eliza.

"Of course. I'll be right behind you." Eliza made one last stitch. "I have an errand to do for Dorothy."

"Tootles." In a cloud of taffeta and fur, Maud whisked Agatha out as quickly as she'd come in.

Eliza took the drinks tray back to the kitchen, fed the cats, and then locked up.

Now, where to find a human skull?

One option was Dead Man's Hole at Tower Bridge on the Thames where bodies regularly washed up from the river. Trouble was those bodies would be in various states of decay and she was in the market for a skull only. Preferably the nice clean skull of someone long dead. A hospital perhaps? The morgue? Maybe an antique shop. Although the war had given her ample unfortunate opportunities to encounter dead bodies, she didn't know where one went to purchase bones. She pushed thoughts of the butcher shop from her mind. Dorothy had distinctly said, human.

Pondering the problem of the human skull, Eliza stopped off at Gambit Chess Rooms to pick up a game. It never hurt to make a few extra quid. And Gambit was on her way home.

Walking across Gambit's threshold always removed a heavy weight from her shoulders. She let out a great sigh of satisfaction. The familiar smells of damp wood, Edith Price's floral perfume, and burnt coffee. She inhaled deeply as she crossed the room and hung up her coat.

The room was packed, every board taken. Men in all shapes and sizes squared off over dark and light pieces, some made of wood, some of silver, and one posh set made of ivory that belonged to Lord Balfour. Death may be the great leveler, but winning at chess could make the poorest man feel rich with pride.

Even as a kid when Eliza had to dress as a boy to pick up

games in the park, every time she won, the reward was greater than the few coins jangling in her pockets.

Leaning against the wall, she watched the game between Theo and Lord Balfour, who played well for a washed-up politician. She held her breath as Theo moved his queen into danger. She hoped his gambit paid off. It was risky. Then again, Theo was an aggressive player. Sometimes too aggressive. She used to be like him. Before the year after the war. Before her recklessness had cost her more than a mere chess game.

After the game, Theo was in a sour mood. He won, but only because Lord Balfour made a blunder that cost the game. Of course, he refused to play Eliza, swearing off chess for good as he blustered out of the Gambit. Eliza followed him.

"I know something that will cheer you up." She poked his back with a finger.

"A long walk off a short pier?" He didn't turn around.

"Next best." She stepped in front of him, forcing him to stop. "A human skull."

"How exciting." His eyes widened. "Do tell."

"We need to find one." She smiled. "Any ideas?"

"Don't tell me." He held up a hand. "Dorothy wants it for the initiation."

She shrugged. "Yup."

"Human skull." Stroking an imaginary beard, he paced a few steps. "What about Basil?"

"Basil?" She squinted at him. "As in Basil Thomson? Scotland Yard's disgraced CID?"

"As in Basil Thomson, writer and want-to-be member of the Detection Club." He smirked. "Author of last year's most forgettable novel: *Mr. Pepper, Investigator.*"

"Quid pro quo." She nodded. "Clever. After the public indecency conviction, he might want to redeem himself by helping us."

"We're not exactly the Home Office or Scotland Yard." He chuckled.

No. But right after the war, when she had worked for Scotland Yard, she'd regularly tussled with Mr. Basil Thomson over women in service. Unfortunately, when she let Billy die on the docks, she'd proved him right.

* * *

They found Basil Thomson at his home in Teddington. His housekeeper led them to his study where, surrounded by bookshelves, he was sitting behind a large mahogany desk strewn with papers. A less sturdy man in his sixties would have been living as a recluse after the public humiliation of an indecency conviction, but not Basil.

"Good to see you again, Basil," Eliza lied. She'd never much liked the mustachioed misogynist. And his conviction for soliciting a prostitute in the park did nothing to soften her views.

The former director grunted in her direction.

"What are you working on, old boy?" Theo approached the desk and held out a hand. "Another humorous Inspector Pepper story?"

"Better than Pepper." Basil stood up. "Serious stuff based on my time at the Yard." His large nose was red like that of a heavy drinker. "To what do I owe the pleasure?" He waved at them to sit.

"You know of the newly formed Detection Club?" Theo crossed his long legs.

"Of course." Basil's eyes lit up. "Dorothy mentioned it." He fingered his mustache. "You know she's using one of my stories for a collection she's putting together." He puffed out his chest.

"Yes, well." Theo paused. "She needs a skull."

"A human skull," Eliza added.

"You've come to me for a human skull?" He shook his head. "Are you mad?"

"The Detection Club would be much obliged for your help." Theo's tone conveyed the implicit promise: *Get us a skull and we'll get you in.*

"I see." Basil paced the length of the room. He stopped in front of a bookcase and reached out for a black leather-bound volume. "*A Study in Scarlet.*" He glanced over at them. "Signed by Conan Doyle."

"Nice," Theo said.

"Can you help us get a skull..." Eliza shifted in her chair. She bit off the, *or not?* She didn't want to waste any more time with Basil Thomson if he wasn't going to help.

Basil didn't answer. Instead, he pursed his lips. "A little birdie told me the Detection Club plans to expel Agatha Christie." The twinkle in his eyes suggested the thought amused him.

Eliza stifled an objection. At Anthony's dinner, the writers were just joking about expelling Agatha from the club. Weren't they? Had something happened in the meantime? Dorothy hadn't mentioned anything. Did Basil know something she didn't?

"As a writer, you know anything is possible." Theo smiled. "Sometimes, even the impossible."

"So, it's true, then." Basil rubbed his hands together.

"I didn't say that," Theo hedged.

"Do you think I've got a chance with the club?" Basil ran a finger along the bookshelf as he crossed back to his desk.

"If you help us get a human skull." Eliza's knee was bouncing up and down. They were wasting valuable time with this pompous buffoon. She wanted to get the blasted skull and get back to find out from Dorothy what was happening with the club and Agatha.

"Alright." Basil wiped dust off his finger. "I'll tell you where you can find one, but the rest is up to you." He turned to Theo. "Understood?"

"Understood," Theo repeated.

Exactly what they were agreeing to, she didn't know. And frankly, so long as they got the skull for Madame Secretary, she didn't care.

"University College Hospital." He waved his hand. "Loads of cadavers and skeletons and such."

"And what?" Eliza rolled her eyes. "They have a lending library for skulls?"

"Sharp-tongued as always, Miss Baker." Basil sneered. "I'm sure your beau will think of some story. He's the next Conan Doyle, after all."

"Beau?" Eliza flinched. Theo was not her beau. They weren't even friends. Not really. More like siblings, including good old-fashioned sibling rivalry.

"Conan Doyle?" Theo laughed. "That will be the day!"

* * *

The University College Hospital was housed in the higgledy-piggledy Cruciform Building on Gower Street. The adorable jumble of buildings, facing this way and that, with its spire jutting out of the middle, looked like it belonged in a fantasy play: the home of whimsical Doctor Frankensteins and Doctor Jekylls rather than real doctors.

After asking directions at the front desk, Eliza and Theo found their way to the teaching wing of the hospital where Basil Thomson had promised they would find their treasure. As it was Saturday evening, the classrooms were empty, and the silence and dim lights made the place eerie. A shiver running up her spine, Eliza glanced around. Now, where to find a skull and get out of there?

"Here," Eliza said, trying the knob on a door marked *Neurology Laboratory*. Damn. It was locked. No matter. She pulled a couple of pins from her hair and inserted them into the lock cylinder.

"What are you doing?" Theo's eyes went wide.

"Getting what we came for." She applied pressure to the pins and the lock opened. Her childhood of petty crime sometimes came in handy.

"How did you do that?" Theo's voice rose an octave.

"Easy." She opened the door and slid inside. "Are you coming?"

"Aren't you worried about getting caught?" He stood in the doorway.

"Only if you continue loitering." She grabbed his sleeve and pulled him inside. "Come on."

Light from high, rectangular windows dimly lit the lab. The smells of chemicals and metal permeated the air. Steel countertops glistened in the ambient light.

"Was Basil right?" She surveyed the laboratory. "Are they going to expel Agatha from the club?"

"I don't know." He glanced around wildly like a cornered animal. "I doubt it. Let's get the bloody skull and get out of here." He ran a hand through his hair. "And for the record, I don't condone breaking and entering."

"Of course not." She smiled. "Now, where do they keep the

skulls?" Probably not in a skull cabinet. She walked the circumference of the lab, scanning the room as she went. Hanging in the corner was a full body skeleton. Its skull very much attached. Beheading a skeleton seemed a last resort. Surely, the neurology lab must have skulls some place.

"Perhaps the archeology department would be a better bet." Theo stopped in front of a shelf of pickled brains. "When I was at Oxford, one of my philosophy professors claimed the mind was nothing more than the brain." Mesmerized, he stared at one large brain floating in a jar of amber liquid.

She narrowed her brows. "We're after a skull, not a brain." Opening a tall cabinet, she peeked inside. Shelves of bound journals. No bones.

"He didn't believe in the Cartesian ghost in the machine. That the mind inhabits the body. Nor the Platonic soul as chariot driver directing the body." Theo reached out and tapped the glass. "Anyone home?"

"Quit playing with the brains." She tried the door to the storage closet. It was open.

"But if the mind isn't distinct from the body, what is it?" Theo continued nattering on about minds and brains. "How can we explain art and creativity and longing? Not animal instincts or cravings, but passionate desire? How can we explain good and evil? Our sense of right and wrong? Does all of that exist in the brain?"

She was only half listening. The closet was dark. Putting one foot in front of the other, her hand outstretched, she fumbled for a light pull. Her hand bumped a string and she pulled on it.

"So, if we dissect the brain, can we simply read off a person's likes and dislikes? Their deepest fears and wishes? Their beliefs?" Theo's voice came from the other room. "Is it that simple? Everything we take to be transcendent is just chemicals in the brain?"

"I'm going to brain you if you don't hush up and get in here." She stood staring at a shelf of skulls, many with holes drilled into them. Inspecting the specimens, she looked for one without any extra holes. What made for an attractive skull? Madame Secretary hadn't given her any criteria.

"Creepy." Theo stood at her side. "I don't know. Doesn't it seem sacrilegious to steal a skull?"

"We're not exactly grave robbing." She shook her head. "These bones have been subject to worse than some crazy writer's initiation ritual." She pointed at one with several holes drilled in the cranium. "Look at that poor bloke."

Theo shivered. "I don't like this."

"Tell that to your pal Dorothy." She turned to him. "Maybe you'd prefer to take one of your new mates? A brain in a vat."

"It's all so morbid." Theo's lips twitched.

"Your writer pals are a morbid bunch." She gave him a playful elbow in the ribs. "What's wrong? Are you squeamish?" She'd seen a lot worse during the war... and after. She thought of Billy and how he'd died. She sucked in a breath. A shudder jolted through her as she grabbed a skull. "Here, take this."

"Me?" Theo blinked at her.

She shoved the skull at him.

He took it and examined it. "Emergency Resuscitation Instructional Cranium." He glanced over at her. "See." He held up the skull. "Read the fine print."

He was right. There it was in tiny cursive letters along the base.

"ERIC," she said, looking into the eye sockets. "Pleased to meet you." The bare teeth and jaw formed a gruesome grin.

"How do you know it's male?" Theo asked, turning the skull over in his hands.

A jangling of keys made her freeze in place. Quickly, she pulled the light string.

"Shh." In the dark, she put a finger to her lips. Ears perked, she listened. Footfalls echoed through the laboratory.

Dammit. They were trapped.

* * *

Theo Sharp was hiding in a storage closet, engaged in criminal activities, about to be caught, holding a human skull for God's sake, and all he could think about was touching Eliza. In the darkness, he could feel her breathing. She was so close and yet not close enough. He took a small step toward her. He leaned into her warmth and closed his eyes. When he died and they dissected his brain, they would see *Eliza Baker* written all over it.

Inhaling the scent of jasmine, the scent of her, inflamed his senses like throwing a match into a stream of petrol. He bent his head toward her neck and took a deep breath as if he could take her into his lungs and keep her there forever. He couldn't help himself. His lips brushed against the back of her neck.

Pain exploded across his face and he fell backwards, dropping the skull. It hit a shelf and sailed toward the floor. His hand flew to his nose where she'd just hit him. Wetness, warm and sticky. The taste of iron in his mouth. He withdrew his hand and stared down at it. Even in the darkness, he could tell it was covered in blood. His blood. Geez. He'd barely touched her.

Before he could process what just happened, Eliza had lunged at the skull and caught it in the nick of time before it hit the floor. Next, she pulled a couple pins from her hair, jimmied them into the lock, and popped the door open. He sputtered trying to get his words out. She bolted out of the closet and slammed the door on her way out. She left him stunned and bleeding, alone in the dark. He heard a commotion in the other room. When he opened the door, he saw Eliza hovering over a man slumped in a chair. She had one boot on the edge of the chair and seemed to be positioning the man into a sitting position.

"What happened?" Theo asked, still holding his nose.

"You're a mess." Eliza tucked the skull under her arm and pulled a handkerchief from her sleeve. "Here."

He held the cloth to his face. "Is he alright?"

"He fainted." Her skirt was hiked up and the hem of her petticoat peeked out from underneath. "When he saw me. Poor fellow." Along with a flash of ankle and calf and... something else. The hilt of a blade caught the light. "He's out." She straightened her skirts. "We'd better hop it before he wakes up."

"Is that a knife in your boot?" Muffled by the handkerchief, his voice echoed through his head like a whiny child's.

Her green eyes were as hard as emeralds. "Let's go before someone else gets hurt."

"Speaking of..." He dabbed at his nose. "Did you intend to break my nose?"

"Why would I do that?" She averted his gaze.

"Because I..." He couldn't say it aloud. *Tried to kiss you.* The throbbing of his nose had nothing on the throbbing of his heart.

"Because you what?" Her eyes darted to his bloodstained shirt, which had come partially unbuttoned.

"Because I..." He fastened the buttons. "Forgive me."

"There's nothing to forgive." She tightened her lips. "Nothing happened." She nodded toward the exit. "We got the bloody skull; let's get out of here."

Bloody skull was right. He wadded up the bloody handkerchief and tossed it in the bin on the way out of the lab.

# 4

## EMERGENCY MEETING

The next morning, Eliza was eating breakfast when she got a telephone call. It was Dorothy. Her voice was full of urgency. "I'm scheduling an emergency meeting of the Detection Club." She breathed down the phone. "Some members are calling for Agatha's expulsion due to that Roger Ackroyd novel." She puffed. "Poppycock and twaddle, but best to deal with it right away before it goes any further. I don't want to spend the entire evening picking at the sore spot." She sighed. "So, the main event will be Theodore's initiation ceremony. That way, the debate over Agatha will be merely a footnote."

Eliza couldn't get a word in edgewise.

"Unreliable narrator, magical use of machines, unfair trickery." Dorothy huffed. "I thought it was rather clever." She sucked in an audible breath. "Well, we'd best get to work. We have a lot to do to get ready." She hung up before Eliza could utter a word.

The dinner was Friday. Eliza had less than a week to prepare the props, order the dinner, and make arrangements for the private room at Café Royal. Her mind spinning, she gave Queenie a Milk-Bone and then returned to her toast and coffee.

"Who was that?" Jane asked, taking a bite of toast.

"Madame Secretary." Eliza raised her eyebrows. "Who else?"

"What did she want?" Jane drained her cup.

"I have to run a lot more errands for an emergency meeting of the Detection Club." She took a bite of toast.

"What have you learned about them?" Jane squinted at her.

"As far as I can tell, it's a supper club for writers who like to dress up in capes and tell spooky murder stories by candlelight." She chuckled. "At least judging by the props I've had to round up. I'd say these writers are just overgrown kids playing at crime."

"Do you trust them?" Jane peeked over the rim of her coffee cup.

"Trust them?" That was an odd question. Eliza worked for them. Did she need to trust them, too? She didn't trust anyone. She'd learned the hard way not to get too close to anyone. Well, no one except Jane, of course.

"As you know." Jane lowered her voice. "There are rumblings in Box 500 about your mystery writers giving away military secrets." Box 500 was how insiders referred to MI5.

Eliza still didn't understand why British Intelligence would concern itself with those silly writers. "I doubt they know any secrets." She smeared a large dollop of marmalade onto her second piece of bread. "They live in a fantasy world, not the real one."

"You'd be surprised." Jane popped a last bite of toast into her mouth. "Keep your eyes and ears open."

Nodding, Eliza sipped her milky coffee. She grimaced and then scooped another spoon of sugar into her cup and swirled.

"Remember." Jane stacked her breakfast dishes in the sink. "You promised to help me."

"I remember." Eliza scratched Queenie under the chin. The dog grinned up at her. "Anything for you, dear sister," she said with exaggerated sweetness.

"You're the best." Jane smiled.

"No, *you're* the best." Eliza moved her fingers to scratch behind Queenie's ears.

"I've got to run," Jane said, brushing crumbs from her wool skirt. "Find out what those writers are up to." She waved. "Ta."

Eliza sat staring into her cup. Did Dorothy's urgent trip to Cowley have something to do with military secrets? And the emergency meeting of the club, was it a cover for sharing those secrets? As much as Eliza disliked the unreliable doctor and his stupid Dictaphone trick in Christie's novel, she didn't think it warranted expulsion from the club. Anyway, who would fall for a Dictaphone? Ridiculous that the doctor, who was also the narrator, not to mention the murderer, used a Dictaphone to create his alibi. Not only was it cheating, but it was downright unbelievable. Still, it was just a novel. For a silly bunch, they took themselves far too seriously. All those absurd rules and the even more preposterous debate over them. Detective fiction was a frivolous pastime after all, not a serious art form.

She thought of Theo. Maybe she shouldn't have hit him so hard. He'd surprised her and her instincts kicked in. She'd learned foot-fighting on the streets too. She'd had to in order to protect herself. She'd learned to kick, bite, or elbow first and ask questions later. Two girls alone in Devil's Acre were like raw meat for the dogs. Still, she felt bad about all the blood from Theo's nose. She'd had to resist wiping a droplet of blood from his smooth chest. She shook her head. Enough wasting time.

She drained her cup and fed Queenie. The dishes could wait.
She had work to do.

* * *

Over the next few days, in between shopping for the club
dinner, meeting Dorothy, and carting supplies to Café Royal in
Soho, Eliza stopped off at Gambit to pick up a bit of spending
money. On Monday, she handily trounced a baron who fancied
himself a grand master. Tuesday brought her a slightly more
interesting match with a class-climbing coal magnet who
played chess to "move in new circles." She managed to squeeze
in two games on Wednesday. And by Thursday, she had enough
coins jingling in her purse to keep Queenie in Milk-Bones for a
couple months *and* help Jane with the rent. Friday afternoon,
she sacrificed a game just to get to Café Royal early enough to
prepare everything for the inaugural dinner.

On her way from Gambit to Café Royal, she carried Eric the
skull in a large handbag she'd brought especially for him. She
stopped to pick up two dozen candles and the red satin pillow
and place cards she'd specially ordered from Harrods. She
arrived early to inspect the room and set up the props. Dorothy
was scheduled to arrive an hour early to orchestrate the prepa-
rations. Eliza preferred to set up the room on her own, free
from Madame Secretary's whimsical demands, which was why
she arrived two hours early.

The Café Royal was the place for London's literati to see
and be seen. With its enormous ornate ceilings, wall paint-
ings, and heavy curtains, it was a cavernous affair with a hint
of scandal hanging in the air like a whisper. Eliza directed the
staff to set up the three long tables in a horseshoe shape as
per Dorothy's instructions. It was the first formal dinner and

Madame Secretary wanted it to be perfect. And since it was Theo's initiation ceremony, Eliza put in extra effort. She even bought fresh-cut flowers and put them in glass vases in the center of each table. After spending far too long at the florists, she'd decided on blood-red spider chrysanthemums. They seemed appropriate for the evening's macabre festivities.

Eliza was arranging the flowers when Neville Lively and Anthony Berkeley Cox strode into the room laughing. Why had they come so early? Dorothy wasn't even there yet. They were like a couple of schoolboys, constantly pulling pranks and cutting up.

"We've come to meet Eric," Neville said. "We've heard all about the handsome fellow." He chuckled.

"Yes," Anthony chimed in. "I've heard Eric is a dead ringer for Neville here." He slapped his pal on the shoulder. Poor Neville nearly toppled over.

To get them out of her hair, she pulled Eric the skull out of her handbag and gently set him up on the red satin pillow.

"I say." Anthony clapped his hands together. "Glad to meet you, old chap." He patted Eric.

"He looks lonely," Neville said.

"Why do you say that?" Anthony adjusted the skull on the pillow.

"Because he has no body." Neville broke into laughter. "No body. Do you follow?"

Eliza rolled her eyes and went back to arranging the tables. Dorothy had given her a seating chart so she could put out the place cards. Of the twenty diners, there weren't nearly enough women to alternate by sex. As far as Eliza could tell there was no rhyme or reason for the seating chart. But no doubt Dorothy had a plan. Although her motives could be as mysterious as her fiction. Running off to Cowley at the drop of a hat and then rushing back to host a slapdash meeting of the Detection Club.

At the stroke of five, in a flowing emerald cape and men's felt hat, Dorothy finally arrived. Like monsoon season, she was right on time. In her tiny, round spectacles, wearing a tie and cufflinks, with her hair pulled back severely, she looked like an Oxford don arriving for his tutorial. At least now Dorothy could entertain Neville and Anthony, who had been pestering Eliza to no end.

Dorothy greeted the men and then rushed around *rear-ranging* everything Eliza already had arranged. Tight-lipped, Eliza watched and resisted the urge to put everything back in its original place. She bit a fingernail. She was just the secretary to the secretary after all. And she was getting paid. Who cared what Dorothy or the other daft writers did at their make-believe parties? And aside from keeping a roof over her head, she'd promised Jane to keep an eye out.

The guests started trickling in. One of Anthony's women— was it the wife or the mistress?—ordered a bottle of champagne. Gilbert Chesterton and Agatha Christie arrived at the same time, although not together. Chesterton looked disheveled and uncertain as to where he was. Agatha was elegant in a plain, pale-green gown, a string of pearls, and perfectly coiffed finger waves. Eliza also recognized Fergus Briggs and Maud Wilkerson from the last dinner party. But there were several others she didn't know.

As the new initiate, Theo had a place at the center of the middle table. Despite the tear on the left shoulder of his jacket and his bruised eye (cringe), he looked sharp in his evening suit. Eliza wondered if he'd purchased it second-hand or perhaps it was a hand-me-down from a relative. She was still wearing the same brown, belted, wool serge she'd had on this morning playing chess. Since she wasn't officially a guest of the club, she figured it didn't matter what she wore. Anyway, what she lacked in colorful plumage was more than compensated by Maud's elaborate outfit. Maud's burgundy dress was skin-tight with sequins, beads, and fringe like you might see in a New York jazz club. Neville had gone all out and looked dapper in an emerald double-breasted pinstripe, set off by a gold silk Ascot cravat. Most everyone wore gloves befitting a night at the opera.

After an hour of mingling and cocktails, Dorothy tapped a spoon against her champagne flute. "Gilbert, as our new president, might you do the honors of calling the meeting to order? Tonight, we have a special lecture by the brilliant Bertrand Russell, professor of philosophy at Cambridge, which will be followed by dinner, and then after dinner, we will have a short business meeting to discuss... to discuss current pressing issues. And finally, the finale of the evening..." She waved her hand dramatically. "The initiation ritual for our newest member, Mr. Theodore Torrent Sharp."

At the mention of his name, Eliza shuddered with a case of sympathetic nerves. Knowing Theo, he did not relish the attention or dressing up like a penguin performing at the zoo.

Professor Russell's speech on the difference between induction and deduction was dreadfully boring, despite his attempt at horrible logic jokes. "Sherlock Holmes is famous for using deductive reasoning," he said. "He is known as a master of deduction." There were nods of agreement around the table. "But in actuality, most of the time, he uses induction or abduction. Not deduction." That got everyone's attention.

Chesterton smiled.

Dorothy grumbled and said under her breath, "He uses a combination of both most of the time."

"For example." The professor continued his stem-winder.

"When Sherlock notices mud on shoes and 'deduces' the wearer is from Cork, or dirt under fingernails and claims the victim was from Sheffield, he draws those conclusions using inductive reasoning based on a combination of keen observation, his knowledge of dirt, and probability calculations." He took a sip of wine. "In the famous scene when Holmes first meets Watson and supposedly displays his deductive genius, again that's actually observational, or inductive, genius. He observes Watson is a doctor with a military air about him. An army doctor then. His face is tanned so he was in a sunny climate. His left arm is injured. Therefore, he was in a combat zone. Where is there a warzone in a sunny climate? Afghanistan." He waved a hand. "In deduction, there are general premises that can be used to draw a specific conclusion. Whereas in induction, and the Holmes-Watson example, it is the other way around. Specific observations are used to draw a general conclusion."

Tuning out the Cambridge windbag, Eliza stared across the room at Theo, who had loosened his tie and unbuttoned his collar, and was listening with rapt attention. Did he really fancy solving crimes with logic? Induction, deduction, abduction. No one ever solved crimes using only the so-called "science" of logic alone. Like good chess, good investigation operated according to scientific principles.

Forensics was the science that mattered when it came to detective work. Any Scotland Yard detective worth his salt would collect physical evidence and base his conclusions on examination of the evidence: hard evidence, not abstract theories. Theo glanced across the room at her. She took a quick sip of wine and looked away.

After the tiresome professor finished his lecture, dinner was served. The main course was wine. The writers drank so much, the food was a mere afterthought. When they finished the pudding course, Dorothy rose and asked the guests to retire to the next room while the club conducted its business. Once the spouses and friends filed out, Madame Secretary introduced Gilbert Chesterton as the club president. She helped him into a huge, flowing, red cape and signaled it was time for him to preside over the business at hand. Namely, whether to expel Agatha from the club.

"Of course, I have the greatest respect for the author herself," Neville said. "But we've all agreed to play fair—"

"There are rules after all," Maud piped up.

"Rules are made to be broken," Anthony said. "And the book in question is a masterclass in plotting." His words were slightly slurred, no doubt from all the wine.

"More like a masterclass in destroying the credibility of all detective fiction." Maud waved a long cigarette holder. "What's next? The victim committing the crime? The baby as the murderer? Priests and presidents as villains?" She cackled like a hen about to lay an egg.

"And why can't priests and presidents be as villainous as anybody else?" Dorothy stabbed the air with her fork. "Isn't the point of it all that anyone can harbor murderous impulses? That we are all tempted to evil? Without temptation, there is not virtue." She dropped the fork. "Good and evil are but tests of our humanity. God gave us the ability to choose. Without the freedom to choose evil, we would be nothing more than automatons."

"Brava," Chesterton said. "Well put." His round cheeks were rosy and his nose red.

"Let's wait until we see her sales numbers," Fergus Briggs piped up from the end of the table. "Let the public vote with their pocketbooks." He cleared his throat. "Will the story sell? That's the bottom line."

"It is my most popular story," Agatha said softly to her empty pudding plate.

"Be that as it may." Neville drained his glass. "It sets a bad precedent. A very bad precedent indeed."

"What precedent?" Dorothy bellowed. "That detective writers can quit their day jobs and make a living writing?" She sighed. "Would that really be so bad?" She wiggled her fingers. "Pass the wine, please. I require fortification to continue this ridiculous debate."

Ridiculous, indeed. Eliza took notes, writing down the pros and cons of expelling Agatha. Poor Agatha. Despite her polite smile, she looked as if she wanted to disappear into the upholstery. After a good forty minutes of debate, they weren't any closer to settling the matter than when they began. If anything, they were merely spinning their wheels and digging in deeper.

What of Theo's initiation? She glanced over at him. Poor lad had his head in his hands, which only made his wild locks even livelier. When he raised his head, two twists of hair stuck up like horns.

"Excuse me," Eliza said. "Might I suggest you vote now or table the discussion?" She tapped her watch. "It's already after ten and you still have Theo, Mr. Sharp's initiation ceremony." She shrugged. "Not to mention the guests waiting next door."

"Hear, hear," Dorothy said, tinkling her glass with a spoon. "I move that we dispense with all this nonsense and move on to the initiation. Agatha stays in the club." She nodded in Agatha's direction.

Agatha blushed and gave her a grateful smile.

"I object," Neville said. "We haven't finished our discussion."

"Roberts Rules indicate that we can discuss my motion,

once we get a second." Dorothy was still standing, presiding over the group as if she were president.

"I second." Anthony nodded.

After discussing the matter for another thirty minutes, the writers were no closer to a decision. A few valent objectors kept the others from voting.

"Can't you see your way to going with the stream?" Anthony asked, twisting his napkin and smiling at Neville and Maud the tag-team arguing against Agatha.

"A dead thing can go with the stream." Gilbert Chesterton stood. "Only the living can go against it. To that end, I'm making an executive decision to table this so we can get on with the initiation of young Theo."

"Hear, hear." Dorothy jumped up and went to fetch Eric, who was perched on his satin pillow atop a chair near the back of the room. "Let the ceremony begin," she said as she lit a taper.

The main players in the group got up and went to join her. Rummaging in a large suitcase she'd brought, Dorothy handed out various weapons to her friends: a butcher knife, a German pistol, a piece of thick rope, a vial of blue liquid, a revolver, a boomerang. She kept a pearl-hilted dagger for herself. They lined up at the front of the room, with Chesterton leading the way carrying Eric on his pillow. With the dagger in one hand and the candle in the other, Dorothy brought up the rear. She turned off the lights.

In the darkness, gasps and giggles erupted from the spectators.

"What mean these candles, this ceremony, and this reminder of our own mortality?" Chesterton said solemnly, his booming voice vibrating the table.

"Sir," Dorothy answered. "We present Mr. Theodore Torrent Sharp for admission into our membership."

Using a candle to light his way, Theo rose and was instructed to lay his hand upon Eric the skull.

"Do you promise to play fair with your readers and never conceal a vital clue?" Chesterton asked.

"I do." The light flickered on his face, creating the eerie sensation of a séance conjuring a ghost.

"Do you promise to observe moderation in use of trap doors, death rays, ghosts, hypnotism, and unknown poisons?"

"I do."

The ceremony proceeded with Theo taking ridiculous oaths while Gilbert and Dorothy presided with the seriousness of deacons.

When the last "I do" was uttered, the participants blew out their candles. The eyes of the skull glowed red from some hidden battery bulb or torch. The club members whooped and hollered and in the dim light, their silhouettes brandished their weapons overhead.

Suddenly, a man screamed. "Agatha. No!"

The skull clattered to the floor, extinguishing the only light in the windowless room.

*Bang!* A shot echoed through the chamber. Eliza gasped and hit the floor. Were they mad? Firing guns inside the restaurant. They really had taken it all too far. Someone could get hurt with this madness.

A loud thud was followed by a woman's scream. All this screaming and drama was over the top. Eliza's nerves couldn't take it. She got to her hands and knees and glanced around in the darkness, hoping her eyes would adjust. But the room was pitch dark.

"Lights!" Dorothy yelled. "Someone turn on the lights."

More screeching and thudding.

"Ouch." It sounded like Maud. It was a wonder they all weren't bruised and bleeding, carrying on like this in the dark.

"Lights!" Dorothy yelled again.

"Where is the damn switch?" It was Gilbert Chesterton's deep baritone. "A bunch of detective writers and we can't even find the lights."

Eliza got up from the floor but in the windowless room, she couldn't see a thing. Slowly, she felt around in the dark, taking one tiny step at a time. Her foot ran into a solid object and she stopped.

"Will someone get the lights for heaven's sake?" It sounded like Dorothy.

Finally, the lights came back on. Theo was standing at the door with his hand on the light switch. The ceremonial weapons were strewn around the floor. Anthony was leaning against the far wall. A flicker of a skirt disappeared around the corner. Someone gasped.

Then Eliza spotted it. The body in the middle of the floor.

One hand over her mouth, Maud Wilkerson had tears in her eyes as she stared down at the floor where Neville Lively lay bleeding. Dorothy knelt next to the body, her face a mask of horror. She looked up at the crowd gathered around and shook her head. "He's dead."

* * *

Theo felt the blood drain from his face. He held onto the edge of the door frame. His head was spinning. He closed his eyes. That only made it worse. But if he opened them again, he knew what he'd see. A pool of bright red spreading across the pale Karnak carpet like a deadly rose blooming around Neville's crown. He dropped back into his chair and allowed himself to float away into oblivion.

# 5

## CRIME SCENE

Feeling for a pulse just in case, Eliza shouted, "Call for an ambulance." She glanced around and waited for a response. The mystery writers were gathered round the body, wringing their hands and mumbling. *Crap!* On top of everything else, Theo had fainted.

She examined the body. Neville Lively had been shot in the head at close range. A revolver lay next to him on the floor: presumably the gun that fired the shot that killed him. For, he was indeed dead. The question was, how? An accident? Or murder? The gun lay near his right hand. In his left, he clutched a knife.

She rocked back on her heels. What was she doing? She wasn't a copper. This wasn't her job. The last time she investigated a homicide, her *partner* had died. She squeezed her eyes shut. She couldn't risk messing up and killing someone again. Not now. Not ever.

She stood up. In any case, she was merely the assistant to the club secretary. Not their resident detective. She glanced around. She couldn't help it. Her Scotland Yard training kicked in and she saw everyone in the room as a possible suspect. Had one of these writers killed Neville Lively?

Dorothy rose and stood as still as a statue, the pearl dagger hanging slack from her hand. Some of them must have dropped their weapons in the commotion, which accounted for the props strewn across the floor. Neville had been shot. So, who was carrying the revolver?

"We should call the police," Anthony said.

"Good idea." Eliza let out a long breath. The sooner the police got there, the better.

"I'll go." Anthony trotted off.

"No!" Dorothy jolted to life. "We need to figure out what happened first."

What? Was she mad? They needed to leave this to the real police. Otherwise, they'd contaminate the crime scene.

"We're not real detectives," Maud said, her hand on her mink collar. "All our talk of unsolved mysteries and fictional crimes." Her lip trembled. "This is real... all too real."

"Indeed." Eliza paced the length of the room, resisting the urge to take stock of the evidence.

"Think of what will happen to the club." Dorothy joined her pacing the floor. "To our careers. To Agatha." She glanced over at the elegant lady, who had dropped into a nearby chair.

"Me?" Agatha clutched her pearls.

Anthony reappeared from the other room. "Agatha?" He narrowed his brows. "Why her?"

"Didn't you hear him?" Dorothy stopped in her tracks. "Neville's last words were, 'Agatha. No.'"

"You don't think I had anything to do with this?" Agatha blanched.

Eliza watched the mystery writers bickering and shook her

head. Now was not the time for baseless accusations. It was a time to gather evidence and piece together clues. Where were those blasted police detectives? She glanced at her watch. Almost midnight. She wished the coppers would hurry and get there.

"He was arguing to expel you from the club," Maud said, lighting a cigarette. "And critical of your latest work." Her hand shook as she held the match to the smoke. "Sounds like motive to me."

"Good grief." Agatha withdrew an embroidered handkerchief from her pocket and dabbed at her temples. "It's just a silly club. Nothing to kill for."

Dorothy scowled. If she disagreed, she didn't say. "You have been under a lot of strain lately, dearest." She gave Agatha a sympathetic look.

"My personal life is none of your concern." Agatha fussed with the lace on her handkerchief. "In fact, I should get home to my husband."

"None of us should leave." Gilbert adjusted his pince-nez. "Not until after the police arrive."

"Agreed," Anthony said. "I called Scotland Yard. They're sending someone right over."

"I'll go see if they're out front." Eliza headed toward the door.

"No!" Dorothy held up her hand. "Wait."

Eliza stopped in her tracks.

"What would you have us do with the body?" Anthony nervously puffed on a cigarette of his own. "Wheel it out on the dessert tray?"

"This is not one of our novels," Maud said. "We all have blood on our hands."

"Original sin aside." Fergus Briggs took a step closer to the body. "It has to be an accident." He stared down at Neville. "What else can it be? Poor lad."

*Murder. That's what.* These writers were going to muck up the crime scene and contaminate the evidence. And why didn't Dorothy want to call the police? She stared over at the pool of blood spreading out around the dead man's skull. Blast it all!

Until the coppers arrived, she was the next best thing. She went to the body. Kneeling, Eliza gently lifted the deceased's wrist and sniffed his hand. It was unlikely she could smell gunpowder, but it was worth a try. If only she could test everyone's hands. Then she would know who fired the gun. Except, everyone was wearing gloves. How convenient. On hands and knees, she examined the gun. A Webley .38. If she had her fingerprint kit, she could dust for prints. Oh right. The gloves. "Was someone carrying this revolver during the ceremony?" She surveyed the writers, who were milling around smoking and sipping on cocktails.

The writers looked at each other. Obviously, they didn't trust their fellow club members.

"Who had the Webley?" Dorothy asked. "Agatha, was it you?"

Agatha's mouth fell open. She shook her head. "No. Not me."

"Maud? Anthony?" Dorothy went down the line.

Everyone denied having handled the revolver.

"Someone shot him."

"What about you, Dot?" Anthony asked. "Didn't you have the gun?"

"No." Dorothy waved the dagger. "This was my weapon." She glared at Maud. "You had it!"

"Me?" Maud whimpered. "Why would I kill Neville? I... I..." Her voice trailed off.

"What happened?" Theo finally got up from his seat and joined the fray.

"Neville was shot. Unburnt grains of powder near the entry wound suggest it was close range," Eliza said. No exit wound. The bullet must have lodged in his brain. "You fainted."

Theo knelt next to the body. "Who was carrying the revolver during the ceremony?"

"No one admits to it." Eliza surveyed the suspects. "But I smell a rat," she whispered.

"Neville had that dagger." Maud pointed to the blade in the dead man's hand. "I had a vial of poison. Dot had a knife, too. Anthony had a thick rope, right Tony?"

"I had that German Luger," Anthony said, pointing to a gun on the table.

How many bloody guns were there?

"Did you shoot Neville?" Dorothy asked.

"Good God." Anthony ran a hand through his hair. "Of course not."

"I had the rope." Agatha perked up.

"What's this?" Carefully, Theo plucked a green thread from the butt of the revolver.

"How'd I miss that?" Eliza unfolded her hankie and gestured for him to place the thread inside. A commotion at the entrance made her turn. Neville's son and daughter stood in the doorway. Their eyes were wide. Alice Lively's hand flew to her mouth.

"Does anyone have face powder?" Eliza asked, looking up at the crowd.

"I do!" Maud dashed back to the table to fetch her handbag. She pulled out a tin and handed it to Eliza. "Why do you need face powder?"

"What... what... how?" Alice Lively screamed. "Father!"

Although she was loath to tamper with evidence, these mystery writers were impossible to control. If she didn't test now, the police may find their crime scene completely in a shambles. "Makeshift dusting for fingerprints." Eliza opened the tin, removed the powder puff, and gently dabbed on the handle of the gun. "Remarkable." Hopefully, when the police arrived they would thank her rather than scold her.

"What is remarkable?" Maud asked.

"Oh my God! Father!" Neville's son Barnaby ran across the room and flung himself atop the dead body. "Oh, Papa! No. No. No."

"Who did this?" Alice hadn't left the doorway. Her shoulders shaking, she let out a long, low moan like an injured animal. Anthony went to her.

"This gun has no prints whatsoever." Ignoring the noise, Eliza returned the tin to Maud. Even if the killer was wearing gloves, the gun should have someone's fingerprints. Dorothy's from when she put the gun in the suitcase.

"What does it mean?" Theo asked, moving to get a closer look at the powdered gun handle.

"It means someone has wiped the gun." Eliza sat back on her haunches. How did the killer have time to shoot and wipe the gun all before the lights came on?

"Who would want to kill Father?" Barnaby dropped into a chair and hung his head. "Why would someone do this?"

The rest of the guests from next door flooded into the room. "We heard a loud noise," one of them said.

"Good heavens," gasped another. "What happened?"

Alice Lively was leaning against the wall, sobbing. Barnaby hopped up from his chair and hurried over to her. Like a drunken bandalore, he dashed back and forth between his hysterical sister and his dead father, all the while mumbling, "Why?"

"Come with me, Alice." Anthony took the young woman by the hand. "I'll escort you out to wait for the police." He led her out of the room.

"We should get our stories straight," Dorothy said.

"What's there to tell?" Maud said. "We were celebrating. A shot was fired. Now, Neville is dead." She waved her cigarette holder like a magic wand that could make it all disappear. "It's as simple as that."

Dorothy went over to Agatha, who was sitting with her head in her hands. "Are you quite alright, dear?" She bent down to get a better look. "Would you like someone to drive you home?"

"None of us should leave before the police arrive." Gilbert was munching on a leftover chocolate biscuit.

"They know where to find us." Dorothy helped Agatha to her feet. "And if not, I'm sure you'll tell them."

"My handbag." Agatha retrieved the bag from under her chair. The clasp came undone and the contents tumbled out. "Oh, dear me."

"Let me help." Dorothy bent down but rather than help, she stared at the floor.

"Good heavens." Maud rushed over to Agatha as Anthony came back into the room. "She has a gun."

"What?" Anthony joined the ladies.

"I don't know how it got in my bag." Agatha had gone white as paste. "Someone must have put it there."

"Who? And why?" Dorothy let out a loud guffaw. "If you didn't put it there, how did it get there?" She stood blinking down at Agatha.

"I have no earthly idea." Agatha's voice was small. Her

shoulders hunched; she suddenly looked much older than her thirty-six years.

Eliza went to examine the gun from Agatha's handbag. Another Webley revolver. How many blasted guns did these writers have at their dinner party? Too many. She helped Agatha gather up the contents of her handbag, which had scattered across the floor. A lipstick, a notebook and pencil, some mints, a broken perfume bottle, and a card for a spa in Harrogate. Minus the second Webley, she laid the contents out on the table.

When Agatha had reclaimed her empty handbag, Eliza turned her attention to the second gun, which Dorothy had placed on a nearby chair. "Let me see it." She picked it up by the tip of the barrel and sniffed. A strong scent of rose perfume masked any other smells. No wonder. When the contents were dumped, the gun fell on the perfume bottle and broke it. She used Maud's face powder a second time to check for prints. None. It too had been wiped clean.

How odd. Shouldn't Agatha's prints be on the gun if she'd put it into her handbag?

"I really don't feel well." Agatha hugged her empty bag to her chest. "Might someone be good enough to take me home?"

"Of course, dear." Dorothy gave Anthony a telling look. "Anthony, be a gent and give Agatha a ride home, would you?"

His lips twitched as he scanned the room looking for someone. Probably his wife or his mistress or both. "I would be glad to, after the police arrive."

"I feel rather faint." Agatha dabbed her forehead with a hanky. "Perhaps you could take me home and ask the police to come around tomorrow?"

Dorothy nodded at Anthony.

"Oh, alright." He huffed.

"No one should leave until the police arrive," Eliza said holding up one hand.

"I need a drink," Maud announced, completely ignoring Eliza. "Would anyone like to come with me to the Dove?"

"I'll join you after I drop off Agatha," Anthony said.

"I prefer my regular haunt, Ye Olde Cheshire Cheese on Fleet Street." Smiling, Gilbert Chesterton gathered up his cape and hat. "If anyone wants to join me, you're welcome."

"We all need to wait for Scotland Yard."

The writers acted like she wasn't there.

"No one should leave." She used her most commanding tone.

"Maud, I'll see you out in any case." Chesterton escorted Maud out of the dining room.

Blasted writers. Did they think they were above the law? She let out an audible sigh. She didn't have the power or the authority to stop them. Instead, shaking her head, she watched them file out, no doubt on their way to have more cocktails.

Blast it! Her Scotland Yard instincts kicked in and she dashed to block the exit. "You will wait in here for the police to arrive." She pointed at the dining room where the other guests had been waiting during the initiation ceremony. "You can eat, drink, and be merry in there." She gestured toward the entrance. "But no one will leave until the police tell you to."

"I'm really quite ill." Agatha leaned into Anthony and grasped his arm. "I must lie down. I'm not at all well." She was pale and her eyes looked glassy. She really didn't look well. "Please take me home." Her voice cracked, as if she might cry. She gathered the contents of her handbag, sans gun, and mechanically placed them one by one back into her bag.

"Yes. Of course." Anthony helped her to the door. "Right

away." He turned back to Eliza. "I'll take her home and come right back."

Eliza nodded. What harm would it do? The police could arrest Agatha tomorrow morning just as easily as they could tonight. It wasn't like she would skip town.

After settling the other writers into the anterior dining room, Eliza returned to the scene of the crime, still grumbling about the blasted writers who thought they could simply leave a murder scene before the police arrived.

Theo stood staring down at Neville's dead body, while Dorothy sat quietly praying. Neville's children were waiting in the other room with the others to avoid the trauma of seeing their father lying in a pool of his own blood.

With most everyone gone from the room, Eliza took the liberty of checking Neville's pockets. She recovered a key ring, a wallet, and a gold pocket watch on a chain. She laid his belongings on the table.

"What did you find?" Theo joined her.

"A set of keys," she said, examining them. The largest was obviously a skeleton key, most likely to his flat. The smallest looked like a key to a locker. It had the number eight engraved on its little bow.

When she returned to the body, she noticed a tiny corner of white peeking out from under the dead man's shoulder. Gently, she lifted his shoulder and tugged it free. A bloodstained handkerchief with the letters *A. C.* embroidered in blue thread. Whose initials? It should be easy enough to find out. The question was, why was the hankie under the body? Had the owner tussled with Neville and lost their cloth in the struggle?

"A. C." Theo eyed the handkerchief. "Anthony Cox or Agatha Christie." He drew his brows closer together. "Like a fork."

"A fork?" Pinning the cloth between her thumb and forefinger, she held it out to him. "Place this with the other evidence, if you please." The evidence was piling up. Too much of it. Eliza had an uneasy feeling. Something wasn't right about this crime scene.

"In chess." He gave her a sly smile. "When one move threatens two pieces."

"Except this isn't a game." Eliza gently loosened the sleeve of Neville's shirt and examined his wrists and hands. If there had been a struggle before he was shot, he could have bruises or scratches on his arms, hands, or face. "This is a matter of life and death." Around the victim's right wrist, a blueish purple bruise stood out against his pale flesh. The way it wrapped around his wrist suggested a hand had grasped him and hard. Crawling around the body, she inspected the area around it, looking for any other signs of struggle and more clues to what happened. The coppers would arrive any minute and shoo her out of the room. She didn't have a second to lose.

Moving in methodical concentric circles centered on the body, Eliza took note of every stained carpet fiber and bit of debris strewn from the body to the doorway. Near the exit, a fragment of a bloody footprint pointed in the direction of a quick escape. Was it possible someone snuck in after the lights went out, disposed of Neville, and then made a hasty retreat? The woman whose skirt she glimpsed for example.

"Do you have a sheet of paper?" She glanced up at Theo, who was staring down at the stuff on the table.

"I'm a writer," he said, pulling a small notebook from his baggy jacket. "Of course I do." He tore out a sheet and handed it to her.

Carefully, she laid the paper atop the partial footprint and then stood up and lightly pressed her own shoe into the paper. A red flower bloomed across the sheet. It came to a point at the toe and formed a rough triangle. A woman's shoe then. One of the family members who had been asked to wait in the next room? Perhaps Neville's daughter, who was still waiting next door with her brother. Or had one of the waitresses entered the room unseen and accidently stepped in the pool of blood on her way out? Unless one of the Detection Club members had snuck away undetected during the commotion. No. Someone would have noticed if one of their own was missing. She lifted the paper and held it up to the light.

"Look." Theo pointed at a dry white spot in the middle of the red mark. "The shoe is worn down just there."

"So not a new shoe." Eliza blew on the paper to help it dry.

"Quite the opposite." Theo took a step closer. "A well-worn shoe." He looked her in the eyes. "Perhaps our killer can't afford to buy new shoes."

"Or perhaps she prefers her old ones because they're comfortable." Eliza ripped another sheet of paper from Theo's notebook, laid it on the table, and placed the bloodstained sheet on top.

"If the bloody footprint belongs to the perpetrator." Theo wiggled his fingers. "Then either our killer is poor or prefers comfort to fashion."

"Are you using deductive or inductive reasoning?" Eliza raised her eyebrows. "What would the professor have to say?"

"The only thing that matters," Theo said, "is that our reasoning is sound."

"You, there." A voice boomed from the doorway. "What do you think you're doing?"

Eliza and Theo both swiveled around.

A large policeman carrying a nightstick approached. "Tampering with evidence, are we?"

"No, sir," Theo said, shaking his head.

"I'm Detective Inspector Robert Leonard Goforth," the copper said and held out his hand.

"Theodore Sharp." Theo shook his hand. "And this is Eliza Baker."

"A pleasure to see you again, Miss Baker." The policeman doffed his cap. Eliza knew D. I. Goforth from the Met. What he lacked in investigative skill, he made up for in chattiness. Still, she liked him. He was one of the few inspectors who'd taken her under his wing (only slightly patronizing) and didn't try to undermine her.

"Now, tell me what you're doing here. Are you related to the deceased?" D. I. Goforth waved his hand at the table. "And what's all this?"

"Evidence." Eliza gave Theo a meaningful look. "But the body is there." She pointed. "And the suspects, er, witnesses, are waiting next door."

"Yes, the other members of the Detection Club are in the dining room next door," Theo said, picking up her cue. "This, is —was—Sir Neville Lively, mystery writer." Theo led him to the body. "You may have heard him on the radio. He did a regular show. And specials, too. The last one was a doozey." Theo shook his head. "The revolution in the streets. *Broadcasting from the Barricades*," he said in a mock baritone.

"Right." D. I. Goforth bent over the body. "Gunshot to the head."

Eliza took the opportunity to scoop up the imprint of the bloody footprint and stuff it into the chatelaine bag. The police could make their own impression. She grabbed the key ring and monogrammed hanky while she was at it. The rest of the scene she committed to memory. Too bad she didn't have more time to study the Webley revolver: two if you counted the one that fell out of Agatha Christie's handbag.

But why were there two guns? And why was one in Agatha's bag? Given Agatha's turn and hasty departure, they'd have to wait until tomorrow to find out.

\* \* \*

While Detective Goforth chatted up Eliza, Theo sat staring over at Neville Lively's lifeless body. Of course, Theo had seen a dead body before. The war ensured pretty much everyone had. Still, seeing someone he knew lying dead on the floor of the Café Royal had been a shock to his system. His father always told him that he was too sensitive. That he needed to "buck up" and "be a man."

Theo put his head in his hands. *Be a man.* Wasn't it man's plight to face his mortality? Among all the animals, man was the only one who knew he was going to die. The only one whose very existence was defined by his mortality. All living beings wanted to survive. But only man could truly live. Only man could choose life. Could choose to live each day as if it were his last. Carpe diem and all that rot.

His father would warn against thinking too much about death. Or thinking too much about anything. Morbid thinking was not only unmanly but also unseemly. His father had objected to his studying philosophy at Oxford. He'd wanted Theo to study something more practical, something that would help him manage the family's affairs and oversee the tenants. His main hope for Theo was that he would "grow up" at college and quit moping around the house with a book in his hand or a chess board in his mind. *Yes, Father. I read detective stories and play chess to escape your tyranny.*

"You can go," Detective Goforth said, finally. With his jet-black hair and steely blue eyes, he reminded Theo of his father. Even his smooth tenor seemed familiar. And like his father, the detective loved to talk. They'd been at it for over an hour already, mostly listening to the detective tell stories. Unlike his father, Detective Goforth seemed kind and jolly. "I may need to question you again, so don't go far. Good to see you again, Miss Eliza. I've missed you at the Yard." He smiled. "Now, on to the next room to question the rest of the *suspects*, er, *witnesses*."

Eliza smiled at the kindly detective.

Too bad he was no longer the best at his job. It wasn't his fault. Theo had read that during the war, the inspector took a nasty blow to the head with the butt of a German rifle. Like so many men, he'd never been the same after the war.

Theo lifted his head. He was both exhausted and agitated. He needed to calm down. To take his mind off Neville, the detective... and most of all his father. It was probably too late to go to Gambit. Then again, some nights players hung around next door at the pub waiting to pick up games and then played until dawn.

"I'm going to Gambit," Theo said, gathering up his coat and hat. "Want to come along?"

"For a game?" Eliza's face lit up.

"What else?" Theo shrugged into his overcoat.

"With you?" She smirked.

"Probably not." Theo couldn't tell her the real reason he didn't want to play against her. "I concentrate better during a game."

"You mean, you concentrate *on* the game." She tapped a close-fitting woolen hat atop her bobbed blonde curls. "I've seen the way you play."

"No. *Everything*. Including the game, of course." Still

thinking of his father, he exhaled a big breath. "Playing helps clear my mind. It helps me see the patterns on the board... and off." What patterns would emerge in Neville Lively's murder?

"Since you like games so much." She tugged on her gloves. "How about we place a little wager on who can solve the mystery of Neville's murder?"

He cocked his head. "You mean a competition?"

"Exactly." She smiled. "If I win, then you play me in chess." She buttoned up her coat.

He couldn't help but return her smile. "And if I win?"

"You name it." She shrugged. "Whatever you want... so long as it's not more than a quid."

*Anything I want?* His mind raced through a catalogue of payments he would love to receive from her—none of them monetary. He blushed. "You're on."

# 6

## MISSING PERSON

Eliza stood at the sink, scrubbing a breakfast plate. Queenie sat next to her looking up with those honeyed eyes, hoping for a scrap.

"Golly." Jane looked up from her newspaper. "Have you seen the headlines?"

Eight years ago, Eliza read her last headline. The one that still held her hostage: *Tragedy at Docks*. She hadn't read the story. She hadn't needed to. She'd been there, a helpless witness. No. More than that. An active participant. The guilty party. The match that lit the fuse. Since then, she wasn't much for newspapers. Anyway, she already knew what this morning's headline was about. No doubt, it was a report on Neville Lively's death at Café Royal during the Detection Club's secret initiation ritual.

"Agatha Christie has disappeared." Jane sat blinking. "Didn't you see her last night? When Mr. Lively was killed?"

"Let me see that." Eliza quickly wiped her hands on her apron and then grabbed the newspaper. Queenie barked. The headline read:

Mystery of Woman Novelist's Disappearance

What in the world? Had she flown the coop to escape the police? Was her illness last night feigned? Eliza quickly read the article.

The paper said her car, a Bullnose two-seater, was found halfway down a bank with its bonnet buried in some bushes above a chalk quarry near Newlands Corner. A fur coat and dressing case were still in the car. Her husband, who had been staying with friends, had no idea of her whereabouts. A witness reported seeing an underdressed woman behaving strangely who may have drowned herself in a nearby river or fallen into a gravel pit. The police suspected foul play.

She glanced down at Queenie. The dog was a respectable scenthound. She was half-tempted to take Queenie out there and join the search. Why would Agatha abandon her car in the middle of nowhere?

Cripes. Had Agatha disappeared because she was guilty of murdering Neville? It looked mighty suspicious. She feigned illness, left the crime scene, and then disappeared the very next morning. Might as well have been a signed confession. And if she didn't run away because she was guilty... was she the second victim? Was someone picking off the members of the Detection Club one by one? A shiver ran through her. In that case, who was next? Dorothy? Theo?

She dashed to the closet and threw on her coat and hat. Queenie spun circles around her as she went.

"Where are you going?" Jane asked.

"I've got to find Theo." She had a pretty good idea where to find him. When she jammed her hands in her coat pockets, she felt Neville's keys. "Don't worry, Queenie." She patted the dog. "I'll be back soon."

"Theo. Not Theodore Sharp, that strange friend of poor Reggie Hall? May he rest in peace." Her sister gave her an odd look. "Where did you run into him?"

"The Gambit." Hadn't she mentioned she'd found Theo? She was sure she had. Their adoptive older brother Reggie used to take her to university to visit. That was how she knew Theo. But Jane only met Theo once when Reggie brought him home on holiday, and that was at least ten years ago now, back when she and Jane were just girls.

"The Gambit." Jane shook her head. "I should have known."

Eliza blew her sister a kiss and then flew out the door.

\* \* \*

As she suspected, when she arrived at Gambit Chess Rooms, Theo was deep in match with a wayward duke. Given chess helped him concentrate, she hoped he was concentrating on who killed Neville Lively and what happened to Agatha Christie, who was, after all, one of the prime suspects in the case.

Without looking up from the board, Theo gave her a wiggly fingered wave. She stood the requisite two feet away so as not to distract the players. She was heartened to see most of the pieces lined up alongside the board. Hopefully, Theo would trounce the duke and get it over with soon so she could find out what he knew about Agatha's disappearance.

*Come on, Theo. Beat him.*

Theo moved his bishop into what looked like a trap. Was he making a strategic sacrifice? Or was he distracted? She held her breath.

While she watched and waited, in her mind, for the dozenth time, she reviewed the evidence she'd found at the scene. The twin guns, the embroidered handkerchief, the bloody footprint. How did they fit together? Better yet, who had a motive to murder Neville Lively? Of course, Agatha was upset he tried to get her expelled from the club. But surely that wasn't a reason to kill him. Could it have been someone from outside? An idea formed in her mind. Perhaps the killer had been harmed by Neville's ridiculous radio prank. *Broadcasting from the Barricades*. The fake revolution had made her angry enough to consider telling him off. But not bumping him off.

"Checkmate!" Theo beamed. "Rotten luck, old man."

Eliza knew it wasn't luck. Theo was the best player at the club. He hadn't lost a game yet. But only because he refused to play her. She could take him. If only he'd play.

"Did you hear the news about Agatha?" Theo asked, setting up the board again.

"That's why I'm here." When the duke stood up, Eliza took his seat.

"Not to play?" He smiled.

"You want to play me?" She cocked her head. "Now?"

"Let's just say I have a different game in mind." His cheeks turned a pretty shade of pink. "What if we think of our murder mystery as a game of chess?" He collected the notes the duke had thrown on the table. "With Neville as the defeated king."

"Interesting idea." Eliza reached across the table and brushed a stray eyelash from Theo's cheek, which went from pink to scarlet.

"The king isn't the most powerful piece on the board, but he is the most important." Theo stuffed the notes into his pocket.

"And the queen is the most powerful piece on the board because of her mobility." She smiled. "Agatha Christie is the queen. The missing queen... and possibly the guilty queen."

"Anthony can be the knight." Theo moved the white knight to square f3.

"Because he moves sideways, is sneaky, and can jump over others?" She moved the black knight. "But not so good at close combat or defense."

"And Gilbert Chesterton is the bishop." He moved the bishop diagonally across the entire length of the board. "Just because he's not close by doesn't mean he's not a threat. He can swoop across the board out of nowhere."

"Clever." She smiled. "How about Fergus Briggs as our rook?"

"Another treacherous piece that can come out of nowhere for an attack." Theo nodded. "That makes Maud and Dorothy our pawns."

"Not necessarily." She raised her eyebrows. "We have two knights and two rooks."

"And two bishops," he added.

"I say we make Dorothy another knight. She's sneaky and loves to wear capes." She fingered the black knight. "Maud can stay a pawn."

He chuckled. "And what's our opening move?"

"Looks like you've started with the King's Indian opening. Bold move." She reached in her pocket and pulled out the key ring. "But don't you think first we should find out whether our king is black or white?" She dangled the keys. "And whether our pieces are on his side or playing against him? And who made the first move? Him or his opponent."

"Find out more about our king." Theo stood up. "Makes sense. Although it's too late to protect him, by working backwards, we can at least find out how he was defeated and, in the process, protect the Detection Club... and find Agatha."

"Madame Secretary would be thrilled if we solve the

mystery before the police do." She adjusted her hat. "Hopefully, we'll find out who took our missing queen in the process. Unless, of course, she killed Neville and that's why she's on the run."

"Shall we?" He held out his hand to her. "The game's afoot."

When she took his hand, dimples formed at the edges of his smile. And she couldn't help but smile in return.

* * *

They hailed a taxi and within twenty minutes, Eliza was standing at the door of Neville's building in South Kensington. She used the large, round key in the outer door lock. It worked. Theo followed her inside. She pressed the buzzer for 4B, Neville's flat. He wouldn't be there, of course. But someone else might. While they waited, she slipped the tiny key off the ring, unclasped her necklace, and slid the key onto her chain. She reclasped it around her neck. Just in case she had to surrender the key ring.

"Does he have a wife?" she asked. "Or a live-in maid?"

"His wife left him last year," Theo said. "Not sure about a maid." He shoved his hands in his pockets. "If I'm not mistaken, his daughter lives in Chelsea and his son is just back from India."

"They were both at the dinner last night." She tried the keys on the ring until she found one that opened the inner door. "Did they both get on well with their father?"

"I know Neville and his daughter were close." Theo shrugged. "Not sure about the son. I think he's been away for years."

They headed up the stairs to flat 4B. When they reached the

door, she fumbled with the keys, searching for the right one. She inserted a clover-shaped number but the door swung open before she'd turned it in the lock.

A petite woman with graying hair stood in the doorway. "Can I help you?" Her eyes were red and puffy. She was wearing a black dress with a starched white apron. "I'm afraid Mr. Neville has..." Her voice broke. "Passed away." Her lip trembled. "And Mr. Barnaby has gone out."

"Probably on a bender," Theo whispered.

"Might we trouble you to answer a few questions?" Eliza peeked over the woman's shoulder, taking in the flat. It was on the top floor and even from the doorway, she could see it had large picture windows. "I know it's a difficult time, but we're trying to help."

"We're friends of Neville's from the Detection Club." Theo gave the woman a disarming smile. "We were with him last night," he added softly. "I'm Theodore Sharp and this is my friend Eliza Baker."

The woman nodded. "I'm Mrs. Green, the housekeeper." She ushered them inside. "Would you like a cup of tea?" She sniffed. "Mr. Neville loved his Earl Grey, he did." She led them into a sitting room. "Have you tried chocolate biscuits?" She shook her head. "Mr. Neville loved his chocolate." Standing next to a high-backed chair, she bade them sit down on a sofa. "He had a real sweet tooth, he did."

"Thank you, no," Eliza said.

Theo shook his head. Although she could tell from his expression he was disappointed.

The sitting room was furnished in dark colors with heavy burgundy drapes. Stale cigar smoke clung to the wallpaper and made the place feel masculine and den-like. Mrs. Green gently laid her hand on the arm of the large chair. "Mr. Neville sat here reading them books for hours on end." She nodded toward the fireplace. "Loved a rip-roaring fire, too." Wrapping her arms around her torso, she went to the fireplace. "Should I light it for you?"

"Not on our account," Eliza said even though the place was freezing.

"I haven't felt much like myself today." Mrs. Green picked at a piece of imaginary lint on her dress. "Ever since I got the news." She sniffled. "Such a good man, he was."

Eliza nodded. "I'm sure he was."

"A darn good writer, too." Theo pointed at the writing desk in the corner. "Is that where he wrote his novels?"

"Reading and writing." Mrs. Green smiled wistfully. "All day and half the night. I'd bring him a cup of cocoa at ten and he was still going at it. Typing away." She crossed to the desk and laid her hand on a typewriter. "Clicky-clack, half the night." She tutted. "But I didn't mind." She stroked the typewriter like it was a favorite pet.

"So, you live here, then?" Eliza asked.

"Oh yes." She went back to stand by Neville's chair. "For over thirty years. Ever since Mr. Neville and Miss Holly were married." She smiled. "Miss Holly, bless her soul, doted on the mister. He hasn't been the same since she went away."

"What do you mean? When did she go?" Eliza hugged herself for warmth. "And how did he change?" She knew first-hand that grief had a way of changing people. Like a tiny weevil, it could eat away until it felled even the strongest tree.

"Oh, about a year ago. That's when the master started leaving his supper untouched." She tutted. "Sometimes, he didn't eat his pudding. Then even his fancy chocolate biscuits couldn't tempt him." Closing her eyes, she exhaled a long sigh. "He plum lost his appetite for life, he did."

*And now he's dead.* Eliza shifted on the sofa, wondering if any of this was useful information. "If you don't mind my asking, where did Mrs. Lively go exactly?"

"Oh, she's living in Cambridge." Mrs. Green shook her head. "Terrible thing, that. She was good for Mr. Neville. I'm sure she intended to come back to him. But now..." She pressed her palms together as if in prayer.

"Do you happen to know why she left?" Eliza picked at the sleeve of her blouse, hoping she appeared nonchalant.

"Oh, I couldn't say." Mrs. Green made a sour face. "Needed a break, I suppose. Poor Mr. Neville missed her so. But Mr. Barnaby coming home cheered him considerably." Mrs. Green smiled. "He's such a good boy."

"I'd heard Neville wasn't too pleased about Barnaby hopping off to India." Theo tilted his head. "Were they on good terms lately?"

Mrs. Green looked pensive. She studied her apron string for a few seconds. "It's a blessing they made up in time."

*Just in time.* A coincidence? "Will the children split the estate, then?" Eliza said cautiously. She knew the answer was most likely "no." During the war, women worked alongside men and took over many important jobs, but the inheritance laws still favored sons over daughters.

"I couldn't say." Mrs. Green refused to make eye contact. *She knows something.* "It's not my place to say."

"I can tell you were very fond of Mr. Lively," Eliza said carefully.

"That I was." Mrs. Green peered down at her. "He was always kind to me."

Eliza cleared her throat. "Someone shot him last night." She looked at Theo. "And we intend to find out who did it."

"And bring the killer to justice," Theo added. "Won't you help us, Mrs. Green?" His dark eyes were soft. "Won't you help us get justice for Neville?"

"How can I help?" She glanced around the room nervously as if looking for something or someone. "I don't know anything." She wrung her hands in her apron. "Except..." A light switched on in her eyes. "Last week, Mr. Neville received something strange."

"What?" Eliza asked.

"A note." Mrs. Green jumped up. "I'll fetch it." She disappeared from the room. A minute later, she was back with a slip of paper in her hands. She held it out to Eliza. "Came in the post, it did."

Eliza read it.

You can't get rid of me so easily. Consider this a warning.

She passed the note to Theo.

He whistled. "A threat from the killer?"

She pointed to the word *rid*. "Look, the letter r is askew." She glanced up at Mrs. Green. "Do you have the envelope it arrived in? Exactly when did it arrive? And how? By courier or by post?"

Theo laid his hand on her sleeve. "Maybe ask one question at a time."

"Sorry." She gazed up at Mrs. Green with expectant eyes. "The envelope?"

She shook her head. "I think Mr. Neville tossed it out."

"A mystery writer tosses out a clue." Theo scoffed. "Not likely."

"Someone was threatening him." Eliza took the note from Theo's hand. She examined it again. "If we could find the typewriter, one with a twisted r-key, we'll find our killer." She turned to Mrs. Green. "May I keep this?"

"Be my guest." Mrs. Green returned to her chair.

"Who might have sent it?" Eliza asked.

"I have no idea." Mrs. Green went back to troubling her apron strings.

"I wonder if you could tell us more about Neville's relationship with his children." Eliza softened her gaze. "Who inherits now that Neville is gone? I'm sorry to be so direct, but it's important to the case."

"I shouldn't say..." She looked around again.

Eliza gave an encouraging smile. "It's alright. We won't tell anyone." *Unless it can be used as evidence by Scotland Yard.*

"Well, years ago." She lowered her voice to a whisper. "When Mr. Barnaby defied his father and left for India, Mr. Neville cut him out of the will." She gave one nod as if that settled it. "Everything was to go to Miss Alice."

"*Was?*" Eliza asked. "Not *is?*"

Mrs. Green dropped into the chair and held onto the arms with both hands. "When Mr. Barnaby came home"—she leaned forward—"and they made their peace." She bit her lip. "Well, Mr. Neville called for his lawyer to change his will."

Theo whipped his head around and gave Eliza a knowing look. He turned back to Mrs. Green. "So, Neville just changed his will to make Barnaby the beneficiary?"

"That's just it." Mrs. Green sniffled. "He didn't get the chance." She troubled her apron string. "His appointment with the lawyer was scheduled for this afternoon."

Blimey. Now there was a motive. The oldest in the book. Miss Alice had all the reason in the world to kill her father. So long as she did it before he made a new will. Eliza leaned over and whispered in Theo's ear, "We need to get a look at Alice's shoes."

"Let's go find our Cinderella," he whispered back.

She folded the threatening note and tucked it into her chatelaine bag.

\* \* \*

Were Alice and Barnaby Lively merely pawns in some greater scheme of their father's? Theo knew the importance of pawns. They seemed unassuming, but they often meant the difference between winning and losing. He thought of his own father's scheme, if he could call it a scheme. More like the way of the world. Rich men inherit from other rich men who pass it on to their sons and so on. But Theo refused to be defined by the title or his father's wealth. He planned to make it on his own. Without his father breathing down his neck.

As he held the front door open for Eliza, a man slipped inside. Despite his bluster and low-brimmed hat, Theo recognized him as Barnaby Lively. The housekeeper had mentioned Barnaby was staying at his father's flat.

"Barnaby." Theo reached out and touched the other man's sleeve.

"Do I know you?" Barnaby jerked his arm away. He smelled of liquor and his eyes were glassy. Obviously, Barnaby thought the answer to his grief could be found at the bottom of a glass. Poor lad.

"We met last night at the Detection Club dinner." Theo wondered if his drinking had impaired his memory. "At Café Royal."

"Oh." Barnaby's shoulders slumped. "Right. Sorry." He gave

Eliza a nod and a weak smile. Whatever his relationship with his father, death had a way of refocusing one's life.

"I realize this is a difficult time for you." Eliza stepped back inside the foyer. "But do you mind if we ask you a few questions?"

"About what?" Barnaby's eyes flashed like a caged animal's.

"About your father." Theo lowered his gaze.

Why was Barnaby so nervous? Did he have something to hide?

"What about him?" Barnaby gritted his teeth.

"Wondering how you found him after being away for so long?" Theo said.

"Found him?" Barnaby scoffed. "I hadn't been home a month and he took to ordering me around like one of the servants." He sighed. "I was always a disappointment to him." His lips spread into an exaggerated grin. "Disappointment is a two-way street."

Perhaps Barnaby wasn't grieving his father. Perhaps he felt relief that his father was dead.

"So, you didn't get along?" Eliza tilted her head.

"Understatement of the century." He sneered. "He ruined my life."

"How so?" Theo was still holding the door open.

"Have you got all day?" Barnaby shook his head. "Let's just say the old man had it in for me from day one. Don't ask me why. I couldn't tell you."

"Is that why you shot him?" Eliza blurted out.

Theo let go of the door. He couldn't believe Eliza had just accused Barnaby of patricide. And if he was a killer, he was dangerous. Not a man to be confronted in a doorway. He gave Eliza a stern look.

"Sorry." Eliza shrugged. "I didn't mean to be so blunt."

Barnaby laughed. A big, guttural laugh that made his shoulders shake. "Are you mad? Why would I kill him? Do you go around killing everyone who annoys you? I certainly don't."

Eliza narrowed her gaze. "What about his will?" She continued her direct line of interrogation despite Theo's hand on her sleeve.

"What about it?" Barnaby shrugged. "You'd best ask Alice about that." He twisted his torso as if he was shrugging a hand off his shoulder. "If you're done cross-examining me, I'm going upstairs for a nap."

"Why did you come back from India?" Eliza asked pointedly. She might as well shine a bright light into his eyes and put toothpicks under his fingernails. What was her problem? Hadn't she ever lost someone she loved? Theo had lost only a pet dog and that was bad enough to send him to bed for a month.

Barnaby scowled. "The old man wrote and said he was dying." He let out an audible breath. "I should never have come. Too late now. I'm here, unfortunately." With that, he turned and entered the stairwell.

Was Neville sick? He'd never mentioned it. Or was the letter a ploy to get his son to return to England?

"We need to get the name of Neville's doctor."

Theo gestured to Eliza. He waited for her to cross the threshold and then followed her out onto the street.

A kid in a newsboy cap hawking newspapers called out, "Reward for finding missing novelist. Read all about it."

Theo reached into his pocket for some change and handed the boy a coin. Sprawled across the front page of the *Daily Mail* were pictures of Agatha with her daughter, men beating the bushes, and a man named Jack with his collie dog who apparently found Agatha's car.

"Any news?" Eliza stood behind him, peering over his shoulder. "Have they found Agatha?"

He felt her warmth behind him and shivered. "Not yet." He pushed dark thoughts from his mind. "It's up to us to recover our queen."

# 7

## KING'S PAWN

Alice Lively lived in a flat above a flower shop on Pont Street in Chelsea. Eliza rang the bell. No answer. She was about to give up when Anthony Berkeley Cox stepped out of the front door. She grabbed the door before it could close.

"Greetings." Theo held out his hand to Anthony. "Fancy meeting you here."

"Why are you here, Mr. Cox?" Eliza asked, still holding the door open.

"Same reason you are, I presume." Anthony shook Theo's hand. "To console poor Alice."

"Not to question her about her father's murder?" Eliza cocked her head.

"Good heavens." Anthony ran a hand through his thick hair, which was unusually disheveled. "You don't think Alice had anything to do with it? My money is on that philosopher chap, Russell. He's quite the womanizer and word on the street is he's having an affair with Neville's wife and that's why she left him." With a tug on the waistband, he adjusted his trousers. "Imagine, the man is young enough to be her son."

"What was the professor's motive?" Eliza looked up into Anthony's smooth face. "Why would he kill Neville now?"

"Neville was a catholic and didn't believe in divorce." Anthony shrugged. "I suppose Russell saw murder as the only option."

"Given the age difference," Eliza said, "would the professor seriously consider marrying a woman a decade older than himself?"

"Seems a bit extreme." Theo raised his eyebrows. "If she's living with him in Cambridge, then what difference does it make if she's divorced? Anyway, I thought Professor Russell was already married."

"Divorce isn't as lucrative as murder." Anthony buttoned his overcoat. "My gut tells me to look for a life insurance policy."

"Are you suggesting the professor killed Neville so Mrs. Lively could collect a life insurance policy?" Theo looked incredulous. "Admittedly, a philosophy professor doesn't make a lot of money, but still... murder? Seems far-fetched."

"Passion and money are the top two motives for murder." Anthony smiled. "The combination is even more potent."

"You and your combinations." Theo smirked.

"Never wear the blooming things." Anthony winked. "Haven't since I was an infant."

Eliza had no idea what they were on about. "Underwear jokes aside, where was the professor during the initiation ceremony?" Eliza turned to Theo. "Was he still in the dining room or had he left with the other guests?"

"I'm not sure, come to think of it." Theo scratched his head. "Maybe Alice will know."

"Alice is distraught," Anthony said. "Please treat her with kid gloves. Poor girl is already sick with grief."

"Of course." Theo nodded.

"You don't happen to know where Agatha's gone, do you?"

Eliza watched his face for a reaction. There was something about Mr. Anthony Berkeley Cox that was too slick, too debonair, too smooth to be believable.

"Another crime of passion." Anthony sighed. "Poor Agatha. Her handsome lieutenant chasing his secretary." He shook his head. "The ways things are going, I wouldn't be surprised if they divorce." He tutted. "Agatha will need all our love and support."

"Of course," Theo said, again. "But where is she? Where has she gone?"

"Probably some place to drown her sorrows." Anthony tipped his hat onto his head.

"Hopefully, that's all she's drowned," Eliza said under her breath. "Before you go." She lifted the chain around her neck to hold up the little key. "Do you recognize this key? It was on Mr. Lively's key ring."

He shook his head. "Never seen it before." He doffed his hat. "*Ciao.*"

After Anthony bounded down the pavement, Eliza gestured Theo through the front door and then headed up the stairs. When she reached Alice's door, she knocked.

"Oh, Tony, dearest, you're back," came the voice from the other side of the door. Alice flung the door open and then stood staring at them. "Apologies." She nervously patted her hair and then picked up a black veil from a side table. "I thought you were someone else." She covered her head with the veil.

Obviously. *Tony, dearest.* How well did she know Anthony Berkeley Cox? With a wife, a mistress, and a girlfriend, no wonder his mind turned to crimes of passion.

Eliza peeked over Alice's shoulder, trying to get a look inside. The flat was decorated in light colors and gave the impression of a sweet shop with all its pastel bobbles and knickknacks. Alice looked out of place in her plain black dress and veil. Even with the veil, it was obvious she'd been crying. If she had killed her father, either she was genuinely remorseful or a darn good actress.

"May we come in?" Eliza said after it became evident Alice was not going to invite them inside.

"Oh, sorry." Alice took a step back. "I'm really not in the mood for visitors."

"We'll keep it short," Theo said. "Just a couple questions about your father, if we may."

"Are you from the police?" Alice bit her lip. "Oh, wait. You're from the Detection Club." She gave a weak smile. "I knew I recognized you." She stood in her entryway and didn't invite them in any further. "How can I help you?"

Eliza peered down at her shoes to see if they fit the bill for the bloody footprint. They did not. Alice wasn't wearing proper shoes. She was wearing feathery pink slippers. Only when staring at her feet did Eliza notice the plain black dress was not a dress at all but a dressing gown. Had Alice just got out of bed?

"Your brother told us he came back because your father was dying." Eliza studied Alice. "Is that true?"

Alice's cheeks reddened. "Barney exaggerates."

"Is it true your father was going to change his will?" Eliza softened her tone. "I know this is difficult for you, but we're trying to help."

"Help?" Alice's lip trembled. "What gives you the right to come to my home and treat me like a criminal?"

"We don't think you're a criminal," Theo said in a reassuring tone. "We just wondered if you noticed anything odd about your father recently. Or, if you knew why anyone might want to harm him." He gave Eliza the evil eye. She took the hint and shut up.

"No one would want to harm Daddy." She sniffled. "He was always so kind and lovable. He loved practical jokes and tricks, but always in good fun."

"Like the radio hoax?" Eliza couldn't help herself.

"Hoax?" Alice narrowed her brows. "Oh, you mean *Broadcasting from the Barricades*." Her face relaxed. "Father was just having fun." She waved the whole absurd thing away. "He was always up to something."

"What of your mother?" Eliza asked. "If you don't mind me asking..." She glanced over at Theo, who was scowling at her.

"Mum?" Alice frowned. "I haven't spoken to her since she left home."

"Did she have any reason to... to harm your father?" Eliza continued her questioning, despite Theo's faces.

"You think Mummy had him shot?" The color drained from Alice's face. "Barney! He's told you about the life insurance."

So, it was true. Neville had bought a life insurance policy. And his estranged wife, Holly, was the beneficiary, provided what Mrs. Green had told them was also true. It was clear that both the estranged wife and doting daughter stood to benefit from Neville's death. Holly Lively was not at the Detection Club dinner. But she could have had her lover do the deed. Alice was there. Could she have shot her father, dropped the gun at his side, and then fled the room? Thus, the bloody footprint.

"Your mother wasn't there," Eliza said slowly, "but you were."

If Alice got any paler, she'd be transparent. She hugged herself and swayed back and forth. "I adored him. I loved my father." Her voice trembled. "I'd never..." She sobbed. "I'm going to be sick." Hand over her mouth, she ran into her flat.

"Eliza, come on." Theo took her elbow. "Let's go and leave

the poor woman alone." He led her out of the flat. "You know, sometimes, you can be cruel."

"Why?" she said once they were outside. "Because I don't beat around the bush?" She tightened her lips. "Because I'm not a whimpering, helpless girl?" She jerked out of his grasp.

"No." Theo let out a loud exhale. "Because *occasionally*, you can be thoughtless and even a bit mean."

"And what if Alice is our killer?" Eliza gave her head a self-satisfied tilt.

"I doubt it." Theo held the door open for her.

"Because she's a pretty woman?" Eliza knew from her own experience what pretty women could get away with. During the war, she'd even once or twice tailed a foreign national to get intel because the captain thought a "pretty girl" with blonde curls and smile could go places a man couldn't. It was a wonder what a tight corset and girly frock could do to a man. She pulled her coat tight against the December breeze.

"Because her feet are too big." He tilted his head. "I mean, they look bigger than the bloody footprints."

She squinted at him. "She was wearing big old fluffy slippers so how could you tell anything?" Perhaps her tone had been a tad bit too sharp. Afterall, why shouldn't he know about women's footwear?

"No need to get snippy." He clapped his gloved hands together as if to chase away the cold.

"I'm not snippy." Eliza tried not to sound defensive. Jane often accused her of being prickly. It wasn't cruelty or meanness but a desire for the truth. Plain and simple. She didn't like playing games, except for chess, of course. And back in the day, pickpocketing had been a game. Even espionage had been a game of sorts. And look where that got her. If losing Billy taught her anything, it was that life was not a game. "Not all chance is a game."

Theo gave her a curious look, and she realized she'd said it out loud. "I prefer games of skill," he said. "Like chess and detection."

"Or catching killers." She turned to face him. In the afternoon light, his eyes looked almost as gray as the sky. "Like our little wager on who can find Neville's murderer." The smell of roasted chestnuts floated on the breeze. "And if one of us finds Agatha too..." She licked her lips. "That's frosting on the cake."

He averted his eyes. "I do love cake."

"For now, how about some roasted chestnuts?" She pulled him toward a street vendor who had a brazier on a cart. "Where are *you* going next?" She was deciding between paying a visit to Holly Lively in Cambridge or seeing Dorothy. She was supposed to go to Dorothy's this afternoon anyway, unless Dorothy wanted to cancel given the circumstances. Knowing Dorothy, she was probably deep into her own investigation of the murder... or with the police out hunting for Agatha.

"Why should I tell you?" His eyes danced. "And give away my strategic advantage." He handed the vendor a coin and in return was given a paper bag full of warm chestnuts. He held the bag out to her.

"If detection comes down to deduction, as you and your writer friends maintain..." She reached into the bag and pulled out a chestnut. She held it between her gloved palms for welcome relief from the cold. "Then the test won't come down to empirical evidence so much as logical thought." Peeling the chestnut, she chuckled. "For my part, gut instincts, logical deduction, and poetic interpretation are all well and good. But I'm putting my stake on cold, hard forensics." She popped the heart of the chestnut into her mouth. The heat of sweet, buttery flesh spread and warmed her.

"So, this is a test of my wits against your evidence." Theo bounced on his heels. "The abstract versus the concrete." He was still holding the bag out to her. He asked the vendor for a napkin and presented it to her.

"Philosophy versus science." She took his arm. "Whether we investigate together or separately doesn't matter as much as our *means* of investigation." She had to admit, strolling down the pavement of the posh neighborhood, arm-in-arm, eating warm chestnuts on a cold winter day was nice.

"Don't you mean our different *philosophies* of investigation?" Theo grinned and gently shook the bag. "Like our philosophies of chess. Art versus science?" He tilted his head. "Why not both? Why does it have to be either/or?"

"My method will involve forensic science." She plucked another chestnut from the bag. "Not hocus pocus."

"I suppose you have some device you can attach to our suspect's temples to extract the truth." He held the bag out to her again.

She shook her head.

"Or some other *hocus pocus*." He folded the bag and stuffed it into his coat pocket.

"I'll have you know, there are machines that detect the truth using blood pressure." She let go his arm. "They're called polygraph machines."

"And don't forget about truth serums," he teased. "We could slip a few drops into our suspect's tea." He giggled. "Although a few strong whiskeys might have more effect."

"An argument for starting our investigation by interrogating the biggest drinkers."

"Not necessarily." He winked. "The regular drinkers can

hold their alcohol and thereby hold their tongues. Give a teeto-taler strong drink and the outcome is less predictable."

"In that case." She glanced at her watch. "I think we should pay a visit to Dorothy." Although Dorothy was hardly a teeto-taler, Eliza was expected there for work in an hour.

"My thoughts exactly." Theo nodded. "My *gut* tells me she's hiding something."

"Such a sensitive gut." Eliza reached up to brush a stray lock of hair from Theo's face. "And why does your gut suspect Dorothy?"

"Let's use a combination of inductive and deductive reason-ing, ala Professor Russell, shall we?" He held up his hand. "First, she didn't want us to call the police. And she seemed in a hurry to whisk Agatha away, number two." He counted on his fingers. "Third, didn't you tell me she ran off to Cowley at the drop of a hat?"

He was right. She had told him about Cowley and he had no idea what was so important to her there either.

A smile cracked his face. "And the green thread. The one I found on the handle of the gun."

"What about it?"

"I'll bet you last month's winnings it came from Dorothy's green cape." He raised an eyebrow. "How about we go find out?"

"You're on!" She took his arm.

\* \* \*

Walking arm-in-arm with Eliza was both enchanting and torture. The touch of her hand on Theo's sleeve made his pulse quicken. Her laughter simultaneously brightened his mood and cut him like broken glass. He imagined himself in a romantic novel, something nineteenth century, maybe *Wuthering Heights*.

He would be Heathcliff and she would be Catherine. Not a fortuitous comparison. Heathcliff was an arrogant arse and Catherine was selfish and cruel, not to mention she died and abandoned Heathcliff to degeneration. Perhaps, one of Victor Hugo's creations would be more felicitous. Or better yet, Jane Austen.

Or better yet, he would write their story. A great love story. How would he start? Would it be driven by rich characters? Or driven by its scintillating plot? And what of its metaphors? Those necessary crutches upon which prose limped behind experience. Writers needed metaphors because words were never up to the task of conveying the warm blood coursing through the veins of life. He longed for a writing instrument that, like a syringe, would inject his prose with the vital fluids of fleshly existence.

How pompous he was. Thinking he could write anything great. Romance or otherwise. The best he could do with his writing was tie experience to a chair and beat the life out of it with a pipe.

# 8

## KING'S KNIGHT

Eliza followed Dorothy into her study. Theo and the three cats trailed behind. The curtains were closed and the room was dimly lit by only a banker's lamp on the desk. Shelves filled with books lined two walls, making the room feel even smaller. Neatly arranged newspaper clippings about Agatha's disappearance were jigsawed across the desk.

"I'm helping the police with the investigation," Dorothy said, blushing. "They think I might have insight into the mind of an author."

"Have you made any progress?" Theo examined the clippings.

"Not really." Dorothy sucked her teeth. "And every passing hour extinguishes hopes of finding her alive."

"What about her husband?" Eliza joined them at the desk.

"I'm afraid Colonel Christie just asked her for a divorce." Dorothy knitted her brows. "He's marrying his secretary, Nancy Neele." She shook her head. "Men. Too bad we can only kill them off in fiction."

"If the last war is any indication"—Theo looked up from the

news clipping—"men are fairly good at dispatching each other. We don't need women to do it for us."

"Do you think Colonel Christie murdered his wife?" Saying it out loud gave Eliza a start. She shivered. "And disposed of her body in some remote location?"

"Dear God." Dorothy clasped her hands together. "I sincerely hope not. Poor Agatha." She crossed the room and dropped into a loveseat in front of the fireplace.

Eliza shifted through the clippings. A photograph of Agatha and her husband Archie stared up at her. She picked up the clipping for a closer look. Wearing swimming attire and holding surfboards, they both sported wide smiles. The caption read:

Mr. and Mrs. Christie surfing in Hawaii

"Adventurous sorts." Eliza laid the paper back onto the desk. "Perhaps Agatha is off on an adventure of her own."

"I hope she is enjoying herself." Dorothy's lips disappeared into a thin line. "She's got half the country out looking for her." Her eyes softened along with her tone. "Poor dear. As long as she's alright."

"Her disappearance must have something to do with Neville's murder." Eliza took a seat in an easy chair across from Dorothy. The outside cold clung to her like a shroud and the proximity to the fire was a welcome relief.

"It's an awful coincidence if it doesn't." Dorothy shook her head.

She'd learned from her short-lived career at Scotland Yard, there were no such things as coincidences when it came to homicide. Technically, of course, as a lowly woman, she hadn't been assigned to homicide. Then again, the Met assumed women couldn't be murderers either.

"If only he hadn't gone on about Agatha's novel not playing fair with the reader." Dorothy waved her hand as if chasing away a bad smell. "And all that rot about kicking her out of the club. Totally ridiculous."

"You think it got under her skin?" Theo asked, not looking up from an article he was reading. "It would mine."

"I suspect Agatha has thicker skin than all of us." Dorothy's hand trembled as she lit a cigarette. "At least I hope so."

"Bad business about Neville." Holding his hands out to the fire, Theo sat on the edge of Eliza's chair. "Did you notice anything unusual before the ceremony?"

"Other than Neville needling poor Agatha and making those absurd arguments to expel her?" Dorothy shook her head. "And the ceremony came off beautifully until that fateful shot." She reached for a notebook on a side table. "We followed my script more or less exactly." She passed the notebook to Theo. "Even Gilbert went along with my script." She sighed. "Then Neville had to go and ruin it by getting himself killed." Fiddling with a pencil, she stared into the fire.

Eliza cocked her head. Lots of people could want Neville dead. He was behind the radio hoax, which no doubt angered a lot of concerned listeners. He had disowned his only son and alienated his wife. He was adamant about Agatha's transgressions and tried to get her expelled from the club. But were any of those reasons to kill him? Money seemed the most likely motive so far.

Dorothy gave Theo a sympathetic smile. "I'm sorry Theodore that your initiation was such a mess."

"It wasn't your fault," Theo said, standing to move closer to the fire. "Let's just hope we're as good at solving murder mysteries as our fictional detectives." His eyes twinkled in the firelight. "What would Lord Peter Wimsey do?" He handed the notebook to Eliza.

From Eliza's limited experience at the Yard, lords and ladies could be awful nuisances when it came to investigations. She thumbed through the notebook, examining Dorothy's notes for the ceremony. "Who is Lord Peter Wimsey?" she asked. She immediately regretted it when she remembered he was Dorothy L. Sayers's aristocratic sleuth. What was with these women writing prissy men detectives? She thought of Mrs. Christie's Hercule Poirot and his precious mustache.

Dorothy gave a half-embarrassed laugh. "He'd hop in his Daimler double-six and waste no time in finding Agatha." She stood and announced, "And I plan to do the same, only on my trusty Ner-A-Car."

Eliza chuckled to herself thinking of Dorothy on her motorcycle wearing those silly goggles.

"I'm just sorry I can't take you two along." She gestured to the door.

"Before you go." Eliza looked up from the notebook. "Did you make any notes of who had which weapon?"

"I didn't." Dorothy troubled the hem of her jacket. "And how did that Webley get into Agatha's bag?"

"Who owns that gun?" Theo asked. "Is it Agatha's?"

"Neville loaned us one Webley but I don't know about the second." She shrugged. "Agatha acted surprised when it fell from her handbag. So, someone else must have put it there."

"Her estranged husband, perhaps?" Eliza asked. Outside war, most killings were crimes of passion. Had Colonel Christie planted the Webley in Agatha's bag to use later? Or did she have plans to use it on him? If she'd used it to kill Neville, she'd been very sneaky and quick to shoot him and get it back into her handbag without anyone noticing. "Or maybe she was lying."

"Agatha doesn't lie." Dorothy furrowed her brows.

"Everyone lies." Eliza closed the notebook and laid it on a side table.

"And everyone has secrets." Theo stood up. "Lies and secrets are the meat and potatoes of detective fiction."

"*Fiction* being the operative word." Dorothy took a heavy woolen coat from a closet near the door. "We're dealing with a real-life murder possibly committed by one of our friends." She pulled on her coat. "And of those friends, Agatha is the least likely to commit murder."

With the closet door open, Eliza spotted the green cape. The one Dorothy had worn the night of Neville's murder. If Theo was right, the green thread on the gun had come from that cape.

"And yet." Theo smirked. "In her stories, the least likely is usually the guilty party."

Eliza got up and went to the closet.

"While the tenet of some detective fiction is that anyone can commit murder under the right circumstances, I don't believe it." Dorothy yanked a leather cap over her slicked-back hair. "Some people would kill themselves before taking another life. Or, like Christ, allow themselves to be spiked upon the gallows like an owl on a barn door."

Eliza glanced at them to make sure they weren't paying attention to her.

"Surely, you can't compare the Bible to detective fiction?" Theo's face was a question mark.

Fingering the cape, Eliza looked for any signs of a tear or rip. She lifted the garment and examined the hem. A pucker along one side suggested a pulled thread. Another strand stood on end. Eliza used a fingernail to nip it off.

"Why not?" Dorothy tugged on her gloves. "The judicial killing of God is certainly as interesting as a body in a coal hole." She tapped the top of her cap then turned and stared at Eliza. "If you two will excuse me, I'm off to find Agatha." She held the door open for them. "And for today's errand, I suggest you come out of my closet and do the same."

Eliza palmed the thread until she could slip it into her pocket. She and Theo gathered their coats and hats and followed Dorothy outside. They watched as Dorothy pulled her motorcycle out from the side of the building. She straddled the machine and started the engine. Sitting straight as a rod like a charioteer, she took off with a pop, pop, pop.

"Now what?" Theo asked once Dorothy and her Ner-A-Car were out of sight.

Eliza opened her palm to reveal the green thread.

"Aha!" Theo smiled. "Very sneaky of you."

She folded the thread into a hanky and pushed it into her coat pocket. "I say we split up."

Theo got a hangdog look on his face. "Tired of me already."

"More efficient." She tugged on her gloves. "We can accomplish double and meet up later to discuss our findings." She smiled. "Over a game of chess."

"If that's what it takes." Theo stuffed his hands into his pockets. "But I won't go easy on you."

"Of course not." She clapped her hands together. "I wouldn't expect anything less than your best effort." She punched his shoulder. "Which, I'm afraid, won't be enough."

He grinned. "I guess I'm the one who should be afraid."

"Indeed." She raised her gloved hands and curled her fingers into cat's claws. "And I intend to win our detection competition too." Baring her teeth, she hissed. "So, I'm already preparing for a rematch."

"Good kitty." He patted her head and laughed. "How about we take one match at a time?"

Eliza slinked off into the mist toward the railway station. Next stop Cambridge to interview Holly Lively and her paramour, the philosophy professor, Bertrand Russell. It shouldn't be difficult to find him. She'd heard he taught at Trinity College and lived at Fellows Bowling Green. She couldn't imagine the college knew Mrs. Lively was living there with him. Surely, they would never condone such an arrangement.

\* \* \*

Walking from the station, Eliza marveled at the quaint shops and charming bridge leading to the college campus. Like the rest of the Cambridge campus, Trinity College was composed of a series of stately brick buildings, embraced by ivy climbing up to the beveled windows, which in turn hugged several neatly manicured green quads. Even the overcast December afternoon couldn't diminish the entrance to Trinity with its distinctive golden stone façade, large bay window topped with a crowning cornice, and square turrets reminiscent of a medieval castle.

A gentleman at the reception desk smiled up at her. "Only last year, the college lifted restrictions against women visiting the men's lodgings," he said, looking her up and down.

"I'm here on business with Professor Bertrand Russell." She flipped her hair over her shoulder.

The receptionist let out a guffaw. "Bertrand was given the boot because he opposed the war." He shook his head. "A more decent fellow you'll never meet too. He always gave me the time of day. Wasn't stuck up like the other dons."

Why didn't anyone tell her the professor wasn't still at Cambridge? Why did Neville's children insist their mother had run off to Cambridge with him? Something was amiss. "Do you know where I could find Professor Russell?"

"Last I heard, he and his wife live in Chelsea." He tapped a pencil on his desk. "They started a school for kids."

*His wife!* "Thank you." Had he married Holly? How could he? She was still married to Neville.

She turned on her heels and headed for the quad. Once outside, she stood shivering on the pavement, wondering where to go next. If Bertrand Russell lived in Chelsea with his wife, it was unlikely Holly Lively had run off with him to Cambridge. Had she run off to Chelsea? Or had she run off with someone else to Cambridge?

Eliza went back inside and asked the receptionist if she could borrow a telephone directory. Aha! There was an H. Lively listed on Barton Road.

Despite the cold, Eliza decided to walk to Barton Road. She asked directions and was on her way. Thirty minutes later, with frost forming on her eyelashes, she was standing in front of an adorable little cottage. She knocked on the door and then shifted from foot to foot, waiting for someone to answer. A plump, middle-aged woman with flowing, flaxen hair and wearing an apron answered the door.

"I'm looking for Holly," Eliza said, wondering whether Holly still used her married surname. "That is, Mrs. Neville Lively." The smell of freshly baked bread wafted out into the wintery air.

The woman's smile faded. "I'm Holly." She wiped her hands on the apron. "If this is about Neville, I've been informed." She closed her eyes. "I still can't believe it." Her shoulders shook and she audibly inhaled and exhaled a few times like she might start to cry.

"You've been separated for a year," Eliza ventured. She had to bite her tongue to resist bringing up the rumors about Holly and Bertrand Russell. "Still, it must be a shock."

Holly nodded. "Yes, poor Neville."

"At the risk of sounding forward." Eliza folded her hands together. "Do you mind me asking why you left him?" She met Holly's dismayed gaze. "I'm only trying to get to the bottom of his death. I'm sure you want to know what happened too."

"Alright." Holly's lips twitched. "I came to finish my degree." She wiped a stray hair from her forehead with the back of her hand. "Neville was supportive... at least at first."

"And, if I may ask, Professor Russell?" Eliza steeled herself for the response. "Was he supportive, too?"

"Professor Russell?" Holly blinked for a few seconds. "Oh, you mean Bertrand, Frank's brother." She chuckled. "Bertrand is the professor. Frank is a solicitor. He owns this cottage. He's my landlord." She blushed. "And my friend."

Frank Russell. Where had she heard that name? *Oh my.* "Frank Russell as in Earl Russell?" Also known as "Wicked Earl" due to his infamous marital troubles and a bigamy charge.

"Yes," Holly said amiably. "Do you know him?"

Eliza shook her head. "I've heard you are the beneficiary of Neville's life insurance policy."

"Dear Neville." Holly's blush deepened. "When he got the diagnosis, he immediately bought the policy. He was thoughtful to the end, dear man. He wanted to make sure I could finish my degree, finally. A dream come true for me. After raising my children, of course."

Eliza continued shifting from foot to foot. She peered longingly over Holly's shoulder at the fireplace in the sitting room.

"Oh, how rude I've been." Holly got the hint. "Come inside. You must be freezing."

"Thank you." Eliza didn't have to be asked twice. She made a beeline for the fireplace. After a few minutes, her tense muscles began to relax. "Very kind of you."

"Would you like some fresh biscuits? I just made them." Holly smiled.

"That would be lovely." Suddenly, Eliza felt exhausted from the effort of getting warm. "So, it sounds like Neville was setting you up for the next phase of your life, a phase without him, after his diagnosis." She didn't try to guess what diagnosis sent Neville out to buy a life insurance policy. "Very considerate and thoughtful of him."

"Even after his death." Holly stared down at her hands. "He wanted to make sure I was taken care of."

Eliza wondered whether the policy covered death by murder.

Holly gave a little wave. "Let me get you some biscuits." A minute later, she returned with a plate of gorgeous, powdered sugar biscuits and a pot of tea. Eliza's mouth watered just looking at them. Her stomach growled and she realized she hadn't eaten since breakfast. She bit into a biscuit and was transported to a realm of the senses, sweetness and softness and warmth. "Delicious." The tasty treat almost made her trip all the way out to Cambridge worth it. Then again, the trip hadn't been a waste. She was now confident she could cross Holly Lively off her list of suspects.

If Neville was dying anyway, then surely Holly didn't need to have him killed to collect the life insurance. And Holly's relationship, if she had one, was with Frank and not Bertrand Russell, which seemingly dissolved any motive the philosopher could have had for wanting Neville dead. Still, at some point, it might be worth paying the professor a visit just to be sure. In the meantime, finding Neville's doctor and confirming the diagnosis was her top priority.

"One last question, if I may." Eliza took a sip and peeked over the lip of her teacup. "What size shoes does your daughter wear?"

Holly gave her a quizzical look. "Size six. Why?"

"No reason," she said smiling as she lied through her teeth. "You've been a great help. Thank you." She glanced down at her own boot, also size six, and the same size as the bloody footprint. Not big at all.

\* \* \*

Theo paid a visit to Detective Inspector Robert Goforth at New Scotland Yard on the Victoria Embankment of the Thames River. The red brick and white stone building featured round capped turrets that gave it a much too festive air for police headquarters. Goforth's office was on the second floor and overlooked the river.

Goforth seemed happy to see him. With a broad smile, he invited Theo to sit down across from a large desk near the window. A chatty fellow, Goforth was all too happy to talk about the Agatha Christie disappearance. He was less forthcoming about what evidence they'd found in the Neville Lively murder case.

"The autopsy report isn't back yet," Goforth said. "That's all I can tell you." He got a twinkle in his eye. "Except." He lowered his voice. "The bullet was a .455 caliber Webley."

"Shot from the Webley found next to the body?" Theo figured by now the police had tested the gun to see if it had been fired recently. "Or the one taken from Mrs. Christie's bag?"

"We don't know yet. And even if I did, I'm not at liberty to say." Goforth smiled. "I'm no Basil Thomson, after all." It was well known there was no love lost between the two Scotland Yard detectives. "Let's just say, it's not an either/or proposition." He winked. "More like both/and."

Was the detective inspector speaking in riddles? Or was he telling Theo both guns were fired? "Both guns were recently fired?" Theo's mouth fell open. So, Agatha could have shot Neville over the Roger Ackroyd feud. He found that hard to believe. "Does that make Agatha a suspect?"

"Everyone is a suspect." Goforth jabbed a boney finger in Theo's direction. "Including you." He tapped his desktop with the same finger.

"Me?" Theo baulked.

"You were there." Goforth tilted his head. "And word on the street is you were jealous of Neville Lively's success."

"Jealous?" Theo scoffed. "No. We were friends... Well, more like acquaintances—"

"But you're an aspiring writer hoping to break into the big time, are you not?"

"I'm an aspiring writer who would be happy just to be able to make a living from his writing." He ran his hand through his hair. "But I'm not about to make a Faustian pact with the Devil and kill someone to make it happen."

"How far would you go?" Goforth smiled. "To become a successful writer? Kidnapping the most famous female writer in Britain might get you some attention." He winked.

"Oh, come on, detective." Theo stood up. Surely, Goforth didn't believe he'd kidnapped Agatha. The very idea was absurd. "If anything, it's Agatha you should suspect. She ran off right after Neville's death." Although he doubted she would have killed Neville over the squabble at the club.

"True. The lady's disappearance does make her more suspect." He cleared his throat and continued drumming his fingers. "We have leads. And just because you don't hear about our investigations doesn't mean they aren't ongoing. We *will* get to the bottom of this."

The way the detective inspector drummed on the desk reminded Theo of his father when he used to lecture him about being a man and doing his duty. Needless to say, his father's ideas of duty and his ideas were as far apart as night and day.

"Is there anything you can tell me?" He was beginning to think he'd wasted a trip. "Anything at all?" Surely, Eliza was having better luck and getting closer to winning their wager. As much as he rooted for Eliza to succeed in all her pursuits, in this particular case, he was resolved to win.

"Well. There is one thing perhaps you could help me with." Goforth opened his desk drawer and pulled out a small envelope. He opened it and dumped the contents on the desk. "Have you seen this before?" It was a button.

"Where is it from?" Theo shook his head. "Can I see it?"

"Sure." He gestured. "Knock yourself out. I found it at the crime scene after you left. It was near a table leg not far from the victim."

Theo plucked the button from the desk and examined it. With a herringbone design engraved in brass around a solid ivory center, it looked like a button off a woman's overcoat or a man's hunting jacket. "Do you think it belongs to the killer?"

"Could do." He shrugged. "The bruises on the victim's wrist suggest a struggle. Perhaps this button came off then. It doesn't match those on the victim's jacket. So, it could be from the killer's."

Theo turned the button over in his palm. He couldn't tell if it looked familiar or not. It was just a button, after all.

"Have you seen a button like this recently?" Goforth leaned forward and picked it up. "Say, on an article of clothing worn by Agatha Christie?"

"Not that I remember." Theo scratched his chin. "Do you have any more clues as to her whereabouts?"

"A witness saw her wandering about last night." His face lit up. "Wearing only a thin dress and no coat or hat."

"No hat," Theo repeated. Like most ladies, Agatha never went anywhere without a hat. And with the temperatures, especially at night, she wouldn't be out without a coat, either.

"And," Goforth continued with the glee of an inveterate gossip, "she was disoriented and confused."

"From an auto accident perhaps?" Theo had read about the damaged car. "At least we know she's alive."

"Was alive yesterday." Goforth nodded. "Sir Arthur Conan Doyle took one of her gloves to a medium who is performing séances to help locate her." He chuckled. "Can you imagine?"

"He might do better with Sherlock Holmes." Theo knew about Conan Doyle's otherworldly pursuits. Ever since the death of his son in the war, Conan Doyle had been desperately searching for a way to make contact, which, of course, meant the charlatan psychics were circling like sharks. "Where do the psychics say to look for her?"

"In a spa taking thermal water treatments." Now he laughed outright. "As if a lady in distress would wander into a luxury spa."

"Quite." Theo made a mental note to check the area around Newlands Corner for health spas.

"I'd love to stay and chat," Goforth said, standing up and extending his hand, "but I've got an appointment with a grieving widow."

"Holly Lively?" Theo hazarded a conjecture.

"No." Goforth shook his head. "Although I couldn't tell you if it was now, could I?"

"No, I guess you couldn't." Theo tapped his hat back on his head and resolved to make the widow Lively his next visit.

**\* \* \***

Ninety minutes later, Theo arrived at the address Alice Lively had given him for her mother. With its thatched roof and stucco walls, it was the typical charming Cambridge cottage. Ambling up the stone walkway, he spotted Eliza. The collar on her wool coat was turned up. And the way her cloche hat tilted to obscure one eye, she looked like a character out of an F. Scott Fitzgerald novel.

"Well, well, well." Theo grinned. "Great minds and all that rot."

"Beat you to the punch, I'm afraid." When she laughed, her chin tilted skyward ever so slightly. "Such as it was."

"What do you mean?" He stood beside her, close enough he could feel the heat emanating from her body. It was so cold out, he wished he could embrace her and wrap himself in her warmth. *Yeah. For survival. Right.* He couldn't fool himself into thinking his desire to bury his head in her neck was merely a survival instinct.

"Not exactly a knockout." She kicked at the ground. "Holly Lively came to Cambridge to finish her degree and with her husband's blessing." She looked up at him with those gold-flecked green eyes and he averted his gaze. "After he got a terminal diagnosis."

"Blimey," he shuddered. "So, Neville was dying. And anyone who knew would have no reason to kill him. They could just wait..." He let his voice trail off. *Wait for the old man to kick the bucket.*

"Unless..." She arched her eyebrows. "He was about to change his will in a way to disadvantage one of his heirs."

*Alice. Had she learned something about Alice?* "Pray tell," he said, trying to sound nonchalant. If she'd gotten some information out of Holly Lively, he could too.

"That's it." Eliza's face was open and bright. "I've told you everything I've learned. What about you? What have you discovered?"

"Uh-uh." He shook his head. "I'm not going to give away my secrets. Especially to my most intractable opponent."

"Me, intractable?" She laughed. "Why, I'm an open book."

*A book I'd very much like to read from cover to cover and back again.*

He felt his cheeks warm and he couldn't help but look away.

# 9

# THE PROFESSOR

The next morning, Eliza spread the evidence out on the kitchen table. The monogrammed handkerchief, the imprint of the bloody footprint, the two green threads (one from the gun handle and one from Dorothy's cape), and the threatening note. Waiting for the coffee to percolate, she went to the pantry and fetched her microscope. Queenie trotted behind her. The weight of the leather case always made her feel more serious. She laid the case on the table, blew off the dust, and unbuckled the locks. She hadn't used the microscope since the war. She smiled to herself as she removed the hefty metal device from its case. Queenie sat next to her, waiting to see the results.

"What's all this?" Jane bounced into the kitchen. "Good to see you back to work." She went to the stove, turned off the burner, and poured two cups of coffee. "Is this related to your assignment?" She sat one cup on the table next to the microscope.

"In a manner of speaking." Eliza placed the two green threads side by side between two glass slides. Gently, she maneuvered the slide into the stage clips. "Evidence from the

Lively case." She bent and looked through the lens. The cool metal against her eye socket was as reassuring as an old friend.

Just as she suspected. The two threads were identical in their twill weave with its characteristic diagonal ridges and dark etched lines like a charcoal pencil retracing its tracks. The thread on the gun came from Dorothy's cape. The question was, how had a thread from her cape become attached to the handle of the murder weapon? Obviously, Dorothy handled all the weapons for the ceremony. Had a thread innocently snagged when she passed the gun to the killer? Or was it more sinister?

Eliza didn't know the brash woman well. Still, from what she did know, she suspected Dorothy would rather demolish her enemies with words than swords... or guns. She recalled Dorothy kneeling next to Neville's body when the lights came on. Is that when her cape caught on the weapon? When she knelt to check on Neville? An idea formed in her mind. The gun had been wiped of fingerprints. What if Dorothy had used her cape to wipe it clean? That would explain the thread. But why? Why would Dorothy wipe the gun? To protect herself? Or someone else? In either case, she must know the murderer.

"Have you learned how Mrs. Christie knows state secrets?" Jane sat down at the table.

Eliza stared across the table at her sister. "What do you mean?" She furrowed her brows. "You didn't tell me Agatha Christie knows something. You just said you suspected the Detection Club members. Why Mrs. Christie?" She scratched Queenie's ears.

"Remember the Zimmerman telegram?" Jane tilted her head.

Of course, she remembered the Zimmerman telegram. In 1917, Dilly Knox and friends had deciphered a telegram from German Foreign minister, Arthur Zimmerman, to the German minister of Mexico offering the United States territory to the Mexican government if they joined the Germans in the war. It was the Zimmerman telegram that convinced the Americans to join the British.

"The Zimmerman telegram is still not public knowledge, and yet a character named Arthur Zimmerman appears in one of Neville Lively's stories—which also just happens to center around a questionable telegram." Jane tightened her lips. "Just a coincidence? Or was Agatha Christie's dear friend Dilly spilling his guts to her and her writer friends? And now, they could be using those radio broadcasts to send out crucial military secrets embedded in code in their detective stories."

"Why not ask Dilly?" Eliza thought a minute. "Dilly may be a silly man, but he's not a traitor."

"I'm not saying he's a traitor." Jane smirked. "Just a blabber-mouth." She took a sip of her coffee. "Anyway, he denies telling anyone anything, especially a 'nosey mystery writer.'"

"I see." Eliza gathered her equipment and carefully placed the microscope back in its case.

"But we need to know for sure." Jane stood up. "We need to know if Mrs. Christie is privy to secret information." She brushed wrinkles out of her skirt. "And we're counting on you to find out."

"Right." Eliza cringed. At least she didn't have a partner this time... unless you counted Theo.

"I'm off to do some errands." Jane blew her a kiss. "But I'll see you this evening for supper."

"Yup." She sat the case on the floor and then took off one of her pumps. She'd intentionally worn the shoes most like the ones that made the bloody footprint. She held her shoe up against the sheet of paper with the imprint from the bloody footprint. Possibly, even likely, the suspect had been wearing pointed-toed pumps. Of course, most women's shoes had pointed toes. But how many had the worn circle in the middle? She had to get a look at the bottom of Alice Lively's shoes.

\* \* \*

Half an hour later, standing in front of Alice Lively's building, Eliza slipped into the entrance behind a delivery man. Quietly, she crept up the stairs to the door of Alice Lively's flat. No answer. She knocked again. Dammit. She should have called and made an appointment. But she wanted the element of surprise. She was the one who got the surprise, along with a wasted trip. As she ran back downstairs, she thought of Professor Bertrand Russell. He too lived in Chelsea. Maybe her trip wasn't wasted after all. She popped into a red phone box to look up the address in the telephone book.

Ten minutes later and she arrived at 31 Sydney Street. The townhouse had an odd bow window jutting out as if from a medieval castle. Through the window, she saw the silhouette of a man. The famous professor, himself? She rang the bell. A petite young woman wearing an embroidered peasant's shirt and a long skirt answered the door. Her chestnut hair hung in two braids like a milkmaid's and her cheeks sprouted adorable dimples when she smiled. Was she a daughter?

She introduced herself as, "Dora, Bertie's wife."

*His wife?* Eliza bit her tongue.

"I'll go see if Bertie is available." She glanced at her watch. "He usually doesn't take a break from his writing until supper time. And I think he already had a visitor this afternoon."

A few minutes later, the professor appeared. His thick hair was tousled and he looked as if he'd thrown on his clothes in a hurry. Perhaps noticing her surprise, he ran a hand through his hair and straightened his collar. "To what do I owe the pleasure, Miss Baker?" He held out his hand.

"I'd like to ask you a few questions about the night of the Detection Club meeting, if you don't mind." Eliza took his hand. It was soft and dry. "Is there a more private place we might talk?" She glanced over at Dora, who was watching from the foyer.

"Of course." He took her coat and hung it on a coat-rack near the door, and then gestured toward the hallway. "If you don't mind a mess, you're welcome to join me and my guest in my study." With his easy smile and intelligent eyes, she had to admit, he was charming. "I believe you know him." He cocked his head. "Theodore Sharp."

"Theo is here?" Drat. He'd beat her to it.

The professor put his hand on the small of her back and led her down the hall. She restrained the urge to elbow him in the ribs and break away. Instead, she asked about his research and his interest in detective fiction. In her espionage days, she'd learned men love nothing more than talking about themselves, and the smart ones were the worst.

"I devour endless detective stories." He smiled. "I can't get enough of them." He stopped in his tracks. "I especially enjoy puzzle mysteries. They remind me of a good maths problem." He continued down the hall. "A good mystery, like good philosophy, contends with the human condition and the mysteries of life."

"So, your interest is philosophical?" Figures Theo would start his investigation with the philosophy professor. They were probably having a grand old time talking about the meaning of life and the human condition. What a waste of time. Why couldn't they just get on with it? The meaning of life was in the living of it. Nothing more. "Might I ask about your brother,

Frank, and Mrs. Holly Lively?" Eliza changed the subject. Yes, her approach was blunt. But it did have the benefit of surprise, an ambush of sorts.

"My, you are direct." The professor chuckled. "My brother and Neville Lively came up together at Eton. They're old pals. Terrible thing, Neville's death." He gestured toward a chair across from his desk and next to where Theo sat smiling at her.

With the large bay window, the study was bright and cozy. Bookshelves lined every wall. Stacks of magazines and journals were piled next to the desk, surrounding it like a moat. The desk was a jumble of papers and books scattered around a typewriter, which was the centerpiece of the messy ensemble.

The professor took a seat behind his desk. "As I was telling Mr. Sharp..." He folded his hands in his lap. "I was in the other room with the other guests at the time Neville was shot."

Theo nodded, chewing on a toothpick.

"Did you witness anything odd?" Eliza asked.

"Life is odd. People are odd." The professor smiled. "Can you be more specific, Miss Baker?"

"Did anyone leave the room before you heard the shot?" She removed her hat and gloves and placed them on her lap.

"As I told Mr. Sharp, Miss Alice Lively excused herself and went to powder her nose." His smiled broadened. "I don't know why ladies insist on such silly euphemisms."

"When did she leave for the toilet?" Eliza met his gaze.

"A few minutes before the shot was fired." The professor looked from her to Theo and back again. "You two should combine forces. Working together is not only more efficient but also more effective. The mind works best in conversation."

"I agree." Theo gave her a warm smile.

She glared at him. "When did Miss Lively return to the

guest dining room?" She wasn't going to let him win their little bet.

"I'm not sure she did." The professor straightened some papers on his desk. "When we heard the shot, everyone was shocked and it was all a bit chaotic. Then everyone rushed into the main dining room. And, as you know, we found Neville shot. I believe shortly thereafter, Mr. Anthony Cox escorted Miss Lively away from the grisly scene."

"Did you happen to notice her shoes?" Eliza pointed to her own boots.

"Her shoes?" The professor gave her a bewildered look. "I don't remember anything strange about them. Regular lady's heels. Brown, I believe. With a little strap."

"Mary Janes," Eliza said more to herself than anyone else. She had to find a way to see those shoes.

If the bloody footprint belonged to Alice Lively, then she could be the killer. She had a strong motive. And given she'd left the guest dining room before the shot was fired, she'd had the opportunity. Did she have the resolve to carry out cold-blooded patricide? Did she do it?

Getting a look at Alice Lively's shoes would require a distraction and clever subterfuge. As much as she wanted to beat him, she and Theo would have to work together.

"Thank you, professor." Theo stood up and held out his hand. "You've been most helpful."

"Yes, thank you, professor," Eliza repeated absently. Her mind was on Alice Lively's shoes.

The professor led them back out into the foyer, handed them their coats, and bid them good day.

"You're welcome any time." Dora waved from the kitchen where she was working at a typewriter. "Next time, I insist you take some tea or coffee." She put aside a notebook. "Today, I was busy preparing my lecture on why marriage is unnatural and a prison for women." Obviously, Dora Russell was not like most ladies. Then again, Bertrand Russell was not like most men.

Theo nodded. "Very kind of you."

"Very kind," Eliza repeated, and followed Theo outside.

On the tree-lined street, they stood looking at each other. "I know what you're thinking," Theo said, flicking his used toothpick into the bushes.

"What?" She took the bait.

"Philosophers make poor witnesses." He exhaled a cloud of breath.

"For a philosopher, Mr. Russell was extraordinarily observant." She sniffed. "I was thinking, we need to get a look at Alice Lively's shoes and I have an idea how to do it."

He took a step closer. "I hope it doesn't involve breaking and entering."

"How well you know me." She smirked. "But no. Not if we plan our strategy in advance."

"And get lucky." He raised his eyebrows.

"We make our own luck." Eliza tossed off the remark with the wave of a hand.

"You do, anyway." Theo hugged himself. "Speaking of breaking and entering, did you hear about the break-in at Neville's flat?"

"No." She stared at him. "What happened? What was stolen?"

"Nothing." Theo shook his head. "Apparently, in the wee hours this morning, someone jimmied the lock and rifled through the papers in his study." He shrugged. "Obviously, someone is looking for something."

"And if we find out who and what…" Eliza patted his sleeve. "We just may find our killer."

# 10

## SETTING THE TRAP

They walked to Alice Lively's flat. Eliza led the way. It was only ten minutes away, but the biting December wind cut through her coat and gloves. Her cheeks stung by the time they reached the building. Shifting from foot to foot, she rang the bell.

*Buzz. Buzz. Yes!* This time, Alice answered and buzzed them in.

Eliza had instructed Theo to keep Alice engaged while she looked for the bloody shoe. As soon as Alice let them in, Eliza asked to use the bathroom.

"If I'm not mistaken," Theo said, following Alice into the sitting room. "You studied literature at the University of London."

"Yes." Alice smiled.

Eliza took that as her cue to "use the loo." From the hallway, she heard Theo chatting up Alice about social class in Dickens and Austen. *Good lad. That should keep her busy.* Eliza followed the hall to the end and opened the last door. Bingo. Alice's bedroom. She dashed across the room to a large mahogany armoire. She flung the doors open and then fell to her knees to investigate. Reaching inside rows of long, lacy evening gowns and summer silk coats, she felt for shoes. Alice's shoes were lined up along the bottom of the cupboard like a battalion of soldiers waiting to be deployed. Eliza looked for a pair of brown Mary Janes. In turn, going down the line, she lifted each shoe and inspected it. The woman had a lot of shoes. And a lot of frocks. Eliza picked up a pair of striped, scarlet pumps sporting blue heels. How very vogue.

Aha! She found a pair of brown Mary Janes. She turned them over. Sure enough, the soles were worn right in the center. Upon closer examination, she saw dark stains on the sole and side stitches of one of the shoes. She'd found her culprit. Glancing over her shoulder, she made sure no one was watching her. She took a small knife and a tiny envelope from her chatelaine bag and scraped specks of dried blood from the sole. Once she had her sample, she replaced the shoe, stored the sample in her bag, stood up, and brushed off her skirt. On the way out of the bedroom, she spotted a ledger open on the side table. She couldn't resist peeking at it. Was Alice already planning how to spend her inheritance?

Glancing around the room, Eliza advanced on the ledger. Towering over it, she stared down at the open page. Golly. At regular intervals for the past year, withdrawals were circled in red. Tucked into the ledger, a receipt from Harrods poked out. Eliza slid it out from between the pages. One hundred and thirty quid for a fur-trimmed coat. Goodness. No wonder Alice Lively needed money. The ledger was practically a smoking gun. Just last week, there was a rather large payment to Maud Wilkerson. *What for?*

Armed with the ledger, Eliza marched down the hall and made an entrance waving the book. It was time to confront Alice Lively and find out the truth.

Laughing together, Alice and Theo were sitting side by side on the sofa. They both looked up as Eliza entered the room.

"You're in debt, Miss Lively." Eliza held up the ledger. "Which is why you need your inheritance now." She bore down on the heir. "I know you left the guest dinner before the shot was fired. And I know it was your bloody footprint leading out of the room after your father was killed."

Theo uncrossed his legs and sat upright staring at her.

Her eyes wide, Alice Lively looked stunned. "No." The color drained from her face. "You can't think *I* shot my father." Her lip trembled. "What are you doing with my father's ledger?" She jumped up, dashed over, and grabbed it out of Eliza's hands. "You have no business." Tears welled in her eyes.

"Your *father's* ledger." Eliza had thought it belonged to Alice. "Why are those withdrawal entries circled in red?" She softened her tone. "Were you making regular withdrawals on your father's accounts?"

Alice shook her head. "It's not what you think."

"What is it then?" Eliza stood arms akimbo.

Theo glanced up at Eliza and gave her a warning look as if to say, *Don't be cruel.*

Eliza softened her tone. "I'm sorry to have to ask, but we all want to find your father's killer." She gave Alice a sympathetic smile. "Can you tell me about the payment to Maud Wilkerson?"

"I don't know anything about why Daddy was paying Maud." Alice dropped back onto the sofa. She thumbed through the ledger. "But Fergus Briggs, my father's bookkeeper" —she glanced up—"he has been embezzling funds... My father found out and confronted him." She fumbled with the ledger. "He forged the books to make it look like I was making the withdrawals. Father got angry..." Her voice trailed off.

"Briggs?" Theo gave Eliza a meaningful look.

If what Alice said was true, then Fergus Briggs had a strong motive to dispose of Neville. "Does anyone else know about this?" Eliza took a seat near Alice. "Did your father tell anyone?"

"That's just it." Alice closed her eyes and let out a long sigh. "We were gathering evidence against Fergus, but father was killed before we could present it to the authorities." She sniffed. "But it's all in here." She patted the ledger. "Fergus doesn't know I have it."

"The break-in," Theo said. "Could Fergus Briggs have gone looking for your father's ledger?"

"Stands to reason." Eliza stood up again and paced the length of the room. "If the ledger is evidence Briggs was embezzling, it could land him in prison." She stopped and looked back at Alice. "Briggs must have been looking for the ledger. And if he finds out you have it, then your life may be in danger."

"We must not tell him then." Alice sat erect and crossed her arms over her chest. She'd regained her composure.

"Actually." Eliza smiled. "That's exactly what we *should* do."

"And put Alice in danger?" Theo scratched his jaw. "Are you sure that's a good idea?"

"It's a brilliant idea." Eliza dropped back into the armchair. "We use the ledger as bait to catch Fergus Briggs in the act." She beamed. "We let it be known that Miss Lively has the ledger. And when Mr. Briggs learns its whereabouts and comes after it, we have our friend Detective Inspector Goforth waiting to nab him."

"Do you think Mr. Briggs killed my father?" Alice blinked.

"Avoiding prison is a strong motive." Theo put his elbows on his knees and leaned forward. "If your father recently confronted Mr. Briggs, the timing is right, too." He gave Alice a reassuring smile. "And if we can trap Briggs and get him to confess, then you're off the hook."

Alice flinched. "I'm innocent." She threw her head back. "I have nothing to hide and I'm not on the hook."

"I'm afraid Scotland Yard might not see it that way, Miss Lively." Eliza pointed at the ledger. "May I?" She held out her hand. "If you're frightened, we could put the ledger elsewhere. The key is to set the trap."

"I'm not scared." Alice fidgeted. "I want to find my father's killer as much as you do... More." She picked at a cuticle. "He wasn't always just, but he always did what he thought was right." She glanced up. "He never compromised his principles."

"Including his insistence mystery writers play fair," Eliza said. At least inheritance and embezzlement were better motives for murder than a silly squabble over Mrs. Christie's unreliable narrator. She flipped through the pages of the ledger. "Now to set our trap. Who is Mr. Briggs's closest friend in the Detection Club?"

Theo thought a minute. "Anthony, I guess."

At the mention of Anthony's name, Alice blushed.

"So, you let slip to Anthony." Eliza tapped the ledger. "You have it on good authority"—she held the book out to Alice—"Miss Lively is in possession of her father's journal, which contains damning evidence against Mr. Briggs."

"And then what?" Alice took the ledger. "We sit here in the dark and wait to pounce?"

"I'll confer with D. I. Goforth and hopefully, he'll go along with our plan." Eliza nodded. "And make sure you're safe in the process."

A knock at the door silenced her. The three of them sat staring at the door as if by talking about him, Fergus Briggs had been summoned.

The knocking got louder.

"Would you like me to go to the door?" Theo asked with concern in his voice.

"I'll go." Alice took a deep breath and crossed the room.

Obviously not realizing anyone else was with Alice, Anthony Berkeley Cox blustered in. "Darling. Are you alright? I heard about the break-in at your father's." He pulled her into an embrace.

She stiffened. "I have visitors." She nodded toward the sitting room.

"Apologies." Anthony ran his hand through his hair. "Theo. Eliza." He cleared his throat. "Good to see you again." He came to greet them.

Clearly, there was something going on between Alice and Anthony. Could their liaison be responsible for Alice's hedging about the bloody footprint? "At the risk of being indiscreet—" Eliza looked from Anthony to Alice.

"When has that stopped you?" Theo interrupted.

"As I was saying." She ignored him and turned to Alice. "I don't mean to be indiscreet, but may I ask if your leaving the guest dining room before the shot was fired has anything to do with your, eh, *friendship* with Mr. Cox?"

A veil of horror covering her face, Alice looked to Anthony. "We are... we are..." She stammered.

"Yes," Anthony said. "I snuck out during the ceremony to meet Alice." He lit a cigarette. "And she left the guest dining room to meet me." He took a long drag. "When we heard the shot, we both rushed into the dining room." He shook his head. "You know the rest. Like you, we were shocked to see Neville lying there, dead."

"Your footprint, Miss Lively, was leading away from the body and out of the dining room," Eliza pointed out.

"I immediately ran back to tell Barnaby, Papa had been shot." Tears welled in her eyes again.

"I can corroborate." Anthony took a step closer to Alice.

"Does that adequately solve the mystery of the bloody footprint?" Theo said. "So, what should we do about the journal?" He gave Eliza a sly smile. "The evidence against Briggs is damning."

"I don't want to do anything until after Papa's estate has been settled," Alice said, following the plan. "And we don't know for sure Fergus is at fault." She was an excellent little actor.

Eliza got up and grabbed the ledger from the side table. "There's enough evidence in here to send Mr. Briggs to prison for a long time." She made a show of flipping through the pages. "Keep it in a safe place, Miss Lively." She handed the ledger to Alice and then went back to her chair.

"I'll put it in my nightstand right now." Alice took the ledger and disappeared into her bedroom.

"What's this all about?" Anthony looked concerned. "I've known Fergus for years. He wants to publish my next book."

"He's been embezzling from Neville's royalties," Eliza said forcefully. "And we need to report him to the police."

"Not so fast." Theo held up a hand. "We don't know if the entries Neville circled implicate Briggs. Shouldn't we ask him before going to the police?"

"And tip our hand?" Eliza shook her head.

"You should at least respect Miss Lively's wishes and wait until after the estate is settled." Anthony's tone was defensive.

"Perhaps." Eliza fiddled with the piping on the edge of her chair. "I guess it wouldn't hurt to wait, as long as no one breathes a word of this to Mr. Briggs." She looked straight at Anthony.

"Of course not." Anthony's dark eyes shone.

Alice returned from the bedroom.

"I should be going." Anthony smiled at Alice. "I'll stop by again tomorrow to see how you're getting on, Miss Lively."

"Thank you." She smiled.

"Before you go..." Eliza unsnapped her chatelaine bag and withdrew the monogramed handkerchief. "Does this belong to you?"

"Where did you find it?" Anthony reached for it. "I must have dropped it."

"Next to Neville's dead body," Eliza said.

Theo gave her a disapproving look, and Alice cringed.

"Next to Neville," she repeated, leaving off the "dead body."

"In the commotion, I guess I dropped it." Anthony ran his hand through his hair again. A nervous habit of his?

What if Anthony and not Dorothy wiped the gun clean? "You weren't using it to wipe prints from the murder weapon?" Eliza asked pointedly.

"Of course not!" Anthony snatched the hanky out of her hand. "Why would I do that?"

"The answer is obvious." Eliza cocked her head. "You were trying to protect someone... unless you did it—" She grabbed the handkerchief. "This is evidence and I'm giving it to the police."

"That's ridiculous." Anthony huffed. "I gave it to Alice after... She must have dropped it. Or perhaps I did." He sounded exasperated. "In the chaos, it landed on the floor. So what?"

"In a murder investigation," Eliza said meeting his gaze, "every detail matters. I would think you detective writers would know that."

He patted his pocket where a matching handkerchief

peeked out. "I suppose you're right." After a few whispered goodbyes to Alice, he took his leave.

Had he been telling the truth? His indignation seemed genuine. Then again, he was a smooth operator. Juggling so many women, he had to be a practiced liar. Still, while she didn't completely trust him, she could come up with no reason why Anthony Berkeley Cox would want to kill Neville Lively. Except perhaps Alice's inheritance. That was if he planned to divorce his wife and then jilt his mistress to marry Alice Lively.

Once Anthony left, Eliza jumped up. "Now, to pay Detective Inspector Goforth a visit and let him in on our plan." She went to Theo. "Perhaps you'd better stay with Alice until the police arrive."

He nodded and then went to the windows and checked their locks, as if the threat from Fergus Briggs could fly in through the windows.

\* \* \*

Theo could have checkmated D. I. Goforth on his last turn. But where was the fun in that? Anyway, Eliza was waiting to challenge the winner and he couldn't face playing her. Chess was too intimate and his emotions were too strong. Sitting across from her, under the intensity of her gaze and the energy of her concentration would be too much for him. He had to shed these inappropriate feelings first. She obviously didn't share his ardor and he wasn't about to risk a broken heart.

She was standing behind him. And although he couldn't see her, he could sense her presence scrutinizing his every move. He was surprised she didn't say anything when he passed up the chance to win. Surely, she saw it, too.

"I'm ready." Alice appeared in the sitting room. She was

dressed to the nines. "Anthony will be here soon. Shouldn't you hide?"

They were counting on Anthony's loyalty to Fergus Briggs. Their plan was working. They'd baited Anthony into taking Alice out for dinner, presumably to enable Fergus Briggs to retrieve the ledger. Hopefully, he'd already told Briggs about the ledger and the dinner date. If so, the plan was already in motion. Briggs would know the ledger was in Alice's flat. And he would know Alice would be out. The question was, would he take the bait?

*Like setting a trap in chess.* The Rubenstein trap worked best if your opponent playing black got greedy and couldn't resist taking the bait, which in that case was a knight. Most players couldn't resist taking a knight with a lowly pawn. But once they did, the trap was set and their queen was pinned, or worse, checkmate.

*People who embezzle are greedy.*

*Briggs embezzles.*

*Therefore, Briggs is greedy.*

*Greedy people always take the bait.*

*Briggs is greedy.*

*Therefore, Briggs will take the bait.*

Deductive logic. Theo chuckled to himself. Carefully, he lifted his chess board and carried it to the kitchen. Nattering on about an elusive ring of pickpockets on the east side, Goforth trailed behind. Eliza dimmed the lights. And then the three of them sat in the dark in the kitchen waiting for Anthony to arrive and take Alice away.

Eliza had convinced them it was best if Anthony wasn't in on the plan. Not only because he would be more convincing when he told Briggs, but also because she didn't really trust Anthony. And Eliza claimed to rely on evidence and not "gut feelings." Then again, she did fancy herself a good judge of character. No doubt based on some evidence from the perceivable world. Her sense of smell, perhaps. She could smell a rat.

After Anthony arrived and Alice left with him, the trio continued sitting in the dark. Theo borrowed a small torch from Eliza, who always carried one in her hip bag along with who-knew-what-else. Shining the torch on the board, he said, "Your move." After a couple more moves, his hand was tired of holding the torch. And it was distracting playing in the dark while waiting for an embezzler and potential murderer. Despite allowing Goforth to play much longer than he deserved, Theo had always kept the path to mate in the forefront of his mind. So, when the time came, he made short work of it.

"Congratulations, old man," Goforth whispered. "Well done."

"Brilliant game." Theo may have exaggerated a bit. But Goforth was such a jolly chap and such a good sport, he couldn't help but encourage him.

The thin slice of moonlight coming through the window was the only illumination. Waiting until his eyes adjusted, Theo replaced the chess pieces in their leather case. He was just collecting a rook when a noise in the hallway made him freeze. "Shhhh...." He put a finger to his lips. "Listen."

Eliza's entire body tensed like a cat ready to pounce. Goforth stubbed out a cigarette and sat motionless. Theo perked up his ears. Silence. Had he imagined it? He held his breath.

*Rattle. Rattle.* No. He definitely didn't imagine it. Someone was jiggling the doorknob. *Creak.* The door hinges squeaked.

Slowly, Theo laid the rook on the table. His heart was racing. As still as a statue, he listened in the darkness. He sensed, more than heard, footfalls approaching from the foyer.

D. I. Goforth quietly got to his feet. He turned toward the sounds. Eliza did the same. A shadow passed by the kitchen, moving toward the bedroom. Goforth shouted, "Stop. Police."

The shadow turned and ran full tilt at Goforth. With a grunt, the inspector fell backwards and tripped over a chair. He uttered a curse as he lay on the floor holding his ankle.

Frozen in place, unable to move, as if his feet were glued to the floor, Theo watched as the figure lunged at Eliza. "No!"

Eliza whirled around and kicked the intruder in the jaw. He staggered back a few steps but not far enough to avoid a second kick to his torso. Eliza's butterfly kick had left the burglar crumpled in a heap next to Goforth.

Theo's mouth fell open. *My God. Where did she learn to fight like that?*

Finally, collecting his wits, he flipped on the lights. "Fergus Briggs," he said. "We've been expecting you."

# 11

## BLACKMAIL

Eliza didn't take her eyes off him. In the bright light of Miss Lively's kitchen, with his three-piece suit, the intruder looked more like an accountant than a burglar. Red-faced and puffing, Mr. Fergus Briggs sat restrained in a chair. The flat was quiet except for his breathing. If he tried to make a break for it, he'd be sorry. He was outnumbered three-to-one, but that hadn't kept him from pushing the detective inspector to the floor and trying to run. Luckily, her ju-jitsu training had kicked in, literally, and she'd stopped him in his tracks.

"I didn't kill him," Mr. Briggs whined for a fifth time. "It wasn't me." His bald pate gleamed under the kitchen lights. D. I. Goforth stood behind him with his hands on the intruder's shoulders. On the condition Theo give him chess lessons, the detective agreed to allow Eliza and Theo to ask a few questions before his partner arrived and he took the burglar back to the station.

Her palms on the table, Eliza leaned in. "You were embezzling from his royalties. He found out and confronted you. So, you killed him."

"No, I swear." Mr. Briggs was practically in tears. "I didn't kill him." He slumped in the chair. "Alright. I did doctor the royalties a bit." He glanced around wildly. "Because of my daughter's medical expenses. Otherwise, I never would... but I was desperate."

"What did you do when Neville found out and confronted you?" Theo asked, chewing on a toothpick.

"Nothing." Mr. Briggs's face was red and blotchy. "I promised to pay him back."

Eliza scowled.

"Really, I did." Mr. Briggs's tone was defiant. "I wish he was alive. You could ask him."

"He isn't," D. I. Goforth said. "And we're not about to take your word for it. You've admitted to embezzlement. You've admitted you were desperate. Why not murder?"

"I'm not a murderer." Mr. Briggs dragged his sleeve across his forehead. "You're looking in the wrong place. Why don't you go pester Maud? She was the one who was blackmailing Neville."

"What do you mean?" Theo asked.

A knock at the door signaled the arrival of D. I. Goforth's sergeant. He entered without waiting for an answer.

"Ready, Gov," the sergeant said.

"Let's get you to the station for a proper questioning." D. I. Goforth looked back at Eliza. "We really need you back at the Yard. No one interrogates like you." He patted the perp on the shoulder. "Come on, Briggs. Let's go. You're just lucky I don't use the techniques of my predecessor, Basil Thomson. He'd have given you a good whack—"

"Wait." Eliza stood up. "What about Maud and blackmail?"

"Everybody knows they were having an affair." Mr. Briggs smirked. "She threatened to tell his wife if he didn't pay."

Eliza doubted Holly Lively would care if Neville had been having an affair. She was off finishing her degree. Theirs was an odd marriage. Although perhaps not as odd as Mr. Russell's or his bigamist brother Frank's. Was Mr. Briggs telling the truth? He might be lying to cover for his own misdeeds. An embezzler and a burglar, he'd already proven himself untrustworthy. Why should she believe him now?

"Up, Briggs. Let's go." D. I. Goforth slapped him on the back.

"Neville's latest manuscript has all the juicy details." Mr. Briggs stood up. "We're publishing it." He rubbed his hands together. "Nothing like a murdered author to boost sales!"

"Are you confessing?"

"Heavens, no!" Mr. Briggs bristled. "Just stating a fact."

Eliza furrowed her brows. "And is this blackmail business a fact or a fiction?" Of course, he'd got it from a story. A made-up story. And he was trying to pass it off as truth. Publishers were as bad as writers.

"Why can't it be both?" Mr. Briggs shrugged. He let out a big sigh. "Take me away, detective."

*Why can't it be both? Fact is fact. Reality is reality. And fiction... well, that's just a bunch of boloney to distract the faint of heart from the truth.*

Eliza watched as the policemen flanked Mr. Briggs.

D. I. Goforth called back over his shoulder, "Thanks to your help, Scotland Yard has once again got its man. The Detection Club will be happy the case is solved and they can move on."

After D. I. Goforth and his partner hauled Briggs away, Eliza and Theo sat looking at each other. What did Mr. Briggs mean about Maud and blackmail? Had he based his supposition on a mystery-novel manuscript? Was he just trying to save his own skin? Or had Maud been blackmailing Neville? If he'd refused to pay her, or ended their affair, that could be motive for murder.

"Should we visit Maud?" Theo asked.

"Or go looking for Neville's manuscript?" Eliza got up and paced the length of the kitchen.

Theo glanced at his watch. "It's getting late." He joined her at the window. "I suggest a quick visit to Neville's flat followed by a nightcap."

"You can get a drink if you want." She tightened her lips. "I'm going to continue with the investigation."

"Why not do both?" He smiled. "Maud Wilkerson and her writer friends regularly meet at The Dove in Hammersmith for cocktails on Sunday nights."

"Well then, a nightcap it is!" Her mood brightened. Nothing like apprehending a burglar and coming up with a plan to lift one's spirits. "After our quick trip to Neville's flat. Hopefully, Mrs. Green can help us find a copy of his latest manuscript." She wasn't sure how reading a mystery book would help the investigation, but Mr. Briggs had indicated the story was based on Neville's experience. Perhaps, it was his only way to tell the world about his blackmailer. And if it was an autobiographical novel, then it might give them other clues as to Neville's state of mind, not to mention his health. "Alright. Let's go." She led Theo out of the flat, careful to leave everything as they'd found it and turn off the lights.

Outside, the night air was frigid. Eliza stayed close to Theo for warmth. They decided to take a taxi to Neville's flat. It would be quicker, and warmer, this time of night.

Huddled next to Theo in the taxi, she rehearsed what they'd learned so far... or at least the parts Theo already knew. She had to keep her advantage in their competition, after all. She hadn't told him the green thread from Dorothy's cape matched the thread from the gun. Although he was the one who found the thread and made the connection. She glanced over at Theo. He hadn't said a word since they got into the taxi.

Silent and sullen, he was staring straight ahead. What was wrong with him? Was he tired of the investigation? Tired of her? Or just plain tired? Maybe he was practicing chess in his head. Or maybe he was hiding something. Had he found some clues he wasn't telling her about? She tried to engage him in conversation, but he only grunted and stared out the window. She gave up and rode the rest of the way in silence, her hands folded on her lap.

The taxi pulled up in front of Neville's building. They had to pool their resources to pay the fare.

She pressed the button and Mrs. Green buzzed them up. The housekeeper answered the door with her hair wrapped in a plain scarf. She was only too happy to help them look for the manuscript. "If it means finding out who took Mr. Neville from us, I'll do anything," she said, pulling out drawers and searching through his desk. "Do you think the book is what got him in trouble?"

Eliza tilted her head. "Why do you say that?"

"That's what the lady writer and Mr. Neville argued about, isn't it?" Mrs. Green stopped hunting and stood there blinking.

Eliza and Theo looked at each other.

"What lady?" Eliza asked.

"When?" Theo added.

"Day before he died, it was. Mrs. Christie comes here accusing him." Mrs. Green stood near the desk wringing her hands. "Quite a row it was too."

"What did they argue about?" Eliza tightened her lips. Why hadn't the housekeeper mentioned the row before?

"Blackmail." Mrs. Green shook her head. "The lady accused

him of blackmail." She put a hand to her cheek. "Can you believe it? Mr. Neville would never..." Still shaking her head, she went back to rummaging in the desk.

*Blackmail?* Eliza's mouth fell open. *Again?* This was the second time tonight someone had mentioned blackmail. So, who was blackmailing whom? Was Maud Wilkerson the blackmailer? Or was it Mrs. Christie? Or Neville himself?

Mrs. Green pulled out an envelope from the bottom drawer. "This is it! The book." She turned it over and read off the envelope: "*Mrs. Crispy's Demise.*"

"Mrs. Crispy." Theo let out a guffaw. "Not very well disguised if he's writing about Agatha."

"And if Mr. Briggs is right about the manuscript"—Eliza nodded—"then perhaps, along with the blackmail, we'll learn more about Mrs. Christie's argument with Neville. Maybe it will give us some clues about her disappearance."

"Should make for an interesting read." Theo tucked the envelope under his arm.

It had better give them some helpful information. She didn't want to waste her time reading when she should be investigating.

"Now what?" he asked.

"Let's stick to our plan." Eliza buttoned her coat. "Next stop The Dove to find Maud Wilkerson." She glanced back at Mrs. Green. "Might I borrow something belonging to Mr. Lively? A small article of clothing perhaps?"

The housekeeper gave her an odd look. "Well, if it will help you find out who killed him." She went to the coat-rack and lifted a silk scarf. "How about this?" She held it up.

"Perfect." Eliza rolled up the scarf and tucked it into her chatelaine bag.

* * *

As they walked from Ravenscourt Park Station to the Dove, Theo pointed out the Bookworm Bookshop on Rivercourt Road. "I live just up there, above the shop."

*Figures he'd live in a bookshop.*

A few more streets and they reached the Dove, a cozy little pub overlooking the Thames River.

A roaring fire in the stone hearth was a welcome sight. Eliza and Theo hung their coats and hats on the coat-rack and then took a seat at the bar. Eliza ordered a glass of Chardonnay and Theo had Scotch whiskey neat.

They'd finished their drinks and were about to have a second round when a commotion at the entrance turned all heads. The familiar, high-pitched voice pierced the air like an ice pick puncturing a tin can.

Maud Wilkerson and her entourage of well-dressed society sorts laughed and waved long-stemmed cigarettes. They took the largest table toward the back of the pub. Flopping into wooden chairs around the table, they fawned and preened like they knew everyone was watching.

With Theo in tow, Eliza descended on Maud. When the older woman saw them, she squealed. "Eliza, darling. Theodore. Join us. I insist." Maud waved to the waiter. "Two more glasses... and keep the champagne coming."

"What are we celebrating?" Eliza asked, wondering if Neville's death was the happy occasion.

"Being alive," Maud said with a flourish. "Seize the night! You never know when it will be your last." She grasped her champagne flute with a gloved hand and took a sip.

"Like poor Neville Lively." Eliza pulled up a chair next to Maud.

"Exactly." Maud sighed. "Poor, dear, Neville. May he rest in peace." She held out a full glass to Eliza.

"From what Fergus Briggs tells us, you didn't give him any peace when he was alive." Eliza took the champagne and handed it to Theo, who was standing behind her chair. Hopefully, the champagne would keep him from breathing down her neck.

Maud pursed her lips. "Whatever do you mean?"

"Mr. Briggs told us you were blackmailing Neville." Eliza cocked her head.

"Blackmail!" Maud laughed. "How absurd."

Eliza leaned closer. "Something about an affair," she whispered. She sensed Theo's body tense behind her. He was such a prude.

"Neville and I were friends." Maud waved her away. "Very good friends." She jerked her head like she might cast away her feelings about her *good friend*.

"Why would Mr. Briggs tell us you were blackmailing him?" Theo asked.

"And what about the large payment he made to you last week?" Eliza took a champagne flute from the table. She held the glass mid-air, waiting for a reply. "I saw Neville's ledger."

"Oh, that." Maud laughed again, this time throwing her head back. "I was helping him purchase a painting." Her heavily made-up eyes sparkled. "A Dora Carrington. Have you heard of her? One of those Bloomsbury bright young things." Her tone turned serious. "She's awfully interesting." She put her hand on Eliza's sleeve. "Even with that terrible haircut."

Eliza squinted at her. Was she telling the truth? Were she and Neville just very good friends? Was the ledger entry a payment for a Carrington painting? Why would Neville buy an expensive painting if he was dying? It didn't tally. "We've also heard Neville was gravely ill." She met Maud's gaze. "That he was dying."

"He died alright," Maud blurted out. "Someone killed him." A cloud passed over her face. After a few seconds, she regained her composure. "Why are you pestering me? If you're so interested in finding out who did it, why not speak to Scotland Yard?" When she shook her head, a lock of flaming hair fell over her forehead. "I'm counting on them." She sneered.

"Don't worry. We will find him... or her." Eliza flashed a fake smile. "In the meantime." She lifted the little key from its chain around her neck. "Do you recognize this key?"

"No." She scowled. "Should I?"

"It's off Neville's key ring." She tucked it under the collar of her blouse. "We're trying to sleuth out what it goes to."

"You're no sleuth. You're just a secretary." Maud held the word *secretary* between her teeth like a dirty rag. "And not a very good one at that." With a sniff, she brushed the hair from her face.

Eliza bit her tongue. She was developing a deep dislike for the woman. She may or may not be a murderer, but she was damned annoying. "Scotland Yard is aware of the claims against you." Still feeling the sting of Maud's words, she turned to Theo. "Let's get out of here."

At the coat-rack, Theo helped her on with her overcoat. As he did, he froze in place, staring at another woman's coat.

"Look." He pointed. "The same brass button with an ivory center D. I. Goforth found at the crime scene."

"What button?" Eliza looked surprised. "You never told me about any button." She stood with her hands on her hips. "Withholding evidence, eh?"

"You're the one who wanted to make it a competition." He lifted the coat from the rack and took a closer look. "It's a match." He fingered the coat. "And look here." He held up the fabric where a couple of threads stuck out in the place where a button was missing.

"I'm pretty sure this is Maud's coat." Eliza glanced back to where Maud and her friends were drinking and laughing. She yanked the coat out of Theo's hands and marched back over to Maud. "Is this yours?"

Maud gave her a perturbed look. "You again."

"Is this your coat?" Eliza raised her voice.

"Yes." Maud grabbed it and clutched it to her chest. "What is it to you?"

"You're missing a button." Eliza pointed at the spot where the button should be.

"What?" Maud held out the coat and looked at the spot. "So I am. What of it?"

"D. I. Goforth found your missing button next to Neville's body the night of the shooting." Eliza raised her eyebrows. She didn't know where the detective had found the button exactly, but it sounded good. "What do you say to that?"

"I wasn't wearing this coat that night. The night poor Neville..." She laid it across her lap. "I was wearing my fur," she said indignantly. "I remember distinctly. That night was a cold one and the club dinner was formal." She held up her coat. "I'd never wear this old thing to a fancy dinner party." She arched her brows. "Anyone who had any fashion sense would know that."

"When was the last time you wore it, then?" Eliza used to follow fashion. But only because it helped with her espionage work. She'd never done it to impress people. Not like Maud.

"Let's see." Maud thought a minute. Her face lit up. "Oh, my word. The last time I wore it was to visit Neville. When I got the payment for the painting."

"How convenient." Eliza wondered if she was telling the truth.

"It must have fallen off in his flat." Maud got a queer look on her face. "So how did it end up at the Detection Club dinner?"

"My question exactly." Eliza nodded. "I'm sure D. I. Goforth will have the same inquiry."

"We should take the coat to D. I. Goforth." Theo held out his hand. "He can confirm that the buttons match."

"Are you mad?" Maud let out a laugh. "And let me freeze to death on the way home? I don't think so." She sucked her teeth. "It's all perfectly innocent, I assure you. I must have lost it at Neville's and perhaps he was returning it to me. Simple as that."

"Possible," Eliza said. "We'll see what the Yard thinks about it."

"Fine. Tell the detective to come around tomorrow afternoon and I'll give him a tour of my coat." Maud turned back to her friends. "A toast." She raised her glass. "To the fine fellows at Scotland Yard." As she went to take a sip, she bumped her elbow against Eliza's arm and dropped her glass. *Crash.* It hit the floor and shattered, sending champagne up Eliza's legs.

"Ouch!" Eliza jumped back. A shard of glass had lodged in her shin. She bent and plucked it out. Blood trickled down her stocking into her boot. She shot Maud a murderous look and then pulled the blade from her boot. In one deft movement, she grabbed the coat and used her knife to cut off one of the buttons. "We'll give this to D. I. Goforth to prove it matches the one he found at the scene." Whether or not the button was evidence, she'd enjoyed slicing it off Maud's coat. She turned to Theo. "Do you have a sticking plaster?"

"Back at my place, I do." He stood blinking at her.

She slid the blade back into its sheath in her boot and then took his arm. "Let's go to your place then."

His mouth opened and closed a few times but no sound came out. Finally, he blurted out, "My place is a bit of a mess." He blushed.

"A disorderly house is the sign of an orderly mind." Eliza grimaced and shook her leg. "And you, Theo Sharp, have a meticulous mind."

"So, you're expecting my flat to be a disaster?" Theo grinned.

She squeezed his arm. "I'll be disappointed if it's not." The cut on her leg stung as she sloshed toward the exit, her boots wet from champagne tinged with blood.

\* \* \*

Eliza had never been to Theo's flat. It was tiny. Much smaller than the one-bedroom she shared with Jane. And it was dark like a cave. Theo seemed indifferent to his surroundings and it showed in his living arrangements. Maybe coming to his place wasn't such a good idea. There were only two places to sit: at his desk or on his bed. She chose the desk chair.

He didn't offer to take her coat, so she slipped it over the back of the desk chair and then sat down to examine her wound. Her stocking was ruined and her leg still stung.

Theo hurriedly gathered up sheets of paper strewn across the desk. "Sorry," he said, collecting the pages and stacking them in a pile. As he did, she noticed her name on one of them. She plucked it out of his hand. What was he doing writing about her? She'd better not show up in one of his stories. She read the lines:

*Seeing Eliza every day is torture. I wish we'd never met up again at Gambit. If only I could exorcise her from my life and my dreams.*

She jerked her head up to look at him.

Even in the dim light, she could see his agonized expression. "I'm sorry," he said, taking the page away from her. "That wasn't for your eyes."

"No, I'm the one who's sorry." She got up. "Maybe I should go." She didn't want to *torture* him any longer.

"But your leg," he sputtered. "Let me get you a sticking plaster."

"I'm fine." She tried to keep her voice steady. "It's just a scratch." A prickly heat spread up her neck to her cheeks. "Anyway, we shouldn't be working together. Not if I'm going to beat you." She tugged on her coat and grabbed the envelope containing Neville's manuscript. On the off chance Mr. Briggs was telling the truth, she wasn't about to let Theo keep it.

When she opened the door to leave, Anthony was standing on the other side with his knuckles in mid-air about to knock.

"Eliza," he said in surprise. He glanced down at her blood-streaked leg. "What happened to you?"

"Nothing." She sniffed. "I'm fine."

"I'm looking for Theodore." He peeked over her shoulder. "Is he here?"

"He's all yours." She jerked her thumb toward the flat. "I was just leaving."

"Stay," he said. "You're going to want to hear this." He pushed past her. "I might know who killed Neville."

After what she'd just read, even Anthony's confession wouldn't get her to stay. Still, why was Anthony there? Was he going to confront Theo?

For the first time since the shooting, it dawned on her that

Theo Sharp could be the killer. She thumped herself on the head. How could she have been so stupid? If Theo shot Neville, then she'd clued him in on her entire investigation.

* * *

Theo's heart was racing. Why did she have to read his journal? She'd probably never speak to him again. Absently, he picked up a notebook from his desk. It was hard enough seeing her. What would it be like *not* seeing her? It wasn't just that she was pretty and smart. There was something mysterious about her. Like her foot-fighting. Where did she learn ju-jitsu? And lock picking? What other hidden skills did she have? The way she went right to the point. Like a dagger through the heart. It was exhilarating.

"Well, what do you think, Theodore, old boy?" Anthony fiddled with a cigarette. "Cat got your tongue?"

"Sorry." Theo laid the notebook down again. "I was distracted."

"About Agatha." Anthony's voice was tinny and impatient. "And my theory about the murder."

"What about her?" Theo dropped into the desk chair.

"Do you think she did it?" Anthony looked exasperated. "And she's hiding from the police. That's why she disappeared the morning after Neville's death."

"I don't know." Theo closed his eyes. *Mistake.* All he could see was Eliza rushing out the door. He opened them again and stared down at his hands. Why did he let her come here in the first place? Now she probably hated him.

*Seeing Eliza every day is torture. I wish we'd never met up again at Gambit. If only I could exorcise her from my life and my dreams.*

The lines from his journal came back to torment him. He let out a breath. At least now she knew how he felt.

"Neville's ten commandments of detective fiction were tongue-in-cheek." Anthony finally lit the bloody cigarette. "Surely, he didn't mean for everyone to take them so seriously." He shook his head. "And now he's dead." He looked skyward. "God rest his soul."

"Maybe it was just an unfortunate accident," Theo said, forcing himself to pay attention. Possible but not likely.

"Yes," Anthony said with a weak smile. "I suppose you're right. It was an accident."

"You and Neville were close." Theo played with a pencil. "How did he seem lately? Was he preoccupied or worried?" If Neville was being blackmailed, maybe Anthony had noticed him acting strange or anxious. And he must know if Neville was ill.

"Well." Anthony picked at imaginary lint on his trousers. "He wasn't quite his old self." He looked over at Theo. "With Holly away at Cambridge and his illness..." His voice trailed off.

"Tell me about his illness." Theo dropped the pencil on his desk and sat upright. "Was it terminal?"

"Afraid so. Nasty business." Anthony knitted his brows. "Bright's disease."

*Bright's disease. What a terrible way to go.* "Who was Neville's doctor?"

"On Chesterton's recommendation, I believe he saw Doctor Johnson at St. Barts in Smithfield." Anthony sucked his teeth. "Such a shame."

"A shame," Theo repeated.

Anthony stood up. "I'd best leave you. It's late. My wife will wonder where I've got to." He flashed a weak smile.

"Yes, quite," Theo said, his mind still on Eliza and his stupid journal.

## 12

### THE DOCTOR

The next morning, Eliza curled up on the sofa in front of the fireplace with Queenie at her feet. She tried to concentrate on Neville Lively's book manuscript. At least she had an excuse to stay indoors. The sleet outside the window looked dismal.

She was on her second cup of coffee. It wasn't helping her focus. She kept thinking about Theo's journal. What did he mean, seeing her was torture? Why didn't he just tell her he didn't want her around? He didn't have to see her every day. Or ever again, for that matter. Why did he tell her to take the job with the Detection Club if he didn't want to see her? No doubt out of some misguided sense of obligation to her adoptive older brother and Theo's roommate, Reggie Hall. He must have promised to look after her when Reggie went to fight on the Western Front.

But she didn't need looking after. She never had. As a small girl, she'd hustled chess and picked pockets and survived on the streets. No. She didn't need Theo or anyone else looking after her. Especially if it was *torture*.

She gazed into the fire, allowing the dance of orange and

yellow flames to carry her thoughts away from Theo. The trouble was, they carried them back to Billy and the night at the docks when he got his foot caught in the anchor ropes racing to save her.

*Come on. Stop it and concentrate.* Shuddering, she forced herself to go back to the manuscript. Scanning the sentences with her finger, she looked for clues. Clues to what? How could this novel tell her anything about Neville's murder? She let out a frustrated exhale and pressed on.

"Taking the day off?" Jane appeared at the foot of the sofa. "Aren't you supposed to be finding out what those mystery writers are up to?" She raised her eyebrows.

"I'll have you know." Eliza uncurled and put her feet on the floor, careful not to disturb Queenie. "I'm doing just that." She held up the thick manuscript. "This is Neville Lively's latest novel. I'm reading it and looking for clues."

"Reading a book with words." Jane winked. "How grown-up of you."

"Make fun all you want." Eliza rolled her eyes. "It's probably a waste of my time."

"Loitering around Gambit Chess Rooms is a waste of your time." Jane kissed the top of her head. "Reading books expands your mind."

"No wonder my head hurts." Eliza smiled.

"See you this evening." Jane crossed the room and gathered up her coat and hat. "Be good—"

"I know. I know." Eliza waved her away.

Once her sister was gone, Eliza tucked her feet up on the sofa, gave Queenie a pat, and went back to the manuscript.

So far, the story seemed vaguely like Mrs. Christie's *The Murder of Roger Ackroyd*. But instead of the protagonist using a Dictaphone as an alibi, in Neville's story, he used it to incriminate an innocent woman and thereby throw suspicions off himself. Her nerves in shambles, the framed woman retreated to her favorite spa in Harrogate for a week-long treatment. *Harrogate, why does that sound familiar?*

If Neville was using a similar conceit with his unreliable narrator, then why did he object so violently to Mrs. Christie's murder mystery? Eliza flipped to the end of the manuscript. Was it possible Neville was jealous of Mrs. Christie's success and that was why he wanted her expelled from the club? Or perhaps he'd been scooped and he resented her? He'd wanted to publish his novel first but she beat him to it?

But Mrs. Christie hadn't been expelled from the club. If anything, Neville's arguments against her just made the other writers more sympathetic. And it was Neville who was killed not her. *Oh God, hopefully not her, too.* So how did his resentment of Agatha Christie come to play in the crime? Really, it made no sense.

Although it was a strange coincidence Neville's framed woman runs away to a spa in Harrogate and Mrs. Christie went missing immediately after his murder.

*Harrogate! Oh, my word!*

In response to Eliza swinging her feet to the floor, Queenie looked up and shifted on the sofa.

The card in Agatha's bag. It was from Harrogate spa. Eliza needed to find that spa. She glanced at her watch. *Drat.* Already after nine. Too late to start the long trip. Harrogate would have to wait. She would go first thing tomorrow on the earliest train. At this point, twenty-four more hours wouldn't make the difference between life and death. Right? Plus, another day would give her time to make amends with Theo and invite him along so she could surreptitiously investigate him. Whether he liked it or not, she was going to see him again, if just to question him about the murder. She'd take the day to hatch a plan. Heck, in another day, the police may have located Mrs. Christie and she'd have no reason to make the trip.

She shook her head. No. There was no way Neville could have predicted Agatha Christie's disappearance. It was mad to think his mystery novel would lead her anywhere, let alone help her find Neville's killer or locate Mrs. Christie. Of course, Mr. Briggs was lying. He was a liar and a cheat and possibly a murderer, too. She shouldn't have believed him. And now she'd wasted a perfectly good morning reading this ridiculous story.

And then there was Theo...

He always acted so strange around her. Like he was hiding something. What wasn't he telling her? What was he hiding? He had a secret. She knew it. But what? Hopefully not that he'd killed Neville. Anyway, why would Theo want to kill Neville? She wracked her brains for a motive. What was the relationship between Theo and the dead man? What had she witnessed between Theo and Neville? She tightened her lips and tried to remember back to that first night at Anthony's flat.

For one, Theo was on the opposite side of the Christie debate. Would he kill Neville to defend Agatha Christie? Seemed pretty extreme. Second, Theo was a true-crime enthusiast. Was he taking the perfect murder game too far? Way too far. Although it could make a good story, even a bestseller. Is that what he wanted? Third, Theo was trying to finish his second novel and make a living as a writer. Would killing Neville somehow help his career? Would the publicity from the case sell books? It all seemed so calculating and cold. Not at all like Theo. Then again, If Theo did kill Neville, his odd behavior would start to make sense. The averted eyes, the blushing and turning away, the half-sentences and awkward pauses. Of course, he acted like he was hiding something. Because he was.

She glanced out the window. The sleet had turned to rain. Alright, not a perfectly good morning. She reached down and scratched behind Queenie's ears.

She wished she could ask Theo about the story. He was a novelist. But he was also a suspect, although it took her long enough to realize it. Not to mention, he hated her.

She flipped another page. Could any of Neville's story be based on fact? Theo was the literary critic, not her. She had an idea. She should invite him to Harrogate. She could use the time to study him, to question him, to interrogate him. A trip to Harrogate would give her a chance to ask him about Neville's manuscript *and* find out whether he was guilty.

Then again, if she *tortured* him so much, maybe it was best to leave him alone. She snorted to get the stupid thoughts out of her head. *Quit being so childish. Who cares what he thinks as long as you find out the truth?*

She padded back into the kitchen to pour one last cup of coffee.

Tomorrow she would go to Harrogate, with or without Theo. Today, she would work on finding Neville's doctor and learn whether Neville truly had been dying. A dying man was capable of desperate acts. Although getting himself murdered was a bit extreme even for the likes of Neville Lively, executioner of daft radio tricks. Now, if she only knew the name of his doctor.

She went to the telephone and rang Neville's flat. Perhaps Mrs. Green had remembered the doctor's name. Anyway, she had something else to ask Mrs. Green.

A man answered the telephone. Surprised, Eliza's brain skipped a beat. "May I speak to Mrs. Green?"

"It's her day off," the man said.

"And who is this?" No sooner had she asked then she realized he must be Barnaby Lively.

"Neville Lively's son, Barnaby," he said.

"Ah, this is Eliza Baker. Do you happen to know the name of your father's physician?" She readied a pencil and paper just in case.

"Do I know you?" he asked.

"We met outside your father's flat." She paused. "I was with Theo Sharp."

"I don't remember you." His tone was matter-of-fact, but considerably more pleasant than the last time he'd spoken to her. Probably because he'd been drunk last time.

"I'm a friend of... your father's," she lied. "From the Detection Club." She took advantage of his not remembering her. "Your papa mentioned he'd found an excellent doctor and I'm looking for a recommendation. So, I was wondering if you knew who he saw."

"Not off the top of my head." He paused and she heard scraping. "But I'll check the drawer where he keeps his diary. He probably has it written down."

Neville kept a diary. She needed to get a look at it. "Thank you."

She heard the flipping of pages. "Here it is," he said. "Dr. Aaron Johnson."

Johnson was a common name. "Do you happen to have his address or telephone number?"

"The address is suite 3003 at St. Bartholomew Hospital in Smithfield."

St. Bartholomew sunk in her stomach like a rock. The last time she'd been there, she'd watched Billy die the death of a thousand cuts. The anchor rope had severed his leg and nearly took off his arm. Bit by bit, he'd disappeared before her very eyes. That was eight years ago and she hadn't set foot in a hospital since.

She heard Barnaby flipping through more pages. He read off the telephone number.

She didn't bother writing it down. Pushing away the painful memories, she said, "Brilliant. Thank you." She closed her eyes. "Can I ask you something else?"

"Go ahead." Hard to believe this was the same belligerent man she'd met outside Neville's flat.

"Do you know your father's friend Maud Wilkerson?" She bit a fingernail and glanced down at Queenie, who was looking up at her as if she thought Eliza was speaking to her.

"Maud is my godmother," he said warmly. "I've known her all my life."

She wrote *godmother* at the bottom of the sheet. "Do you know anything about a painting she was helping your father purchase?" Maud had said it was a painter by the name of Dora Carrington. Eliza wrote that down too.

"Painting. Hmmm." She could hear Barnaby breathing into the receiver. "Maud's always been a great collector." He paused. "I say. There was a painting delivered yesterday. Could that be it?"

"Is it by Dora Carrington?" She reached down and petted Queenie.

"Let me check." She heard the receiver click against something. A minute later, he was back. "Yes! How did you know?"

"Maud told me." So, it was true. She was helping him buy a painting. "Were you at the flat when Maud visited your father last week? She came by to collect the funds for the painting. Did you by chance see her?"

"I may have done," he said. "I've seen Maud several times since I've been back. From what I gather, she used to visit Papa regularly, especially after Mama moved to Cambridge." He sighed. "I've been away in India, you see."

"And you returned at your father's request." She continued taking notes on the conversation.

"Yes. I say, how did you know?" His voice lifted.

"You told me." She smiled.

"I guess I did." He chuckled. "I sometimes suffer from brown-bottle memory lapses, I'm afraid."

"Speaking of memory." It was a long shot, but she had to ask. "Do you remember Maud wearing a cream-colored wool coat with brass and ivory buttons?"

"Why would I?" He laughed. "Eliza Baker, you ask a lot of questions. You're a nosy little thing, aren't you?"

That was her cue the interview was over. "Thank you, Mr. Lively. Good day." She hung up and immediately went to the closet. Queenie followed her every move.

She put on her heavy boots and then fetched her warmest wool coat and winter hat. On her way out, she grabbed an umbrella from the stand next to the door and tucked it under her arm. She tugged on her gloves, took a deep breath, and then plunged outside into the gloom. Next stop, St. Bart's in Smithfield.

* * *

St. Bart's hospital smelled of bleach and desperation. Eliza's palms started sweating the minute she crossed the threshold. To say she didn't like hospitals was an understatement. The terrible memories of her last visit to St. Bart's threatened from around every corner. She swallowed hard and kept her eyes trained on the reception desk. With a steady stride, she crossed the foyer to the receptionist.

"I'm looking for Dr. Aaron Johnson."

"Dr. Johnson," the receptionist repeated, running her finger down a clipboard. "Urology. Third floor. Suite 3003." She pointed. "The lifts are just around the corner."

She took a deep breath and made a beeline for the lifts. The sooner she got this over with, the better. She pressed the button to call the lift. *Come on!* She pressed it again. And again. *Click, click, click.* Finally, the doors opened and she stepped inside. At least she was alone with her thoughts.

The lift stopped on the first floor. Her solitude was about to be interrupted. The doors opened.

*What's he doing here?*

Theo did a double-take and then stepped inside. The scent of cedarwood and lime followed him in.

"Fancy meeting you here," he said, blushing.

"You're here to see Neville's doctor." Eliza took a step backwards. If he was guilty, he was doing a pretty good job of hiding it. In that case, this whole investigation and their wager was a ruse.

He nodded. "Anthony told me Neville was suffering from Bright's disease."

"That's a kidney disease." She glanced at Theo, wondering if she should mention the journal entry. Of course not. Whether or not he was the killer, she shouldn't be sharing evidence with him. *Especially* if he was the killer.

"Look." He turned to face her. "I'm sorry about last night... I didn't mean for you to read—"

"No." She shook her head. "I'm sorry. I shouldn't have... Really, I feel terrible. But I'm going to make it up to you." She tightened her lips. "I promise. From now on, I'm going to try to be kind." *If that's what it takes to weasel the truth out of you.*

"You *are* kind." He averted his gaze. "You're just forthright—"

"Blunt to the point of cruelty." She looked up at the ceiling as if that could make the lift move faster. He had called her cruel. And he was right. She was impatient, and as a result often lacking in social graces. Funny. Because when the captain sent her to gather intelligence for the War Office, she could flirt and flit with the best of them. It had been her job to be charming. But after the "tragedy" on the docks, all that changed. She changed. Life was cruel. What was the point of pretending it wasn't? "You were right about me."

"You're not cruel. I shouldn't have said it." He stared down at his shoes. "It's just that..." He sputtered. "I've been wanting to tell you for the longest time..." His voice trailed off. He looked over at her with something like sadness in his eyes. No. Not sadness. Longing. Longing for what? To get away from her, no doubt. Or longing to get away with murder.

The lift doors opened.

"We're here." *Thank goodness.* She didn't know how much more proximity she could take. The scent lingering just under the cedar notes, the scent of him, was making her head swim. She pointed to the urology suite, which was straight ahead. She'd better get a grip on her feelings about Theo if she was going to get to the truth. The first lesson of her wasted Scotland Yard training had been *stay objective.*

"Right. Some other time, then." Theo stretched his arm across the lift door. "After you."

They sat in the waiting room of the urology suite until Dr. Johnson could see them. Several patients waited too. Many of them suffered from dropsy and had swollen legs and feet. Eliza looked away. She'd never been able to handle illness. The help-lessness of watching her mother die of tuberculosis had been enough sickness for a lifetime. Her mother told her it would be alright, but she'd seen the terror in her eyes and knew it wasn't.

Finally, the receptionist called them back. Dr. Johnson was an affable, middle-aged man with sunken cheeks. He gestured to two chairs across from his desk and then sat down himself. Theo introduced himself and then explained what had happened. Eliza *may* have mentioned she worked for the Metropolitan police. She *may* have forgotten to put it in the past tense.

"I don't usually discuss my patient's medical records," the doctor said. "But under the circumstances." He sighed. "Yes, Mr. Lively was suffering from incurable Bright's disease. We tried warm baths, dietary restrictions, even leeches." He shook his head. "It was no use. He was dying."

So, it was true. He was dying. "How did he take the news?" Eliza asked. Any normal person would have been shaken by such a diagnosis. And his attempt to reconcile with his son before he died was natural too. Virtuous even.

"He kept his good humor all through the treatments." The doctor smiled. "Mr. Lively was quite a character. Once, he played a practical joke on my nurse, who thought he'd lost several fingers." He chuckled. "But it was just some prank glove he bought at a magic shop." His smiled faded. "In the end, he was a believer and thankfully, he found solace in his faith."

"Thank you, doctor." Theo stood first. "You've been very helpful." He turned to go.

"Yes, thank you." Eliza followed him out.

The first few moments back in the lift were filled with agonizing silence. Eliza inhaled. "I'm going to Harrogate tomorrow to investigate." She turned to look at him. "Do you want to come with me?" Given the awkwardness of the ride up in the lift, she didn't know if she hoped he'd say yes or no.

"Yes." He smiled.

"It will probably be a worthless trip and come to nothing." She shrugged. "You can bring your chess board and practice on the train." *While I interrogate you.*

"Or we could play." His cheeks turned the color of a pale-pink rose. "A game."

"Really?" Her spirits brightened.

He nodded. "Why not?"

Maybe he didn't hate her so much after all. Riding in silence down to the ground floor, she smiled to herself. *Maybe* this trip to Harrogate wouldn't be a waste after all.

* * *

The next morning before dawn, Theo waited for Eliza at Kings Cross Station. They would take the train to York and then switch for one to Harrogate. He still didn't know why they were making the trip. But after the incident with his journal, he was happy she still wanted his company. He wouldn't have blamed her for never speaking to him again.

He paced back and forth on the platform. The train was leaving in ten minutes. Where was she? Had she changed her mind? He glanced at his watch for the tenth time. Perhaps she was already on the train? Why hadn't he asked where exactly to meet? Should he get on and try to find her? Or continue waiting? A paralyzing anxiety seized in his chest. He stood still as a statue, not knowing what to do next. As a writer, how would he describe this scene? How could he make the reader feel what he felt? What exactly did he feel?

A tightness in his chest. But an odd expansion too. As if he might explode. And his throat seemed full of cotton wool. A slight tingling pricked his palms. And an invisible cage ensnared him and kept him from moving. Yes. That was it. Trapped. He felt trapped. Like an animal. And yet, unlike an animal, he knew *what it meant* to be confined. Not just the physical sensations and pain, which humans shared with animals. But mental anguish. Did animals feel mental anguish? He thought of Dorothy's cats following her from room to room... and his father's dogs.

When he was a boy, his father kept dogs for hunting. Once, Theo brought a puppy to his bedroom and snuggled him all night. When his father found out, he put the puppy in a cage and locked it with a key. Theo had searched everywhere for the key to that lock. In the middle of the night, he'd crept into his father's library and searched the drawers of his desk. He'd searched the bookshelves and his father's pipe stand. When his parents were away, he'd escaped his governess and searched in his father's nightstand. No key. Whenever he visited the stables, the puppy would look out at him from the cage with those sad, accusing eyes.

"There you are!" Eliza's voice brought him back from his memories. "I've been waiting for you on the train."

He blinked, wondering if he could capture in writing the puppy's point of view.

# 13

## THE SEARCH

As the train pulled out of the station, Eliza settled into the seat next to Theo. The train car was chilly and she pulled her coat tight around her torso. A cup of coffee wouldn't go amiss.

"This is exciting," Theo said. "I've never been to Harrogate."

Funny. He still didn't know why they were going to Harrogate. He never asked. He'd simply said, "Yes." She liked that about him. Then again, he could be a killer trying to catch her off guard.

"Don't you want to know why we're going to Harrogate?" she asked, rubbing her hands together for warmth.

"Why are we going to Harrogate?" He smiled.

She told him about Neville's manuscript and the mysterious spa in Harrogate.

Theo laughed. "So, we're following a hunch?" His eyes sparked. "I thought you didn't believe in gut feelings." He leaned his shoulder against hers. "What happened to cold, hard evidence and forensic analysis?"

"When you run out of evidence"—she shrugged—"educated guesses are all that's left."

"Are you admitting facts only get you so far?" He sloughed off his overcoat and folded it onto his lap.

"Facts are the goal." She tugged on the finger of her glove. "But the means to attaining them may require—"

"Imagination," he offered cheerfully.

"You could call it that." She glanced at him and then averted her eyes. The way he looked at her was unnerving. And that lock of hair that fell across his forehead. She had the urge to brush it out of his face. And his soft cheeks. She'd never seen a man with such soft cheeks. Didn't he have to shave like all the others?

"Facts are useless without interpretation," he said. "Through imagination, we assemble the facts into a coherent story. The story is the key."

"You and your stories." She stole a quick glance.

"Aren't we piecing together a story?" His voice was full of passion. "Trying to figure out motives, who killed Neville and why? Where Agatha went and why?"

"I suppose so." She picked at a loose thread on her coat.

"The trip to Neville's doctor, the questions of Neville's children: Aren't we trying to construct a story to explain his behavior before he died?" he insisted.

She nodded.

"Everyone has a story—"

"But are they true?" she interrupted. "Not all stories are true stories."

"And what is *the truth* but a story that is repeated and has solidified over time?" He ran his hand through his hair and the tempting lock disappeared from his forehead. "The truth is nothing but a story that has taken root."

*Truth is truth.* She stared out the window. Something was either true or false no matter how many times it was repeated.

*Solidified over time.* "Truth isn't like resin or glue. It doesn't start out soft and then harden or set up." Cold, hard facts were true from the beginning.

"Isn't that how detection works?" He grinned. "Clues solidify into a theory and a theory turns into a hypothesis that with enough evidence becomes the solution to the crime?"

His badgering was getting on her nerves. Who was interrogating whom? She shifted in her seat. She should bide her time. Be patient. Eventually, he would crack and tell her what he was hiding. Argh. She couldn't stand it. "Speaking of crime and truth. What about you? What's your story?" She turned to face him. "Did you have a reason to want Neville dead?" As soon as she blurted it out, she regretted it. As she'd learned at the Met, a good investigator takes her time and builds suspense to get a confession. But patience never was her strong suit.

"Me?" He got a look on his face like a scolded puppy. "Since when am I a suspect?"

"You're hiding something." She held his gaze. "I know there's something you're not telling. Did you kill Neville? Is that why you're always acting so mysterious?"

"No!" He squirmed in his seat. "I'm sure you're hiding things from me too." He tightened his lips. "It's this stupid competition. The wager. It's made you paranoid."

Paranoid? Who was the one who was paranoid? She bit her lip. Why did it hurt so much when he criticized her? What did she care what he thought?

When she didn't respond, Theo must have got the hint. He pulled a book from his satchel and started reading. She watched as the buildings disappeared and fields of green and gold fell over the landscape like an undulating quilt. The motion of the train made her drowsy. Her head bobbed to the rhythm and she could barely keep her eyes open.

When she woke up, her head was on Theo's shoulder, his warmth enveloping her in comfort and ease. She inhaled his scent and closed her eyes again. *Clack. Clack. Clack.* The train swayed to a song in her head, "The Caterpillar," one her mother used to sing when she was a girl. She drifted off to the familiar refrain.

The next time she awoke, Theo was gently pushing her off his shoulder. "We're in York," he whispered. "Wake up, sleepy head."

She yawned and stretched herself awake. She really hoped he wasn't a murderer.

Less than an hour to go and they'd reach Harrogate. Time for a quick game of chess. He'd promised after all.

After they changed trains and settled in, she turned to Theo. "How about that game now?"

"Game?" Theo blinked.

"Chess." She shook her head. "Don't be coy. You promised."

He patted his satchel. "Darn. I left my board at home."

"What!" She scowled and then she remembered she'd promised to be nice and she still hadn't wheedled the truth out of him about whatever he was hiding. "No matter." She smiled. "We can review the case and make a plan for Harrogate."

"What's the plan for Harrogate?" Theo nudged her. "What does Neville's novel tell us to do?"

She opened her bag and pulled out a newspaper clipping. "We ask around." She held out the front page of the *Daily Mail* with its large picture of Mrs. Christie and her daughter. "Find out if anyone has seen Agatha Christie."

"Remind me again why you think she might be in Harrogate?" He gave her a playful look that made his eyes dance. "A hunch, was it?"

She crossed her arms. "The card in Agatha's bag." Truth be told, she had her doubts. "And then Neville's manuscript—"

"Foretold Agatha's disappearance?" he teased.

"Alright. I admit it's a long shot." She rubbed her neck. "But what else do we have to go on?" She exhaled. "Agatha is still a prime suspect and we need to get to her before the police do if we want to clear her name."

The train slowed to a stop at Harrogate Station. A brisk wind met Eliza as she stepped onto the platform.

"Now what?" Theo stuffed his hands in his pockets.

"We start asking questions." Eliza approached a porter. "Excuse me, sir."

The porter stopped pushing his cart. "Yes, miss?"

"Have you seen this woman?" She showed him the clipping.

He studied the picture and then shook his head. "I don't think so."

"Are there any health spas in town?" She folded the clipping and slipped it back into her bag.

"Well, let's see." He thought a moment. "There's the Royal Turkish Bath House."

"And where is that?" She took a piece of paper and pencil from her bag. She really needed to get a notebook to keep all these scraps of paper in one place.

"Parliament Street." He pointed and gave her directions.

"Do you know of any others?" She wrote down the address.

"Sorry. No." He smiled. "But I've heard wonderful things about the Turkish Baths."

"Thank you." Theo nodded. "I'm sure we'll enjoy it."

\* \* \*

The Royal Turkish Baths was a beautiful brick building topped with a Moorish dome. Upon entering, they had three choices: the winter gardens, the hospital, or straight through to the Turkish baths. They stopped at the kiosk and Eliza showed the clipping to the attendant.

"I'm not sure." Her mouth twitched as she studied the picture. "So many ladies come for the waters and treatment."

"Can we take a look around?" Eliza asked.

"For three shilling apiece," the attendant said.

"We just want a quick look." Eliza narrowed her brows.

"Of course. That will be three shillings each."

Eliza looked at Theo.

"That's a week's wages." Grumbling, he dug into his pocket and produced the coins.

"We're the best spa in Harrogate." The attendant handed Eliza a brochure. "Internationally renowned."

"Are there other spas in Harrogate?" Eliza asked.

"I wouldn't know." The attendant handed them each a ticket. "The baths are just through there." She pointed down an arched hallway. "Women and men split off at the end of the hall. Women to the right and men to the left."

When they reached the split, Eliza patted Theo's arm. "You wait here while I question the women." She held up the clipping. "Then you can take the photograph and ask the men."

"I paid," he said. "Why don't we take the waters?"

"We don't have time." She turned toward the women's changing room. "The last train back to London leaves at five."

"But—"

She left him standing there gaping at her. Not bothering to remove her clothes, she marched through the changing room to the baths. The bathing room was lovely with decorative arches and mosaic-tiled floors. Several women soaked in a large pool.

The room was hot and steamy and she started to perspire just crossing over to the pool. The humidity made her hair stick to her face and her clothes stick to her skin. The newspaper clipping went limp in her hand.

"Excuse me." Eliza stood at the edge of the pool. "Might I ask you ladies a question."

They all stared at her. This was the first time she was embarrassed about wearing clothes. "Have you seen this woman?" She went to each lady and showed them the photograph. None of them had seen Mrs. Christie.

"I love her books!" one of the women raved. "I want a Christie for Christmas, that's what I told my husband."

By the time she got back to the hallway, she was damp and sticky and her cheeks felt inflamed. Maybe coming to Harrogate wasn't such a good idea. What had she been thinking... making the trip on impulse to chase a silly hunch, all because of Neville's novel?

Eliza paced the hallway waiting for Theo to get back from checking with the men.

When he returned, his hair was damp and his cheeks were red. He shook his head. "No luck with the men either."

The cold air outside was a welcome relief. As they walked toward the town square, they stopped at every hotel and spa along the way and asked about Agatha Christie. No one had seen her. After three hours of walking and inquiries, they stopped at a pub to grab a quick bite before heading back to the train station. The trip had been a complete bust. No one anywhere had seen Mrs. Christie, although many knew of her widely publicized disappearance.

Eliza ordered a pot of tea and a plate of fish and chips and Theo did the same except he had beer instead of tea. They sat near the fireplace to warm up. After traipsing around in the cold slush and still damp from the Turkish bathhouse, she was chilled and her boots were soaked through.

"I'm sorry I dragged you on this fool's errand." She rubbed her hands together.

"I've enjoyed it." He smiled.

*Was he mad? Did he actually enjoy a long train ride where she accused him of murder followed by a dismal day slogging through slush?*

He took a sip of his beer. "And we got to see Harrogate."

"Such as it is." She poured herself a cup of tea. "This will teach me to follow a hunch."

"Let's not give up quite yet." He held out his hand. "If it's worth wanting—"

"It's worth working for." She finished his sentence.

"That's right." He drained his glass. "Give me the photo."

She reached into her bag and pulled out the clipping for what felt like the hundredth time. It was smudged and looking worse for wear.

He circled the pub showing Agatha's picture around to the other patrons and staff. The result was the same as before. Head shaking, expressions of admiration and worry for the mystery writer. After making the rounds, Theo dropped back into his chair. "Sorry mate, no luck."

The waiter delivered their food. Eliza realized she hadn't eaten all day. She'd skipped breakfast to get to the station on time. Her stomach growled. The smell of the crispy fish and golden chips made her mouth water. She tucked in with gusto.

"Waiter," Theo said. "I wonder if you've seen this woman by any chance?" He held out the news clipping.

The waiter tilted his head and examined it. "May I?" He took the photograph and held it up to the light. "She does look familiar."

Of course she looked familiar. Her picture was plastered across every newspaper in the country.

"I think I've seen her at the Hydro." He looked down at Theo. "I'm filling in for the regular drummer in the Miff Mole band. After I get off here, I go down the street to the Hydro to play for posh visitors from London and Edinburgh."

"Where is this Hydro?" Eliza's spirits lifted. "And *what* is it?" Her pulse quickened. Could it be? Did they finally have a lead?

"Don't you know?" The waiter gave her an odd look. "That key around your neck." He pointed. "It's a key to a locker at the Hydro spa." He looked from her to Theo and back. "I figured you must be staying there."

She fingered the key. "So the Hydro is a spa?" Why would Neville have a key to a locker at a Harrogate spa? Was he taking the waters as a treatment? They needed to get to this Hydro and open that locker.

"It's a hotel and lodge with Turkish baths and entertainment." The waiter handed the clipping back to Theo. "Just up the street in the center of town. You can't miss it."

Eliza glanced at her watch. "But we *will* miss our train."

# 14

## HARROGATE HYDRO

The Harrogate Hydro Hotel was indeed in the town center. Outside, it was an unassuming gray building. In the summer, no doubt the ivy climbing the brick added charm. Now, brown and withered, it added an air of decay and foreboding.

Inside, with high beam ceilings and stone fireplaces, the hotel resembled a rustic lodge. Unlike the Royal Turkish Baths, where the focus was on treating the body, the Hydro seemed more tailored toward treating the soul. Although not as colorful as the baths, it offered swanky dining options, healing waters, and massage treatments, along with speakeasy-style entertainment. A billboard in the lobby advertised tonight's entertainment as Miff Mole and his jazz orchestra.

Eliza asked directions to the spa and then speedwalked across the lobby to get there.

"Wait for me," Theo called from behind her.

The spa was lovely... and expensive. She grimaced as she turned over her last coins to gain entrance. As she stood at the door to the women's locker room, she realized that Neville's key would be for a locker in the men's. Reluctantly, she pulled the chain over her head and handed the little key to Theo. "I guess you'll have to do the honors."

He smiled, snagged the key, and trotted off to the men's locker room.

She paced back and forth in the hallway waiting for him to return. It didn't take long. Within a few minutes, he was back.

"Well?" She looked intently at him. "What did you find?"

He held out his hand. In his palm sat another little key. This one had the letter V engraved on its bow.

"Another key?" She took it and turned it over. Not just another key: another locker key. "Why would Neville have a locker key in his locker? What else was in there?"

"Nothing." Theo threw up his hands. "Here is your chain." He held it out to her.

She slipped the new key onto the chain and put it around her neck for safekeeping. The mystery of the first key led them to the mystery of the second. Did this key have anything to do with Neville's murder? Was he hiding something? Something the killer was trying to find? And how did Agatha's disappearance fit in? Was Mrs. Christie looking for this key? Had she skipped off in search of whatever Neville had hidden in this locker?

Eliza tucked the key into her blouse. "Let's continue our search for Agatha." She led the way.

For the next two hours, Eliza and Theo wandered around the hotel asking staff and patrons if they'd seen Agatha Christie. Apparently, their waiter was the only person who'd seen her. Eliza was beginning to wonder whether he had imagined it, or perhaps seen someone who resembled Mrs. Christie. Surely, if she was here, others would recognize her.

They took a seat in the supper club and waited for the band to come on. If they didn't find Agatha, or another witness to her whereabouts, Eliza could question the waiter-cum-drummer before the show. While she waited, she ordered a Chardonnay and Theo asked for whiskey neat. She turned her chair toward the entrance so she could scan the guests as they entered. Soon the lounge was filled with well-dressed men and women, most in couples or groups. No sign of Mrs. Christie. And no sign of the drummer. As the tables filled up, the room exploded with chatter.

The lights dimmed. The crowd hushed. And the band walked on stage. Sure enough, there was the waiter from the pub. He took a seat behind the drum set. Eliza would have to catch him during intermission or after the show. Then what? What if he couldn't tell them any more about Agatha's whereabouts? What if he'd been mistaken? She drained her wine and ordered another while Theo nursed his whiskey.

The dance floor was quickly packed with couples swinging and swaying to Miff Mole's orchestra. The little man with round spectacles sure could play the trombone. The music was so peppy, Eliza couldn't help but sway. Still, she kept alert and on the lookout for Mrs. Christie.

Theo sat blurry-eyed as if in a trance, seemingly mesmerized by the music.

"I don't see her," Eliza said between tunes. "Do you?"

Theo shook his head.

"I'm going to ambush our waiter friend." She got up from the table. "Wait here."

Eliza stood near the stage waiting for the band to take an intermission. After ten minutes, she went to get another glass of wine. The band kept playing upbeat numbers until nearly midnight. By the time they finally stopped, and after two more glasses of wine, Eliza felt a bit woozy. With Theo in tow, she made her way backstage. Why was the room tilting? She grabbed Theo's arm.

"Are you alright?" he asked.

"Perfectly fine." She stumbled over the word *perfectly*.

The band was nowhere to be seen. Eliza spotted a rear entrance and made a beeline, a buzzy beeline, zigging and zagging. Outside the entrance, some band members, including Miff Mole, stood smoking and laughing. But the drummer was gone.

"Have you seen this woman?" Eliza asked, whipping the clipping out of her chatelaine bag.

"No," Mr. Mole said. "She's a doll. She your sister?" He had an American accent.

"A friend," Theo said.

Eliza showed the photo around. But the other musicians hadn't seen her either. She followed Theo back inside. The last train back to London had left long ago. They couldn't sleep in the street. They'd freeze to death.

"I'm sorry I led you on this wild goose chase." Eliza's shoulders sagged. "And I'm sorry I torture you and you wish you'd never met me."

"That's not true." Theo leaned against the wall. "Running into you at the Gambit was the best—"

Her head was spinning. She needed to lie down. "I'm completely knackered." She could barely keep her eyes open. "Can I just go to sleep now?"

He pushed himself off the wall and took her by the elbow. "We'd better get you a room."

"And a bed. I need to lie down." She stumbled and he caught her. "Please, take me to bed." Her voice echoing through her head sounded strange. Like her words were being stretched on a loom.

"Come on. Let's get you a room." He led her down the hallway toward the lobby. "This place looks expensive. I wonder if we should find some place cheaper."

"I'm too tired to walk another street." Eliza held onto the sleeve of his overcoat and let him pull her along.

When they reached the lobby, Eliza skidded to a stop. "You can tell them I'm your sister." Yup, she was definitely slurring her words. Perhaps she shouldn't have had that last glass of wine. She hiccupped.

"Alright." He went to the hotel clerk and asked for two rooms. One for himself and one for his sister.

She stood next to him, hiccupping.

"That will be twenty pounds for two rooms for the night," the receptionist said cheerfully.

"Blimey." Theo fished in his pockets and then turned to her. "How much money do you have with you, *sister*?"

Leaning against him, she opened her bag and withdrew her purse. When she pried it open, she was confronted with a dozen little scribbles to herself and zero notes. One lone penny was hiding in the crease. She dumped it out into her palm and held it out to him.

"Please excuse us a moment." Theo took her by the elbow and led her a few feet away from the reception desk. "Between us, we only have enough for one room."

"Fine, let's get one room." Her words seemed to drool down her chin. "It will have a bed, won't it?"

"Are you serious?" He straightened bolt upright like he'd been struck by lightning. "Both of us, together, in one room?"

"Why not?" She suppressed a giggle. "You can sleep on the floor... *brother*."

Shaking his head, he went back to reception. A minute later, he returned with a key and then shepherded her off and into the lift.

When they got to the room, she leaned against the door frame while he worked the key. Inside, the room was small but pleasant with a four-poster bed, upholstered easy chair, and floral curtains. If only it would stop spinning. She clung to Theo's arm and let him lead her across the threshold.

"You smell good." She leaned into him and inhaled the scent of lime and cedarwood... and something else. The scent of him. Of Theo. On tiptoes, she sniffed his hair. "You smell too good to be a murderer," she whispered into his ear. Suddenly, she had the urge to kiss him. She kissed his earlobe and then let out a long breath. She kissed his neck. His skin tasted slightly salty but sweet. She shifted position so she could kiss his lips.

His dark eyes looked wild and fierce. He put his arms around her and pulled her into a tight embrace. Pressing his lips onto hers, he let out a soft moan. "Eliza, Eliza, Eliza," he whispered into her mouth.

A buzzing sensation coursed through her body all the way to her legs, which were shaking. She giggled. "Hold still." She put her arms around his neck and held on. Why was he swaying? Everything was swaying.

"Eliza." He took a step back and held her at arm's length.

She reached out to brush that adorable lock of hair from his forehead.

"We shouldn't," he said softly. "I shouldn't."

"Why not?" She gave him her best pout. "Don't you like me?"

He let out a snort. "Like you?" He cleared his throat. "Yes, Eliza. I like you." He tucked a stray lock of her hair behind her ear.

"Don't you find me attractive?" She tilted her head and

gazed into his eyes. His eyes. Midnight and dark oceans. Pulling her in.

"If you only knew." He ran a hand through his hair. "But this isn't right. You've had too much to drink." He shook his head. "I know this is just the wine talking."

She took a step closer and leaned into his torso. "You smell good."

"So you've said." He let out a tortured sigh. "Eliza. I know this isn't you. As much as I want to, I won't take advantage of your... your... intoxication." He kissed the top of her head and then inhaled into her hair. "You smell good too." He removed her coat and hat and then led her to the bed and sat her down. "Too good."

"Argh." She held onto the edge of the bed. "Why is everything spinning?"

He laid her back onto the pillow and then lifted her legs onto the bed.

"Theo." She reached out her arm, but he wasn't there. "Theo." Where was he? Why had he abandoned her? "Theo, don't leave me."

A few seconds later, he returned with an Afghan and gently covered her. "Sweet dreams, Eliza."

"Theo." She looked up at him. "Tell me a bedtime story."

"Once upon a time." He tucked her in and smiled. "There was a fair-haired girl who grew up to be a brilliant chess player and passable sleuth."

For once in her life, she felt safe. Really safe.

She closed her eyes and let herself drift away.

\* \* \*

Theo stood watching her sleep. The soft sound of her breathing tormented him. He ran a hand through his hair. What did it mean? Why had she kissed him? Because she was drunk. It didn't mean anything. She was drunk. It was the wine talking.

He dropped into the easy chair and buttoned his coat. The room was chilly. And yet his face was hot. He put a hand to his cheek. How he wished he could touch her cheek. So beautiful. He sighed and closed his eyes. There was no way he was going to be able to sleep. Not with her only a few feet away.

He took his journal from his satchel and opened it to the first blank page. Hovering his pen over the page, he planned his attack against its overwhelming whiteness. What was this compulsion to fill the page? To fill the void with his ink? Why did he need to write? Yes. He needed it. Like a drug. Like nourishment. Like breath itself. He had to write to live.

At the top of the page, he wrote *Eliza*.

He couldn't even adequately describe his pen. How could he describe her? He stared at her hand, which was atop the Afghan. How was it different from every other hand? Slim fingers, pale-peach colored, pink and white nails, delicate wrinkles at the knuckles, bluish veins laced across the top. He gritted his teeth. Was he writing a biology textbook? How would a poet describe that hand?

He thought of Shakespeare:

I will live in thy heart, die in thy lap, and be buried in thy eyes.

He tried again. *Your hand is like the wing of a dove, carrying me to the edge of the infinite sea of my love for you. Your hand is like a precious pearl, smooth and perfect and attached to your body.* He grunted. Ridiculous exercise. Trying to describe what makes her hand special. It is special because it belongs to her. How to describe her?

He looked at her sleeping. Her blonde curls. Her slim body shrouded in the knitted blanket. Her lovely face. His senses weren't at fault. He took her in with his eyes. Meditated on her, as if she were poetry in repose. The very meaning of life. No. It wasn't his senses that weren't up to the task. Unfortunately, they were all too aware of his desire for her. Her scent. *Jasmine.* Her touch. *Soft and warm.* Her taste. *So sweet.* Her lips. *Absolute loveliness, a red rose bud, a valentine's heart.*

Words were inadequate. They were at fault. Granted, he was no Shakespeare. Not even close. And yet, were The Bard's words really up to the task? When he wrote of love, did he feel the words betray him too?

Eliza stirred.

He tucked his pen into his journal and closed it. Leaning his head back against the chair, he shut his eyes and hoped his dreams could do better than his pen.

## 15

### REGRETS

The next morning, Eliza woke up with a pounding headache. *What happened?* She sat up in bed. Big mistake. A wave of nausea hit her like a tsunami. She took a deep breath to quell the queasiness and held her head in her hands. "Ouch." She whimpered.

*Wait.* Where was she? Why was she dressed? She opened one eye and glanced around. With his coat thrown over him like a blanket, Theo was asleep in a chair. *Right.* It was all coming back to her. Unfortunately.

She'd drank too much and she... No. She hadn't. Had she? *Crap.* She had. *Oh no!* She'd kissed him. Her cheeks burned. What would he think of her? How could she face him? Her heart plunged to the pit of her stomach like a runaway lift.

She'd kissed him and he'd pushed her away. She didn't know which was worse: her forwardness or his reluctance. She thought of what he'd written in his journal: *Seeing Eliza is torture. Touching me must be even worse than seeing me.* She groaned. She'd really messed up. Maybe she could sneak out without waking him and catch the first train back to London.

What a disaster. The whole trip. They hadn't found any trace of Agatha. They'd missed their train. She had a horrible hangover. And she'd thrown herself at Theo and probably ruined their friendship.

*Blimey. Could things get any worse?*

"Good morning." Theo stretched and yawned. His coat fell to the floor. He was wearing only his smalls. His elegant muscular arms were bare. His shapely legs stretched out from under his union suit, which hitched up when he stretched.

*Yeah. They could.*

She looked away. Could her face get any hotter? She was probably as red as a beetroot. She pulled the Afghan up to her chin and peeked over it.

Theo scrambled to cover himself with his coat. "Sorry." Holding his coat in front of his torso, he gathered his clothes off the floor. "I can't sleep in my regular clothes."

"I don't usually either." Eliza didn't know what to say. "If we'd planned to stay the night, I would have brought a night-gown." If they'd planned to stay the night, she would not be in this awkward situation. If they'd planned it, they surely would have gotten separate rooms. And she wouldn't have... kissed him.

Remembering the kiss sent a tiny pulse of electricity through her body. His lips were so soft. Unforgettable, unfortunately. She put her fingers to her lips. She had to admit, it had been nice. Very nice.

"How do you feel?" he asked, tugging on his trousers from under his coat. "You might have over-indulged last night." He chuckled. "I think the wine snuck up on you."

"About that." She swung her legs off the bed. "I hope you don't... think—"

"I don't." He threw on his shirt. "You weren't yourself."

"I'm really sorry—"

"Don't give it another thought." He smiled at her. "I don't plan to."

She bit her lip. Obviously, it meant nothing to him. Why didn't she feel relieved? "I know how you feel about me. And I —" Her voice trailed off. What could she say? She knew how he felt and she kissed him anyway.

"Oh." Theo's cheeks were rosy. "I doubt that." He slid his arms into his coat. "You'll feel better after some coffee and breakfast." He slipped his feet into his shoes. "Then we can head back to London and forget all about Harrogate and the Hydro."

She nodded. She doubted she could forget that kiss. Hopefully, some coffee would help her forget her horrible headache. Like trying to remove a sticking plaster little by little to avoid the pain, she crept around the room, gathering herself up to leave.

The scraping sound of the lift was like fingernails on a chalkboard. She closed her eyes and held onto the wall.

The breakfast room was no better. With its canary-yellow wallpaper, it was cheery and bright. Too cheery and too bright. She groaned. The bright, jacquard pattern on the walls was probably to compensate for the fact that the room had no windows.

They took a table near the buffet. After the waitress delivered their coffees, Eliza staggered to the buffet table. Not quite able to face a real breakfast, she placed a small Danish pastry in the center of her plate and headed back to the table. Theo returned with a heaping plate filled with bacon, eggs, sausage, tomato, mushrooms, fried bread, toast and a slice of black pudding. She cringed and pushed her plate away. When the waitress returned, Theo ordered a beer.

"Bit of the hair of the dog." He smiled. "You should try it. You look like you need it."

"No thanks." She leaned her chin into her hands. "Just let me die in peace."

He chuckled and then tucked into his hearty breakfast.

Eliza ever so carefully sipped her coffee and hoped she could keep it down.

The waitress delivered the beer. The smell was enough to do her in.

"Do you happen to have any aspirin powders?" Eliza stifled a moan.

"Sure thing, love." The waitress trotted off toward the kitchen. "Back in a jiff." A few minutes later, she was back with aspirin powders and a glass of water. "Drink this down and you'll be right as rain."

Eliza nodded. She forced herself to gulp down the aspirin. As she sat the empty glass back on the table, she squinted toward the buffet where a woman was filling her plate. She could only see the woman's backside, and her elegant lavender wool skirt set, but it looked familiar. "Don't look now." She leaned across the table and whispered, "Is that who I think it is?" She pointed her head in the direction of the buffet. "Don't turn around."

"How am I going to answer without looking?" Theo stopped chewing and turned his head ever so slightly. His head snapped back like a rubber band. "It is! It's Agatha." He dropped his fork on the table and then stood up. He threw his napkin onto the table and marched to the buffet.

Eliza didn't have the energy to follow him. Plus, he was a friend of Mrs. Christie's whereas she was only an acquaintance. She watched as Theo approached his missing novelist friend.

"Agatha, fancy meeting you here." Theo beamed. "Won't you join us?"

Mrs. Christie gawked around, a confused look on her face.

"Is everything alright?" Theo took her plate. "Here, let me help you."

"Thank you." Mrs. Christie followed him to the table.

"You remember Eliza Baker?" Theo laid the plate at an empty place on the table.

"Good to see you again." Mrs. Christie smiled weakly and then sat down. She still had the look of a deer in the headlights. Her complexion was wane and her eyes looked glassy and distant. Perhaps she was ill and she'd come to the spa for treatment. Judging by her plate heaped with Danish and sweet rolls, her appetite was healthy. In her hand, she carried a jug of what looked like cream. She took a sip. "It's from a cow, you know," Mrs. Christie said with a smile.

Eliza nodded as if the comment made perfect sense. "Are you quite alright, Mrs. Christie?"

"I'm not sure." She blinked. "To tell the truth, I feel a bit off."

"Off in what way?" Eliza's coffee was tepid but she drank it anyway. She needed something to wake up.

"Not quite myself." Mrs. Christie nibbled on a sweet biscuit.

"Would you like some marmalade?" Theo asked, taking a small pot from the center of the table.

"Oh, yes please." Mrs. Christie's face brightened. "I'm sorry, I've forgotten your name."

"Theo. Theodore Sharp." He glanced from Mrs. Christie to Eliza and grimaced. "Don't you remember me? From the Detection Club."

"Detection Club," Mrs. Christie repeated thoughtfully.

"Yes." Theo looked at Mrs. Christie with concern. "The club met under a week ago and the next day, you disappeared."

"I disappeared?" she repeated in a daze.

He tilted his head. "Don't you remember how you got here?"

Mrs. Christie's lips receded into a thin, red line. "I drove?" It came out as a question.

"Mrs. Christie, the police found your car over two hundred miles from here." Eliza snatched a piece of toast off Theo's plate. "So you couldn't have driven."

"Oh." She blinked. "I see." But it was clear she didn't see.

"Will you excuse us a moment." Theo laid his napkin on the table and stood up. He gave Eliza a knowing look and beckoned her to follow him. He led her to a nearby alcove. "She's clearly delusional," he whispered. "Do you think she has amnesia?"

"I don't know." Eliza leaned against the wall. The headache powders were helping but she still felt a bit queasy. "There's definitely something wrong with her."

"How did she get here?" Theo ran his hand through his hair. "If she's ill, did someone bring her? If so, who? And why was her car found in the bushes near Newlands Corner?"

"Maybe she's faking it." Eliza wouldn't put anything past these writers. "To get publicity for her book."

"No." Theo scowled. "Agatha wouldn't do that. She's an adventurer to be sure but not a practical joker like Neville."

"We need to get some answers out of her." Eliza pushed off the wall. "I'm going to give it a try."

Theo caught her arm. "Be careful with her." He quickly removed his hand as if he just realized he'd touched her and she was made of molten lava. "She seems very fragile."

"Yes, sir." She held up her hands. "See. Kid gloves."

When they got back to the table, Mrs. Christie was slathering marmalade onto a sweet biscuit. After using half the pot of jam, she started on the pitcher of cream. She poured it straight from the jug into her cup and drank it like a cat. For someone who couldn't remember how she got here, she seemed content, if a wee bit pale.

"Mrs. Christie." Eliza refolded her napkin. "The night of the Detection Club meeting, Neville Lively made a motion to expel you from the club. An hour later, he was dead from a gunshot. Do you remember?"

Mrs. Christie stopped midbite and nodded. "Terrible accident."

"Yes, well." Eliza glanced over at Theo, who gave her the evil eye. "It appears Neville was murdered."

"Murdered!" Mrs. Christie's mouth fell open. "Dear me."

"Do you know who might have wanted Mr. Lively dead?" Eliza held her gaze.

"Let's see." Mrs. Christie's eyes darted back and forth. "He and Gilbert didn't get along." She paused. "And Dorothy wasn't a fan either. And don't get me started on Fergus Briggs, the scoundrel. According to Neville, the unscrupulous publisher was a liar and a thief."

*So she did remember!*

"We know about Mr. Briggs. In fact, he's been arrested. But what do you mean about the others?" Eliza rummaged in her bag for a pencil and a piece of paper. She found an envelope. On the blank side of the envelope, she wrote, *G. Chesterton and D. Sayers*. "Why didn't Mr. Chesterton and Miss Sayers care for Mr. Lively?"

"Gilbert didn't appreciate Neville's jokes about God." Mrs. Christie tutted. "You'd think they worshipped different gods, they were so unalike, Gilbert and Neville. Gilbert is jolly and kind, if a bit addlebrained at times." She chuckled. "I'm a fine one to talk, aren't I?"

"Go on," Eliza said encouragingly.

"Neville insisted God has a sense of humor. Gilbert thought

Neville's sense of humor sadistic." Mrs. Christie's eyes sparkled. "He was what I'd call a naughty Catholic."

Eliza agreed, especially after Mr. Lively's radio broadcast, *From the Barricades*. Eliza scribbled, *Neville Lively, naughty Catholic*. "And Dorothy? Miss Sayers?" She hovered her pencil over Dorothy's name. "Why didn't she like Neville?"

"I guess she liked him well enough." Mrs. Christie shrugged. "She just disagreed with him." She smiled. "Dorothy is very protective of me," she said with a sigh. "Thinks I'm not tough enough. That I have a thin skin. But she's wrong."

Eliza tilted her head and considered what Mrs. Christie had said. She suspected the woman was tougher than she looked. She wrote *protective* next to Dorothy's name. "Neville criticizing your latest novel and arguing to remove you from the Detection Club didn't bother you?"

"Of course it bothered me!" Mrs. Christie let out a guffaw. "But he is... was... asinine."

"Was that a motive to shoot him?" Eliza leveled her gaze. "Because he was asinine?"

"Eliza." Theo reached out and touched her arm. "Enough."

"I didn't shoot him." Unfazed, Mrs. Christie took a sip of cream. "Shooting is not my style." She got a sly twinkle in her sage-green eyes. "Poison is usually my method: a dose of strychnine in the medicine, a drop of arsenic in the tea, cyanide in the champagne flute, an overdose of morphine, even too much nicotine will do the trick." She smiled innocently.

There was no evidence Neville had been poisoned. Still, Mrs. Christie knew an awful lot about poisons. "Mr. Lively's housekeeper overheard you arguing with Neville the day before he was killed." Eliza tapped her pencil on the table. "What were you arguing about?"

"We weren't arguing." She jerked her head back. "That's

nonsense. I visited to try to talk him out of the Detection Club claptrap." She waved her hand in front of her face. "When he saw my distress, he recommended I visit the Hydro."

"Distress over the Detection Club?" Eliza folded the envelope and stuffed it into her bag.

"Heavens no." Mrs. Christie waved her away. "I'm used to people criticizing my books. You can't please everyone and that's alright with me."

"Why were you distressed?" Eliza pressed on despite her nausea and Theo's warnings. "Just to rule out any homicidal animosity toward Neville." She leaned her forehead into her palm.

"Personal troubles." Mrs. Christie stared down at her folded hands. "My marriage. Neville told me a trip to the Hydro would take my mind off..." Her voice trailed off. "I'm sorry." Her lip trembled. "I should go now." She had tears in her eyes. "I'm not feeling well."

Eliza wasn't feeling well herself.

"Of course." Theo stood up. He shot Eliza a withering look before taking Mrs. Christie's elbow and leading her away from the table.

Mrs. Christie turned back to Eliza. "Please don't tell anyone you saw me, especially not my husband, Archie." A tear rolled down her cheek. "We had a terrible row the night I left and I can't face seeing him."

"Don't worry." Theo patted her arm. "We won't tell a soul."

*Except for Detective Inspector Goforth*, Eliza thought, plucking another piece of toast from Theo's plate and slathering it with marmalade.

# 16

## THE ARGUMENT

The next morning, still a bit tired from the long trip to Harrogate and back, Eliza slept in. Queenie did too. By the time they got up, Jane had already eaten breakfast and was on her way out the door.

"You're up!" Jane flashed a smile. "Just in time to say good-bye. I've got to run." She dashed over and kissed Eliza on the cheek. "Be good—"

"Don't worry." Eliza grinned. "I'll be careful." She thought of that night with Theo at the Hydro. She'd been anything but careful. And she hadn't been good either. She cringed. At least Theo hadn't made it into a big deal. Hopefully, they both could just forget about it. "I'd better get going too." Dorothy was expecting her to work this afternoon and she had a couple of stops to make beforehand.

After her sister left, Eliza quickly dressed, fed Queenie, grabbed the dog's leash, and downed a cup of coffee before heading out the door with the dog in tow.

The sun was shining for a change. But it was still brisk in the winter breeze. She tightened the belt on her coat and turned her face upward toward the sun. The rays felt good as she walked to the railway station. Tail wagging, Queenie was enjoying it too.

First stop, South Kensington.

The housekeeper, Mrs. Green, buzzed her up and let her into Neville's flat. As usual, she was wearing a black dress and white apron with a little cap atop her gray head. "Miss Baker, I'm afraid Mr. Barnaby is out this morning." Her lips twisted. "Or should I say, he isn't home yet. Keeping late nights, he is." Judging by the scowl on her face, she didn't approve.

"Actually." Eliza unbuttoned her coat. "I'm here to see you."

"Me?" Mrs. Green's cheeks flushed and she glanced down at Queenie. "Whatever for?" She gestured toward the sitting room. "Won't you come in? Would you like a cup of tea?"

"That would be lovely." Eliza wasn't much of a tea drinker, but she'd learned in her espionage work that greasing the wheels of sociality usually made people more comfortable. And when they were more comfortable, they talked. She took off her coat and Mrs. Green hung it on a hook by the door.

Mrs. Green led her into the sitting room and left her in an easy chair by the fire. Eliza gave Queenie a hand command and the beagle sat quietly next to her. A few minutes later, Mrs. Green returned with a tray loaded with plates of biscuits and tea paraphernalia. She poured a cup and handed it to Eliza.

Eliza took a sip and then said nonchalantly, "When was the last time you saw Maud Wilkerson?"

"Mrs. Wilkerson." The housekeeper thought a minute. "Let's see. She came by the week before... before Mr. Neville passed." She troubled the hem of her apron. "She was helping him purchase a birthday present for Mrs. Lively." She tilted her head. "A picture, I think it was." She nodded. "Yes, a special picture that Miss Holly had admired."

"Do you happen to remember what she was wearing?" Eliza figured the housekeeper for a woman with keen powers of observation.

"What she was wearing?" Mrs. Green dropped into a chair and poured herself a cup of tea. With her employer gone, in a sense she was now the lady of the house. At least until the will was finalized and Alice Lively took charge. "Mrs. Wilkerson is always well dressed." She beamed. "Such a lovely lady." She thought for a minute. "Yes, I remember. She was wearing a lavender and white striped day dress with cream-colored boots and a purple scarf."

Eliza smiled. *Bingo.* This woman noticed everything. "And was she wearing a coat?"

"Of course she was." Mrs. Green jerked her head back. "It's freezing outside. She wouldn't want to catch her death." She pursed her lips. "It was a very fine ivory wool coat with brass buttons, it was."

Eliza dug in her bag and retrieved Maud's button from a small side pocket. "Like this one?" She held out the button she'd sliced off Maud's coat. Queenie watched with interest.

Mrs. Green took it and examined it. "Why yes!"

"I don't suppose you noticed whether the coat had all its buttons when she left, did you?" It was a long shot but couldn't hurt to ask.

"Now that you mention it." Mrs. Green's face brightened. "I fetched her coat when she was about to leave. I handed it to her. And I did notice a thread sticking out where a button should have been." Her eyes went wide. "Is that important?" She turned the button over in her hands. "Where did you find it?" She handed it back to Eliza. Queenie's nose followed the button back and forth.

"Scotland Yard found one like it near Mr. Lively's body."

Eliza tucked the button back into her bag. She didn't mention that she'd cut if off Maud's coat. "How it got there is the question."

"Oh, I see." The color drained from her face. "You don't think Mrs. Wilkerson had something to do with Mr. Neville's death, do you? Such a nice lady."

"I don't know." Eliza took another sip of tea. "Can I ask you again about Mrs. Christie and her visit to Mr. Lively the day before he died?"

"Certainly." Mrs. Green nodded. "But I told you everything I know."

"Do you recall anything more about the argument?" Eliza removed a receipt and a pencil from her chatelaine bag.

"Like I told you before, it was a terrible row with Mrs. Christie accusing Mr. Neville of unthinkable things." She continued fiddling with the hem of her apron. "Blackmail, she said."

"Do you happen to remember her exact words?" Eliza readied her pencil. Surely if this woman remembered a missing button, she remembered a terrible row. Observant was one word for it. Nosey, another.

"Let's see." Mrs. Green narrowed her eyes. "Mrs. Christie asked Mr. Neville to forget the nonsense at the Detection Club. She said, 'Come on, Neville, it's just for fun. We're all writers. We must support each other.'" She paused. "Later, when I was passing by the door to Mr. Neville's study, collecting the laundry, I heard her say something very odd. Very odd, indeed."

"What was that?" Eliza put her hand on Queenie's head.

"Something along the lines of a cold-blooded killer wouldn't be sentimental and then she mentioned repentance. A woman wouldn't repent." Her face brightened. "Yes, that's what she said: a woman who killed wouldn't be sentimental or repent." She shook her head. "Can you imagine? A woman committing murder." She shivered. "Her voice was strange, too. Almost like a man's."

Eliza was busy writing. She took down every word in the smallest handwriting she could manage to fit on the receipt. "Sentimental... repentance," she said under her breath as she wrote. Sounded somehow familiar. Had she heard Mrs. Christie say it before? "Did you hear anything else?"

"I'm not an eavesdropper or a busybody, Miss Baker, if that's what you think." Mrs. Green sniffed.

"Of course not." Eliza folded the receipt and slid it into her pocket. "You've been extremely helpful, Mrs. Green." She dropped her pencil back into her bag. "One last question." She held up the little key from the Harrogate locker. "Do you know what this key goes to?"

Mrs. Green studied it for a few seconds and then shook her head. "Sorry, I don't."

"Thank you." Eliza glanced at her watch. She gave Queenie another hand command and the dog stood to attention, waiting for the next.

Eliza had just enough time for her second stop before work. Ye Olde Cheshire Cheese Pub on Fleet Street. A favorite of Gilbert Chesterton.

**\* \* \***

Situated in a narrow alleyway, the entrance to the pub was unassuming, deceptively so. For, once inside, its dark paneling gave way to enormous ceilings and at least a half-dozen rooms warmed by open fireplaces. Eliza stood in the foyer, waiting for her eyes to adjust to the dim light. Queenie stood stock still at her side.

She spotted him. It wasn't just his size that made Gilbert Chesterton hard to miss. He had a buoyancy and liveliness, a presence, filling up the space. He sat at the end of a table with several other men huddled around him. Everyone seemed entranced by his stories as he waved his pipe in the air for emphasis. Eliza watched for a few minutes from the sidelines, wary of interrupting the great man and his audience. After listening to the tale of a time he ended up in Brighton when he was supposed to be giving a lecture in Birmingham, Eliza ventured over to the table.

"Miss Baker. What brings you to our neck of the woods?" Mr. Chesterton said with a flourish. He reached out and patted Queenie on the head. "What a pretty puppy," he cooed.

"I wondered if I could ask you a few questions about the night Mr. Lively died." Despite odd looks from the men, she took a seat next to him. She held her hand palm down and Queenie lay down near her feet.

"Hmmm," he said between his teeth, which were clamped around his pipe. "Rum do, that."

"If you don't mind me asking, how was your relationship with Mr. Lively?"

"How?" He chuckled. "Not the metaphysical question of *what* but the procedural question of *how*." He smiled. "Perhaps you should be a barrister, Miss Baker." He puffed on his pipe. "Neville and I were friends. He was a prickly fellow, but I always enjoy a good debate." He pointed his pipe at one of his admirers. "Just ask Joe, here."

"It's true." Joe laughed. "Gilbert is the only man I know who can make lifelong friends by disagreeing with absolutely everything the other fellow says."

"And what was your disagreement with Mr. Lively?" Eliza said. "If I may ask."

"Oh my." Mr. Chesterton chuckled again. "Neville and I argued about the nature of God, the afterlife, right versus good, the philosophy of Immanuel Kant." He waved his hand. "You name it, we probably disagreed about it."

"Mrs. Christie called Mr. Lively a naughty Catholic." Eliza steadied her gaze. "And said you didn't appreciate his sense of humor."

Mr. Chesterton let out a hoot. "Naughty Catholic. I love it."

"Is it true you didn't approve of Mr. Lively's sense of humor?"

"It isn't up to me to approve or disapprove." When he shook his round head, his mop of curls danced up and down. "Let's just say, I didn't always find his jokes very funny. But humor is a strange faculty. Everyone's is different. And what's funny one day might not be the next."

Eliza shifted in her chair. Having an audience was unnerving. Queenie must have sensed her uneasiness. The dog raised her head. "One last question, if I may." She fingered the necklace at her throat and held up the key. "Do you recognize this?"

Mr. Chesterton leaned closer. She could smell beer on his breath. He lifted his spectacles and leaned closer still. Instinctively, Eliza jerked back.

"Looks like a Victoria Station locker key." He sat back in his chair, *thank goodness*. "Why do you ask?"

*Of course. The letter V.* "It belongs—belonged—to Neville Lively." She replaced the key under the collar of her blouse.

"Ahhhhh." Mr. Chesterton's countenance became serious. "And you think Neville is hiding something." He nodded. "I see. Yes. It makes sense." He cocked his head. "I wouldn't put it past Neville to have planned this whole charade." He waved his pipe again. "It would be just like him to make a practical joke out of his own death."

Eliza blinked. Could it be? Could Neville Lively have planned his murder? Thereby framing Agatha Christie? What an absurdly preposterous idea. "Thank you, Mr. Chesterton." She stood up. "I'll let you get back to your... admirers."

"Admirers. My goodness." When he laughed, his belly jiggled and his cheeks turned pink. If only he had a white beard and a red suit, he could be Santa Claus. His friends joined in the laughter.

It was a relief to leave the jolly group behind. The cold, fresh air did her good. With renewed vigor, she and Queenie strode to the station. Next stop, Bloomsbury and Dorothy's flat where—she glanced at her watch—she was supposed to be ten minutes ago.

"Blast it!"

She picked up her pace.

\* \* \*

"You're late," Dorothy said without looking up from her desk.

"Apologies." Eliza bustled in, unbuttoning her coat as she went. "I have news. We found Agatha Christie in Harrogate." She knew that would get Dorothy's attention and distract from her tardiness. "Sit," she commanded Queenie, who obediently did as her mistress bade.

"I heard." She continued with her papers. "D. I. Goforth found her at the Harrogate Hydro."

"Because I rang him and told him she was there!" She unclipped Queenie's leash from her collar.

That got Dorothy's attention. "You?"

"Theo and I went to Harrogate." Laying her coat on a chair, she pushed memories of that kiss from her mind. She removed her hat. "We found Agatha at the Hydro," she said, patting her hair. "And *I* called D. I. Goforth." She glanced at Queenie, who hadn't moved a fur-covered muscle.

"And what was she doing in Harrogate?" Dorothy got up from her desk. "Besides taking the waters?" She stopped in her tracks. "And *who* is *that*?" She pointed at Queenie.

"My dog, Queenie." Eliza motioned for the dog to sit next to her. "The odd thing was, Agatha didn't seem to know why she was there." She dropped into a chair and positioned Queenie next to her. "She was confused and out of sorts." She shrugged and opened her palms skyward. "I don't know what was wrong with her, but something surely was." She tugged on the fingers of her gloves. "She got better by the end of our visit."

"Do you think she had a nervous breakdown, poor dear?" Dorothy came over to give Queenie a pat on the head. "You're not going to eat my cats, are you?" she said, giving Queenie a faux scolding.

"Some of the newspapers called Agatha's disappearance a publicity stunt." Eliza pursed her lips. "My gut tells me it wasn't. She truly seemed unwell."

"She's been through a lot lately." Dorothy held Queenie's ears out. "What big ears you have my friend," she said using a baby voice this time. She glanced over at Eliza. "What with her mum passing away and then Archie's wandering eye. Poor thing. It's a wonder she can function at all."

Death and betrayal. Eliza knew what that was like. In her case, they could be pseudonyms for Mum and Dad. "Well, at least the speculations about her drowning or her husband murdering her were unfounded."

"Thank goodness." Dorothy returned to her desk. "The important thing is Agatha is alright." She shuffled some papers. "And we will welcome her back with open arms and no prying questions." She glanced up. "I'm sure she has her reasons. And she is well within her rights to keep them to herself." She gave a quick nod. "If she's out of sorts, the Detection Club should be a place of solace and comradery."

Laying her gloves on her lap, Eliza took a deep breath. "She told me there was no love lost between you and Neville Lively."

Queenie barked.

"Queenie!" Eliza barked back.

Dorothy stared over at the dog. "I don't think my cats—"

No sooner had she got the word out of her mouth, than two cats slinked toward Queenie. Their eyes wide, they moved slowly with their fur sticking up. One of them hissed and lunged at Queenie. Eliza held up a hand and Queenie sat perfectly still, enduring all the abuse the cats had to offer. When they realized they wouldn't get a reaction, they retreated to a corner where they kept watchful eyes on the dog.

"Neville was an acquired taste." Dorothy tightened her lips. "One I never acquired." She went to the cats and bent down to caress them in turn.

"She also said you were protective of her." Eliza raised her eyebrows. "Is that why you wiped the handle of the gun with your cape?" She held Queenie by the collar. The dog was well trained, but she was still a hound.

"I did no such thing." Dorothy's cheeks reddened. She huffed. "If I did, it was by accident." She came to stand in front of Eliza's chair. "You really can't blame me..."

"An accident. Honestly?" Eliza sneered. "You wiped fingerprints off the gun handle because you thought your friend Agatha fired the gun."

"You have some nerve accusing me of being in cahoots with Agatha." She stomped her foot. Queenie growled. The cats scattered. Dorothy snorted. "The nerve..."

"Alright, calm down." Eliza held up her hand. Queenie

perked up her ears. "I'm sorry. I was just testing you." She let out a long exhale. "I know you wiped the gun to protect Agatha. But I don't think she did it."

"No, she didn't. She couldn't." Dorothy put her hand over her mouth. "Could she?"

"Neville's housekeeper told me he and Agatha argued the day before he was killed." Eliza sat upright on the edge of the chair. "Agatha mentioned blackmail and then said... Hold on..." She pulled the receipt from her pocket and squinted at it for a moment and then read. "Something along the lines of a cold-blooded killer wouldn't be sentimental and wouldn't repent, especially if she was a woman."

Dorothy got a funny look on her face. She squinted at Eliza. "Read that again." She plunked into a nearby chair.

Eliza repeated it.

"I know where it's from." Dorothy jumped up and went to her desk. She picked up a book and thumbed through it, scanning the pages as she went. "Here!" She returned to Eliza, shivering with excitement. She read from the book. *Oh my word. Dorothy was right.*

Eliza tilted her head to see the book's cover. Queenie did the same.

No wonder it sounded familiar.

It was from *The Murder of Roger Ackroyd.*

## 17

### VICTORIA STATION

The next morning, Eliza met Theo at Gambit Chess Rooms. They both needed cash after the expensive trip to Harrogate. Eliza opted for speed chess against three blokes at once, while Queenie watched from a corner near the fireplace. Theo took on the duke for a handsome purse. An hour and a half later, they both had spare change in their pockets and smiles on their faces. Their smiles disappeared when they stepped outside into the freezing rain.

"How about a trip to Cairo?" Theo jangled a few coins together.

Queenie shook the cold from her fur.

"Any place would be better than this today." Eliza turned up the collar on her coat and tightened her belt. "I'd settle for another trip to Harrogate," she said under her breath, thinking of that kiss.

Theo smiled. "Me too." He opened his umbrella and held it over her head.

She huddled closer to him for warmth. Would winter never end?

"Since we're going to Victoria Station..." He made sure to keep the umbrella above her head. "Why don't we hop on the Orient Express?"

"Yeah, right." She quickened her pace to get out of the rain. Queenie stayed close at her heels. "We'd have to pick up more than a few games of chess to afford that trip." She sighed. "Someday, maybe..."

Since she was a little girl, she'd dreamed of *someday, maybe* having the resources to feel secure enough to think beyond tomorrow's dinner. *Someday, maybe.*

"*Someday, maybe* my novel will become a bestseller." Theo grinned. "If not, I can raise the stakes with the duke at Gambit."

"The duke is an idiot to play you for money." She brushed rainwater off her sleeve. "He has more money than sense."

Queenie tugged at the leash, obviously in a hurry to get out of the rain.

"Thank God for wealthy idiots." Theo smiled, but it didn't reach his eyes.

\* \* \*

By the time they reached Cannon Street Station, Eliza's boots were soaked through. At least the railway station was a reprieve from the rain. The railcar was only slightly warmer than the outside air. But it was dry. Queenie curled up at her feet and took a nap.

"Poor dog must be freezing," Theo said, reaching down to pet Queenie. The smell of wet dog wafted up from her coat.

"Queenie has a job to do." At the mention of her name, the dog lifted her head. Eliza smiled down at her. "Good girl." Eliza pulled Neville's scarf from her bag and held it out to Queenie. The dog sniffed it and looked up at her mistress as if she knew what she had to do. Eliza was confident the dog did know. She wasn't a scenthound for nothing.

When they arrived at Victoria Station, Eliza sloshed off the train and into the station. The station wasn't exactly warm, but it was dry, which was more than she could say for the left sleeve of her coat and her feet and legs.

After asking an attendant, they learned the storage lockers were in an alcove behind the cashier's kiosk.

"How do we know which locker?" Theo asked, trotting along beside her. "We'll have to try every one."

"We have another plan." She led the dog into the alcove. "Right, Queenie?"

"What do you think we'll find?" Theo's voice was full of excitement.

"We're about to find out." Eliza held out Neville's scarf to Queenie again. The dog sniffed it and then looked up at her with what appeared to be a smile.

"Don't you want to speculate?" Theo dashed after her.

"Why bother speculating?" Eliza removed the key from around her neck. "It's an empirical question." She glanced over at him. "And we'll have our answer soon enough." She gave the dog a hand command. "Queenie, find him."

Tail wagging, Queenie sniffed the floor around the perimeter of the lockers. She made two passes, and then stopped in front of number 23A. She sat to attention and looked over at Eliza as if to say, *This is it*.

Eliza joined the dog at the locker. "Good girl." She patted Queenie's head. She waited for Theo to join them and then inserted the key in the lock and turned it. The locker popped open with a click. Slowly, as if she might find a poisonous snake inside, she swung the door open. A corduroy jacket met her gaze. It was thrown over something. Carefully, she lifted the jacket. It hid a rather large rectangular black case. She reached in, clasped her hand around its handle, and pulled it out. It was very heavy. A typewriter maybe? Why would Neville keep a typewriter in a locker at Victoria Station? She grabbed the jacket, stuffed it under her arm, and then carried the case to a nearby bench.

"Is that all?" Theo peered inside the empty locker and then shut its door. He joined her at the bench. "A typewriter?"

She unlatched the locks and opened the case. Inside was a large machine with a thick carriage, several levers, and a long cord. "Not a typewriter." She picked up the cord. At the end was a mouthpiece like you'd find on a telephone. "What is it?"

"A Dictaphone." Theo glanced around. "We need to find an electrical outlet."

"Why would Neville keep a Dictaphone in a locker at Victoria Station?" She examined the mouthpiece.

"As a friend of mine says, that's an empirical question." Theo flipped a lever on the machine.

"Actually, it isn't." Eliza replaced the mouthpiece and then closed the case. "*What* is on it is an empirical question. *Why* it's here is a psychological question, which is more your bailiwick than mine."

"Are you saying we make a good team?" Theo smiled.

"I wouldn't go that far." Eliza picked up the case. "I'm sure I'd do just fine on my own."

"Why do you always do that?" His expression became serious. "Why do you always insist on being alone and doing everything yourself? Never asking for help." He huffed. "Pushing people away. What are you trying to prove?"

"I'm not trying to prove anything." She stood up and tightened her belt. "I'm trying to figure out who killed Neville and why."

"And you made it into a competition rather than a collaboration." Theo ran his hand through his hair. "Why are you so afraid of relying on someone else?"

"We're collaborating now, aren't we?" She picked up the case. "Let's *collaborate* to find an outlet." She smirked. "Happy now?"

He shook his head. "Why do you put up defenses against everyone?" He stuffed his hands in his pockets. "Against me. Are you afraid of getting close? Of being vulnerable? Of someone actually getting to know you?"

"I'm not afraid of anything." She jerked her head. "Stop psychoanalyzing me." She took off at a brisk pace. She wasn't going to let him get to her. She had to concentrate on finding an outlet and learn what was on the Dictaphone.

He caught up to her. "I think you're afraid of abandonment. That's why you don't want to get close—"

"Stop badgering me!" She stopped and whirled around, nearly hitting him with the case. "I told you to stop."

"I'm sorry." Theo bit the inside of his cheek. "But you're your own worst enemy."

Her lip trembled. "From my perspective, you're the problem." She couldn't meet his gaze.

"Eliza." He touched her sleeve.

She flinched.

"Eliza, I'm sorry." There was gentleness in his voice. The way he said her name was disarming like a verse. "It's just..." He paused. "It's just..." He looked down at her with soft eyes. "I want us to be closer."

She brushed her eyes with the back of her hand. "Be careful what you wish for." She adjusted the case to her other hand.

The blasted thing was heavy. "Now, let's go find an outlet and discover what's on this bloody machine."

Theo took the case out of her hand. "Let me."

"I suppose if I don't, you'll accuse me of having some sort of psychological complex." She let him take the case.

"I would never presume—"

"Oh, yes you would." She marched to the exit.

* * *

For the sake of privacy and ease, they decided to take the machine elsewhere. They ended up at Theo's tiny flat since it was closer than her place. He cleared off space on his desk and put the case down. "Let's see what's on this, shall we?" He plugged it in.

Eliza unbuttoned her coat and removed her hat and gloves. She tossed them over the back of a chair. She joined him at the desk.

"The moment of truth." She held her breath.

Theo fiddled with the levers until the cylinder began humming. Agatha Christie's voice filled the room: "And we don't want any eavesdropping either. What's all this about blackmail?"

Mouth open, eyes wide, Eliza looked at Theo. She felt like she was looking in a mirror. He too had a look of shock on his face. "What in blazes?" She listened. Although the voice was definitely Agatha's, it sounded off, like she was imitating a man. The recording continued with the line from *The Murder of Roger Ackroyd* about sentiment and repentance.

"She's reading from her novel," Eliza said, baffled. "Why does Neville—"

"It's from her BBC radio performance of *The Murder of Roger*

*Ackroyd*." Theo scratched his head. "Neville must have recorded it."

"But why?" She shook her head. "And why lock it up in Victoria Station?" A lightbulb went off in her brain. "This must be what the housekeeper heard the day before Neville's death." She gasped. "It wasn't a row at all. It was a recording from Agatha's BBC performance." *Oh, my word!* She put her hand to her mouth. What did it mean?

"Good old Neville." Theo let out a guffaw. "Up to his old tricks." He turned off the machine. "Don't you see? The Dictaphone. It's central to the plot of Agatha's novel. It's how the doctor gets away with murder."

"Gosh. You're right." Eliza paced the length of the room, which amounted to three steps before she turned and stepped over a pile of chess magazines. "But why?" She puzzled over the clues, trying to piece them together. "The endgame. Until then, the king hides." She looked up. "But he becomes most powerful during the endgame."

"And we've got Neville in mate?" Theo pursed his lips.

They'd already established Dorothy had used her cape to wipe the gun because she was afraid her friend Agatha had done it; that accounted for the green thread on the gun handle. The monogrammed handkerchief belonged to Anthony Berkeley Cox. The bloody footprint was Alice Lively's when she surreptitiously left the guest dining room for a secret rendezvous with Anthony and then rushed in to find her father dead and rushed out again to fetch her brother.

But what about the Dictaphone hidden away in a locker at Victoria Station? And the button that went missing from Maud Wilkerson's coat a week before the murder but turned up at the crime scene? And the second gun in Agatha's bag? And the threatening note at Neville's flat?

"Good God." A chill ran up her spine. "I think I know who killed Neville." She turned to Theo. "Yes. We've got him in checkmate. We need to get back to Neville's flat to confirm my suspicions."

# 18

## THE USUAL SUSPECTS

What Eliza and Theo found at Neville's flat was damning. It proved her hypothesis. She was right. She knew who killed Neville Lively.

At Eliza's request, Dorothy called an emergency meeting of the Detection Club. Once again, they met at Café Royal, although this time in a different private dining room. No one could face the room where Neville had been killed. This time, rather than a debate or an initiation ceremony, they were gathered for real live detecting: to expose who killed Neville and why.

Except for Fergus and Neville, of course, all members were present. Waiters delivered cocktails while the writers mingled before dinner. Along one wall, spare chairs lined up like soldiers waiting for battle. Given the sparse furnishing and lack of décor, Eliza suspected it was a storage room converted into a dining room just for the Detection Club. The same U-shaped table arrangement had been constructed in the center of the room. This time, no one dimmed the lights.

The mood was more subdued than the last time they'd

met. Both in black mourning clothes, Neville's son and daughter had joined them. Dorothy had exchanged her green cape for a gray jacket. And Eric the skull was locked in the closet. Gilbert Chesterton wore his usual black cape rather than the club's red one. Even Maud Wilkerson's two-piece evening dress was a muted crème brûlée. Agatha Christie wore the same elegant suit and pearls she'd worn to the last Detection Club dinner. Her complexion and demeanor were much improved from the last time Eliza saw her in Harrogate. In fact, she seemed fully recovered from the ordeal and back to her usual pleasant self.

The rest of the club members welcomed her back with open arms and no questions just as Dorothy had no doubt instructed them to do. Except for Maud, who made a point of rushing over and dramatically throwing her arms about poor Agatha.

"Oh dear. We'd thought you'd drowned or been kidnapped." Maud kissed Agatha's cheek.

"No, I... I..." Flustered, Agatha took a step away from her assailant.

"We're just glad you're back safe and sound." Maud raised an eyebrow. "You are sound, are you not?" She tittered.

Agatha blushed and nodded.

Dorothy intervened. After giving Maud a sharp look, she took Agatha's arm and led her to the dining table. "There, there, dear." She waved to a waiter. "Let's get you a drink and you'll be right as rain."

Too nervous to make small talk, Eliza fiddled with the place settings and darted around the tables making sure everything was just right. Tonight, *she* was on the agenda. In a room full of would-be detectives, she would be the one presenting the evidence to solve the mystery of who killed Neville Lively. Of course, to make it more "interesting," Dorothy suggested they go around the room and each present their own theories first. Naturally, the writers had to make sleuthing into a game.

Dorothy tapped a spoon against the edge of her glass. "May I have your attention." She paused. When the crowd didn't quiet, she tapped again. "Ladies and gentlemen." She raised her voice. "Please take your seats."

Conversations trailed off and the writers took their places at the table. Standing at the center table, Dorothy called the meeting to order. "We are gathered tonight for a special emergency meeting of the Detection Club. Miss Eliza Baker claims to know who killed Neville Lively." She gestured toward Eliza.

Eliza gave a weak smile and then took a quick sip of water. At the mention of her name, the butterflies in her stomach started multiplying at an alarming rate.

Dorothy nodded toward Detective Inspector Goforth, who was sitting to her left. "Which is why we've invited Robert to join us this evening." She chuckled. "It seems Scotland Yard needs our help."

"As far as I'm concerned, we've got our killer locked up." D. I. Goforth smiled and threw up his hands. "Unless, of course, you can prove it wasn't Fergus Briggs."

"Before we cede the floor to Miss Baker, to hone our detection skills, I'd like to propose we offer our own theories about Neville's murder." She gestured to Gilbert Chesterton. "And I'd ask our esteemed president to start the proceedings." She sat down.

Gilbert stood and cleared his throat. "Neville's death is a tragedy. We've lost a friend and a talented writer. I ask for a moment of silence to honor his importance to our group and to pray for his everlasting soul." He bowed his head. The rest of the writers did the same. After a minute, he raised his head. "And now, we do what we do best. We get to the truth!" He stabbed the air with a chubby finger. "Someone in this room may be a murderer."

Chatter from the crowd interrupted him.

"If so." He held up his hand. "If so, we will get to the bottom of it. And justice will prevail." His booming voice echoed through the sparsely furnished room. "If not here and now, then we leave it to God's justice. For, in the end, we will all be subject to His almighty and infinite righteousness."

"Amen." Maud crossed herself.

"Anthony, why don't we start with you," Gilbert said. "What's your theory? Who do you think killed Neville and why?"

"Why me?" Anthony coughed into his napkin. "Oh, alright." He stood up. "In any murder, my first thought turns to a crime of passion. Specifically, to the person closest to the victim, namely his or her spouse." He glanced over at his own soon-to-be ex-wife. "In Neville's case, that is his estranged wife, Holly Lively, who left him for a Cambridge philosophy professor." He raised his eyebrows. "And to top it off, Holly Lively has a financial motive. I know for a fact Neville took out a substantial life insurance policy two months ago." He shrugged. "So, in my humble opinion, our murderer was our esteemed visitor, Bertrand Russell."

"May I respond?" Eliza laid her napkin on the table. Her palms were sweating as she stood to give her rebuttal. "First off, Holly Lively moved to Cambridge with her husband's blessing. Second, Neville Lively purchased the life insurance policy because he knew he was dying of Bright's disease. And finally, the Russell you're imagining has a relationship with Mrs. Lively is the wrong Russell. It is her landlord, Frank Russell, who is acquainted with Mrs. Lively, not his brother, Bertrand. And for that matter, we have no reason to believe she is having inappropriate relations with the brother either."

"He is a known philanderer," Anthony interrupted.

"If we suspected every philanderer of murder, half the country would be under scrutiny." Eliza's voice was strong. "Present company included." She didn't mention Anthony Berkeley Cox was among that company.

"Well, so I was wrong." Anthony shrugged. "Not all detective work yields the right answers." He glanced at Gilbert. "Sometimes, the truth stays hidden in the shadows and is never brought out into the light of day."

"But one day," Gilbert said, "God's light will illuminate even the darkest shadows of the human soul."

"Perhaps there are some things that should remain hidden in the shadows." Anthony sat down.

Gilbert pursed his lips and nodded toward Dorothy. "Would you like to go next?"

Dorothy stood up. "I must admit..." She paused to look at Agatha, who was sipping her cocktail. "Given all the hullabaloo over Agatha's latest novel, and Neville's motion to expel her from the club, at first, for only a moment, mind you, I half-thought it might be Agatha." She shook her head. "Of course, I knew it wasn't and couldn't be. Agatha would never seek revenge, especially in the form of murder, for something as trivial as the reception of her novel." She chuckled. "If we all resorted to murder every time one of our books met with a bad review, we'd be so busy killing, we wouldn't have time to write!"

Titters rippled through the audience.

"In those first minutes after the shooting, all reason fled my body and I wiped the gun handle of fingerprints. But only out of an instinct to protect my friend. A misguided instinct, but nonetheless motivated by my love and concern for Agatha." She bowed her head in Agatha's direction. "I'm sorry I doubted you, my friend."

Agatha gave her a smile. "Without your friendship—all of you—I couldn't have got through the last few months." Her lip trembled. "Thank you."

"Agatha, dear," Dorothy said. "Would you like to go next? Tell us your theory about who killed Neville?" She sat down.

Agatha dabbed her mouth with her napkin. "Alright." She remained seated. "With the help of the young people, Scotland Yard has the killer in custody." She twisted around to look at D. I. Goforth. "Isn't that right Detective Inspector?"

"That's right." He beamed. "Mrs. Christie, I appreciate your vote of confidence."

"You see," Agatha continued, "Neville told me that his publisher, Mr. Fergus Briggs, was embezzling from the royalties owed to Neville." She tutted. "I would never stand for my publisher doing such a thing. And when Neville found out and confronted him, Mr. Briggs threatened him." She shrugged. "He used our Detection Club dinner to make good on his threats."

Eliza piped up. "Mr. Briggs claims Maud Wilkerson was blackmailing Neville Lively."

"I never." Maud huffed. "I was not blackmailing Neville." She fanned herself with her napkin. "I simply procured a painting for him. A birthday present for Holly. Naturally, he paid me for the painting. And now this little... *piece* is accusing me of blackmail."

"I didn't accuse you," Eliza said. "Mr. Briggs did."

"Whoever." Maud waved her hand in front of her face. "Neville was a very dear friend. I would never do anything to hurt him." Were those tears forming in her eyes? "I loved him, the dear man."

"How did Holly feel about your relationship with Neville?"

Anthony jeered from the end of the table. "I tell you, it was a crime of passion." He took a drag of his cigarette.

Maud glared at him. "That's rich coming from you." She jerked her head toward Alice Lively. "Everyone knows you've been cheating on your wife—and your mistress—with Neville's daughter."

Alice blushed all the way to her fingernails.

"Not to mention the inheritance." Maud was on a roll. "With Barnaby back in the picture, Neville planned to change his will. But you and Alice made sure he didn't get the chance. Next to your precious crimes of passion, money is the oldest motive in the books."

"In your books, maybe." Anthony chuckled.

"And wasn't that your handkerchief our young friends found near Neville's dead body?" Maud's voice was getting shrill. "Monogrammed with your initials? Perhaps you too were wiping the gun? Tampering with evidence. To protect your lover."

"I didn't kill my father!" Alice was on her feet. "I loved him." She threw her napkin on the table and marched out of the dining room. Anthony ran after her.

"The lady doth protest too much," Maud said under her breath.

"Come now," Gilbert said. "Let's all calm down, shall we?" He glanced around the room, giving each person a scolding look. "We will discover the truth. But we must be patient and show each other a little empathy."

Maud nodded.

"Love thy neighbor and all that rot." Anthony was back with Alice in tow. He returned her to her seat.

"Shall we continue?" Dorothy said. "Gilbert, it's your turn."

Gilbert cleared his throat. "If no one else wants to take a

stab at it, so to speak." His round cheeks turned pink. "Why don't we turn the floor over to our young detectives, Theo and Eliza." He stretched out both arms as if literally presenting them with the floor. "I cede my turn to them."

Eliza looked at Theo.

"Ready?" he whispered.

"As I'll ever be." Eliza stood up and brushed the wrinkles from her skirt. "Enough speculation." She surveyed the diners. "Let's start with the physical evidence. And there's a lot of it. Too much even."

# 19

## CHECKMATE

To help her concentrate, Eliza stepped back from the table and began pacing. "First, there was the gun found next to Neville's body. But there was an extra gun in Mrs. Christie's bag." She stopped and furrowed her brows. "Why the second gun?" She glanced around at the diners. "And then there was the button from Maud Wilkerson's coat." She nodded to Theo.

"Exhibit A." Theo pulled the button from his pocket and held it up.

"Yes!" Maud interjected. "My missing button."

Theo laid the button on the table.

"D. I. Goforth found it at the scene." Eliza gestured toward the detective, who smiled. "But most likely Mrs. Wilkerson lost it a week earlier when visiting Neville at his flat to make arrangements to deliver the painting." She walked to the end of the table and then turned back. "And Anthony's handkerchief. Also apparently misplaced sometime before the killing."

"My handkerchief?" Anthony tightened his lips. "Not again."

"Let us see it." She gestured to Anthony. He shrugged and pulled the handkerchief from his breast pocket and held it up. It was exactly like the one Eliza had eventually handed over to the police. "You know what." A look of revelation lit up his face. "I remember now. I gave one exactly like this to Neville, that night at the dinner at my house."

"And Neville put it to good use." Eliza went to the center of the table where Dorothy was sitting. "And then there was the green thread on the handle of the gun. Dorothy has already admitted she wiped it using her green cape."

"I'm terribly sorry about that." Dorothy blushed. "Bad instinct, I'm afraid." She chuckled. "Probably from reading too many detective novels."

The diners snickered.

"We know Mr. Fergus Briggs was embezzling," Eliza continued.

"And he wrote the threatening note," D. I. Goforth interrupted. "The one found at Neville's flat."

Eliza squinted at the detective inspector. "I take it, Scotland Yard supposes Mr. Briggs typed the threatening note after Neville confronted him." She took two steps and then stopped. "But did Mr. Briggs type that note?" She tightened her lips. "Mr. Briggs is indeed a criminal, but not a murderer."

She paced the length of the table again. This time stopping in front of Alice Lively. "And while Miss Lively stood to gain from Neville's untimely death, and she did leave the guest dining room before the shot was fired and left a bloody footprint fleeing the room after the shot, she loved her father." She raised her eyebrows. "And although she may be guilty of indiscretions when it comes to her love life, she is not guilty of killing him.

"No." Eliza put a finger to her cheek. "None of the people in this room have committed murder." She smiled. "At least not in real life." She joined Theo at the end of the table. "To complete the presentation of physical evidence, Theo will read off a list of items confiscated by the police in their investigation." She gestured to Theo.

He pulled a piece of paper from his pocket and read. "Two Webley revolvers. No fingerprints found on either one." He looked up meaningfully. "A financial ledger belonging to Neville Lively containing evidence of Briggs's embezzlement and the payment to Maud for the painting." He nodded to Maud, who smiled in return. "And the threatening note, which read, 'You can't get rid of me so easily. Consider this a warning.'" He looked at Mrs. Christie. "With all due respect to D. I. Goforth and the Met, given the circumstances, what immediately comes to mind is not Fergus Briggs and embezzlement but Neville's motion to expel Agatha from the club. The note appears to be a response from Agatha."

Eliza took over. "Couple that with Neville's housekeeper overhearing him argue with Mrs. Christie the day before he was killed." Eliza exhaled. "Not to mention her disappearance, and Agatha Christie becomes the prime suspect."

Agatha pursed her lips but didn't say anything.

"And yet," Eliza continued, "just yesterday, Theo and I confirmed that the threatening note was typed on Neville's own Underwood."

Murmurs broke out among the diners.

Theo held up his hand. "How do we know the note was typed on that very typewriter?" Theo opened his palms. "Because Eliza's sharp eyes noticed the letter r was askew." He removed another sheet of paper from his pocket. "Exhibit B."

He passed it to Gilbert Chesterton, who lifted his spectacles and stared at it before passing it on to Dorothy.

As the paper passed through their hands, the diners muttered. On it, Theo had retyped the threatening note, complete with the tilted letter r.

"The suspense is killing me!" Dorothy slapped her palms onto the table. "Who did it already?"

"Neville." Eliza stood arms akimbo. "He planted the clues. He framed Agatha. He shot himself and made his suicide look like murder. Anthony's handkerchief, Maud's button, the gun in Agatha's handbag. The incriminating note. Even the bruise on his arm. All planned and planted by Neville."

Gasps erupted from one end of the table to the other. Surprised chatter drowned out Eliza's voice. "Suicide," Eliza repeated.

"How?" Maud asked. "How did he do it?"

Theo went to the nearby closet and brought out the Dictaphone. "Neville's housekeeper heard Agatha threaten her employer with blackmail and talk of cold-blooded murder." He flipped a leaver and Mrs. Christie's voice burst out of the machine.

"That's Agatha's BBC performance," Dorothy said. "It's *The Murder of Roger Ackroyd*." As if an anvil of realization hit her on the head, she stopped and her mouth dropped open.

"The Dictaphone," Eliza said. "The author reading her novel on the air. The planted clues to implicate every one of his friends." She paused. "In death as in life, Neville Lively was playing an elaborate practical joke."

"But why?" Gilbert asked. "Why such a deadly game?"

Agatha's performance still played in the background.

"Because." Eliza met his gaze. "Neville Lively was dying of

Bright's disease and he knew it. He didn't have long to live. So rather than fade out into oblivion, he went out with a bang... literally." She surveyed the room. "Maud, he kept your button and made sure to drop it nearby before shooting himself." She turned to Anthony. "Same with your handkerchief." She pointed at the articles Theo had placed on the end of the table. "All the evidence was planted, which explains why there was so much of it and why it led in all different directions." She walked back to the center of the room. "The Dictaphone was the coup de grâce, the exact machine Mrs. Christie's fictional murderer used to construct his alibi in *The Murder of Roger Ackroyd*. The very same damning clue her detective Hercule Poirot used to solve the crime."

"Neville always did like a good murder mystery," Chesterton said, crossing himself. "God rest his soul."

Suddenly, Agatha's performance ended and Neville's voice boomed out of the machine.

Eliza looked at Theo. The diners glanced around at each other and went silent.

"Dear friends." Neville's voice was loud and strong. "I hope you enjoyed solving my murder as much as I did preparing it, down to my self-inflicted bruise. Ouch. I applaud you all, especially whichever clever soul found this marvelous machine. Don't you agree, Agatha? Bravo. You've solved the mystery and can now call yourselves a proper Detection Club. Next time you meet, have a drink in my honor, especially once my book sales skyrocket. Perhaps with my newfound notoriety, they'll surpass even yours, Agatha."

*What in the world!* "A confession." Eliza hadn't realized there was more on the Dictaphone than Agatha's BBC performance. If she'd listened to the end, she wouldn't have had to present her case. And yet, it was satisfying to be proved right.

"I was right. He did commit suicide as part of an elaborate hoax."

"Hoping the infamy would sell books." Theo sucked in breath. "Pretty extreme marketing ploy." He shook his head. "Who needs life insurance when they can make the bestsellers list?"

"I can't believe he put us through this." Dorothy wiped her forehead with the back of her hand. "The bounder continues to vex us from beyond the grave." She sighed. "And why? For sales? Royalties for his heirs?" She threw up her hands. "I suppose we should give him credit. He had us fooled."

"Indeed." Gilbert huffed. "If this was his idea of a joke, it was in damned poor taste and not a bit funny!"

"I agree." Maud snapped her fingers. "Waiter. I say, waiter." When the waiter dashed over to her side, she ordered a gin cocktail. "Neville had no business scaring us all half to death. And for what, to sell books? I don't know about you all, but I need a stiff drink."

"I'll have one too," Anthony said, raising his hand.

"Drinks all around," Gilbert said, waving to the waiter. "Make mine a whiskey."

Theo gathered up the evidence and presented it to D. I. Goforth. "What do you think now, Detective Inspector?"

"I think I'll consult you lot on every homicide case." He slapped Theo on the shoulder. "Well done, old son. Thank you."

"Eliza is the one you should thank." Theo glanced back at her.

"Of course." The inspector smiled over at Eliza. "I know all about Miss Baker's talents for detection. She's an ace."

"She solved the case." Theo shrugged. "I only tagged along to keep her out of trouble."

"To keep me out of trouble?" Eliza grinned. "Or so I'd have a partner in crime?"

"Shh." Theo put his finger to his lips and nodded toward D. I. Goforth. "You'd better hush or he'll haul us off and we'll be sharing a cell with Fergus Briggs."

"Mr. Briggs has signed a full confession to the blackmail," D. I. Goforth said. "He will be spending his golden years in prison."

"What about Neville's latest manuscript?" Theo turned to Eliza. "Will it be published? It's what led us to Harrogate."

"If it is, his bet might pay off." Eliza shrugged. "With notoriety about his case and what the newspapers will do with this, no doubt the book will sell." She let out an audible breath. "It will probably be good for business at the Hydro, too."

"I wondered what you two were doing at the Hydro," Agatha said with a shrug. "But at the time, I didn't know what *I* was doing at the Hydro." She gave a weak smile. "Sometimes, truth is stranger than fiction."

The waiter returned with a tray of cocktails.

"Indeed," Eliza said, taking a drink from the tray. Once everyone had their cocktail, she raised her glass. "To clearing Agatha and all the rest of you armchair detectives."

"You heard D. I. Goforth." Dorothy held her glass in the air. "We aren't just armchair detectives. We're official consultants to Scotland Yard."

*Official consultants to Scotland Yard under investigation for exposing state secrets.* Eliza took a sip of her cocktail. As far as she could tell, the writers' only threat was cooking up new ideas for murder.

* * *

Theo marveled at how Eliza had captivated the Detection Club members with her prowess by solving the mystery of Neville's death. She was a force of nature. Smart, beautiful, fearless, and blunt. He'd never met another woman like her, not even close. If only she hadn't been drunk the night she'd kissed him. Then he might believe he had a chance with her.

This last week working with her on Neville's case had been stimulating. Now, thanks to her inspiration, he might be ready to finish his novel. Sitting at his cluttered desk, he stared down at the blank page in his typewriter. He smiled. He had an idea how to finish his book. He would fictionalize their adventures and make them the perfect sleuthing team.

The wonderous thing about fiction was he could create the world as he wanted it to be and not as it actually was. In fiction, justice wasn't just an unattainable ideal or a dream for some undetermined future. He could write a world where justice prevailed and art and beauty triumphed over the base desires for power and wealth.

He thought of his father's last letter chastising him for choosing a life of "poverty and deprivation," and the closing paragraph written by his mother, begging him to come home. No matter how much they begged or shamed him, he would never go back to their inane and useless lifestyle. Unlike his father, he wanted to create something meaningful, not senselessly build a fortune on the backs of others. A beautiful life of books and adventure... and Eliza.

What was he thinking? He could never tell Eliza how he felt. He hit the return carriage on his typewriter. As a poor mystery writer, making a few quid playing chess, he could never give her what she needed: security. He put his head in his hands. If only he could finish this novel. Maybe it would sell and he would have the resources to declare himself to her. Then again, maybe

he'd be living alone in a shoebox for the rest of his life. He
stared down at the blank page.

Then it hit him. Suddenly, his fingers were flying across the
keys. His brain was on fire. And the escapades of the last week
were flowing onto the page, taking on a second life in words.
His words. Words dedicated to her. To Eliza.

# 20

## MYSTERIOUS ADVENTURES

On her way home from an evening of work at Dorothy's place, Eliza stopped off at Gambit to pick up a game. She was still trying to repay Theo for the expensive trip to Harrogate. And it was an excuse to get in out of the rain. She shook herself off like a dog as she crossed the threshold. Rubbing her hands together, she looked for an opponent. She'd win a few quid and then head home. She had to win. She was tired of worrying about money. Even with her wages from the Detection Club, she wasn't any closer to moving out of her sister's flat and getting her own place.

The chess rooms were busy with multiple games. She recognized most of the regulars: Herb, Michael, the duke, and of course, Theo. Shaking off the cold, she hung up her coat and hat on the stand near the doors and ventured towards the tables. As she approached the game between Theo and the duke, she rubbed her hands together and blew into them. The duke had Theo's rook pinned.

"You're making me nervous," Theo said, his eyes focused on the board.

She took a few steps back. Weird. Theo never got nervous. The duke must be giving him a run for his money.

"Should we call it a draw?" the duke said.

"No," Theo shot back. "Taking a draw as white is criminal. Let's keep playing."

"Hey ho, Eliza." Herb waved from the end of a table as he collected his winnings from his last game. "How about a rematch?"

"Why not?" Easy money. She sauntered over to his board, pulled up a chair, and started setting up the black side. Last time she played him, she'd used the French Defense to open, claiming the light-colored center squares and trapping his bishop. But last time, she was playing white. And Herb hadn't had an annoying bag of walnuts next to him like he did now. *Crunch. Crunch. Crunch.* "Should we up the ante to two quid?" She flashed an innocent smile. If she won, she could at least repay Theo.

An hour later, she was jangling two quid in her palm. Smiling to herself, she headed to the kitchenette to make a cup of tea. As she turned the corner, she saw Herb leaning on his umbrella and staring into the sink with a sick look on his face. It was all the more troubling given his usual bright spirits.

"Are you alright?" She approached cautiously.

"I can't go home." His voice trembled.

"Why not?"

"I just lost my last quid and my wife will kill me." He bit his lip.

"You bet your last quid?" How stupid was that? She shook her head as she put the kettle on to boil.

"I was desperate." His face was ashen. "I needed to win to get enough money to buy my daughter's medicine. Poor little mite is sick with bronchitis and the doctor says she needs a medicine called salvarsan." He wiped his brow with the back of his sleeve. "I just need to win one game to afford it."

*Good grief.* "How about a rematch?"

The kettle whistled and Eliza removed it from the burner.

"I don't have any money!" Herb sniffled.

"Double or nothing." She poured dark tea leaves into the strainer.

"I told you." He closed his eyes and exhaled. "I don't have anything to bet. And I'm not taking your charity."

She poured water into the teapot and then looked him up and down. "How about your umbrella?"

"You want my brolly?" He let out a guffaw. "It's not worth much."

"When it's raining, it's worth a lot to someone who doesn't have one." She handed him a cup of tea. "And it's not charity. I just don't want to get wet on the way home." She took a sip of tea. "If you win, I pay double our two quid from the last game." She winced. Four quid would wipe her out. "And if I win, I get your umbrella."

Herb's face lit up. "You're on."

Steaming cups of tea in hand, they returned to the board and set it up again.

Eliza had to concentrate even more than usual. It was hard to look like you were playing to win when you were trying to lose.

After another thirty minutes, Herb had her king pinned.

"Check," he said gleefully.

She pointed to his rook. "Don't you mean checkmate?" She toppled her king and then dug in her purse for her last coins. She handed them to Herb.

"Thank you, Eliza." He blushed. "I won't forget this."

"You won." She averted her gaze. "What's there to forget?"

He held out his umbrella to her.

"No." She shook her head. "You won fair and square."

He nodded and then took off.

She watched him gather his coat and head out the door. What kind of idiot was she? Purposefully losing and giving him her last few quid. At this rate, she'd never pull her weight with the rent.

After resetting the board and cleaning up Herb's walnut shells, she went back to watch Theo mop up what was left of the duke. Somehow, Theo always managed to pull himself out of even the tightest spot.

"Me next." She sidled up to him.

"I'm done for the day," Theo said, gathering up his winnings. "Time to go home."

"What?" She poked her finger into his shoulder. "Did the duke almost beat you?"

"Let's just say, it was too close for comfort." He shook the coins in his palm before pocketing them. "Do you fancy a drink?"

"What I fancy is a game of chess." She stared down at him, her hands on her hips.

"I told you before." He stood up. "I'm not going to play you." His voice was hoarse, like he had swallowed gravel.

"Our wager." She smirked. "I won and you owe me a game." She bumped his leg with her hip. "You promised if I solved the case first, you'd play me." She raised her eyebrows. "Well, I did, and you will. Right now." She plopped into a chair. "You are a man of your word, are you not?" She gave him a sly smile. "Or are you afraid you'll lose?"

"Alright." With a huff, he dropped back into his chair. "But don't start crying when I beat you." He pulled a toothpick from his pocket.

"I don't cry." It was true. She hadn't cried since her mother died. Plenty of tragedies since then had warranted tears. But she just couldn't produce any. Sometimes, she wished she could. "Anyway, I'm not planning on losing."

"No one ever *plans* to lose." He arranged the black pieces. "But one of us *will* lose. It's the nature of the game."

"Look, I can handle it." She jammed the pieces into place. "I've been handling it since I was ten." She kept her eyes on the pawns in her hand.

Tidying his pieces, Theo glanced over at her. "You don't always have to do everything on your own, you know."

She put her elbows on the table. "You want to take care of me now?"

"No." His cheeks flushed. "I just mean..." His voice trailed off. "Never mind." He nodded at the board. "Your move. Let's get this over with." He clamped his teeth down on the toothpick and started chewing.

Two hours later, they were both down to half their pieces and Edith Price was shooing people out.

"We're closing in ten minutes," the proprietress warned. "Record your positions and resume tomorrow." She bustled around the rooms sweeping up stray cigarette butts and sweet wrappers. "Wrap it up, fellows. We're closing."

"I'm tired." Theo leaned his chin into his hands. "Should we call it a night?"

"What? And break my momentum?" She shook her head. "Never." She grinned. "Let's continue at your place. It's nearby."

"I don't know if that's such a good idea..." Theo got an odd look on his face.

"Oh, right." She tightened her lips. "Because being around me is torture." She stood up. "I forgot."

"That's not it." Theo reached out for her but she moved out

of his grasp. "Alright, if you insist on finishing the game tonight..." He sighed. "I guess we can go to my place." He took out a notepad and started recording the position of their remaining pieces. "Let's go." He snapped the pad shut.

\* \* \*

Theo's flat seemed even smaller and messier than last time. The only tidy spot in the whole room was a small table with a chess board: a very fancy rosewood chess board with ebony and ivory pieces.

"Where did you get this?" Eliza ran a finger down the cool smooth ebony of the black queen.

"My folks," Theo said sheepishly. "For my eighth birthday." He sat at the table and gestured for her to do the same.

But she didn't sit. Instead, she meandered around the tiny room looking at his books and magazines. "Wow! Pretty nice for a kid's chess set." She picked up a copy of *British Chess Magazine* and flipped through it, not really looking at the pages.

"Nothing but the best for Theodore Sharp," he said in a self-mocking tone.

"You never talk about your childhood." She glanced over at him. "How come?"

He answered with a shrug. "Nothing to tell." He set up the pieces as they were when they left off at the Gambit. "Ready?" He looked over at her with tired eyes and yawned.

Still wandering around his room touching his things, she glanced at her watch. It was midnight already. She didn't remember the last time a chess game had taken so long. It was exhilarating. It had been a long time since she'd played someone so skilled and sneaky. As much as she was enjoying the game, and making Theo squirm, even more, she reveled in moving through Theo's space. The scent of lime and cedarwood and dust and books and, well, Theo. The Theo-ness of it was a thrill. Odd. Being there with him was exciting but also calming. She thought of the time a bullet grazed her forehead and she got morphine in the hospital. Theo was like morphine, only better. Being with him made her more clear-headed instead of less.

"Do you want to play or not?" He sounded impatient. "I guess I should offer you a drink." He glanced around the flat. "All I've got is whiskey, I'm afraid."

"That's fine." She ran her finger across the edge of his desk. A thick stack of pages made her stop. She picked up the top page. "What's this? Your novel?" She smiled and read the first paragraph:

Emily and Leo made quite a team. She was all science and facts and he was dreams and imagination. Together, there was nothing they couldn't do. Science and art combined.

"Can I read it?" She looked over at him.

"It's not done yet." He poured two glasses of whiskey.

"Can I read what you've written so far?" She caressed the top page as if it were a favorite cat.

"Maybe when it's finished." He handed her a glass. "Can we finish the game now?" He took her hand and led her to the board. "I'm tired and want to go to bed."

She thought of the night in Harrogate... and the kiss. Her cheeks warmed. She sat across from him and moved her pieces when it was her turn. But it was difficult to concentrate on the game. There was just so much Theo in this room. Maybe he'd been right. Coming here was a bad idea.

An hour, and three whiskies later, Theo got up and stretched. "How about we call it a draw?"

"Never." She bit her fingernail and stared down at the board. "Wasn't it you who said taking a draw as white was criminal?"

"I'm exhausted." He ran his hand through his hair. "How about we continue in the morning?"

"I'm going to beat you." She hovered her hand over her knight.

"Well, I'm going to bed." He slipped off his shoes. "You do whatever you want." He unbuttoned his shirt and threw it over a chair. He grabbed a blanket from a messy daybed. He wrapped it around his shoulders and then climbed onto the bed. Curled in a ball, he looked like an adorable dormouse.

Shivering, she stood watching him. He looked so cozy and warm. She slipped off her shoes and snuggled in next to him. He put his arm around her and she drifted off to sleep.

\* \* \*

Theo held his breath and tried not to move. With Eliza asleep in his arms, there was no chance he would sleep. His entire body was electrified. He pressed closer and inhaled the scent of her hair. If only they could stay like this forever.

\* \* \*

Where was she? Her heart leaped into her throat. She was at Theo's place. In Theo's bed. With Theo's arm around her. Gingerly, she slipped out from under his arm and sat on the edge of the daybed. Once she calmed down, she wanted to crawl back into Theo's warmth and feel soft rhythms of his heart against her back. She'd felt safe in his arms. She gazed down at him sleeping and took a deep breath, inhaling the scent of him. She glanced around the room. Should she wake him? Or just leave?

There it was stacked atop the desk. Theo's unfinished manuscript. She was dying to read it. As she slipped off the bed, she glanced back to make sure he was still asleep. He looked so sweet with an unruly lock of hair cascading across his forehead and his pouty lips slightly parted.

On tiptoes, dodging stacks of magazines and discarded clothing, she made her way to the desk. She slid into the chair and leaned over the desk, peering at the first page of Theo's novel.

*The Mysterious Adventures of Emily and Leo.* Carefully, she lifted the title page and laid it atop the desk. Her eyes raced through the first page... and on to the second. As quietly as she could, she turned the pages over as she read them.

Was it a coincidence that Emily had her same hair, complexion, and clothes? She even talked like her, played chess, and knew how to foot-fight. Like MI5, Eliza didn't believe in coincidences. And what about Leo? The want-to-be mystery writer and chess lover? She couldn't wait to learn more about him.

Sipping the dregs from a stale whiskey, she read on. She couldn't turn the pages fast enough. Emily and Leo were investigating the mysterious murder of a writer at the Crown Café. They were closing in on the killer. Halfway through, a question formed in her mind. Was it detective fiction or a love story? Three-quarters of the way through, she let out a gasp. *Oh my word!* Theo, er Leo, was writing in his diary about how Emily tortured his every waking hour and haunted his dreams. "Holy crap." Her heart was racing. "He's in love with her."

She had to stop reading and breathe. She glanced over at Theo. He was still sound asleep. What did it mean? She padded over to the kitchenette to get a glass of water. Was it true? Was Theo's book based on reality? Did Theo fancy her?

Watching to make sure Theo didn't wake up, she hurried back to the desk and rushed through the rest of the manuscript. When she got to the last page, the story stopped mid-paragraph. Theo, er Leo, had just found the damning clue and he and Emily were celebrating with a bottle of champagne. Leo reached out and caressed Emily's cheek. And then the rest of the page was blank. Good grief. Talk about a cliffhanger. She let out an audible breath and neatly restacked the pages on the desk.

Not bothering to be quiet, she slid across the room to the bed.

"How does it end?" She sat on the edge of the bed. Forget about chess. She needed to know how Leo felt about Emily. And did they ever figure out who murdered Nathan Lightly? She gently shook Theo's shoulder.

He opened his eyes and smiled up at her. "You're still here."

"Your book. How does it end?"

"What?" He propped himself up on his elbow.

"Your manuscript." There was more urgency in her voice than she intended.

*Bang. Bang. Bang.* Knocking at the door startled her. "Someone is at your door."

His thick curls stood on end as he padded over to answer the door. He opened it and the visitor flew past him like a whirlwind.

"Jane." Eliza jumped up off the bed. "What are you doing here?" Her head was spinning. Was it from the whiskey or Jane's surprise visit? "How did you find me?" Silly question. Jane worked for British Intelligence.

"We need to talk." Holding the end of Queenie's leash, Jane surveyed the messy room and made a sour face. "As usual, you're neither good nor careful." She didn't move from the spot near the door despite Queenie tugging on the leash. "You must be Theo."

"Right." Theo threw on his shirt. "And you're Jane, Eliza's sister." He stared for a minute. "You look so much alike, it's uncanny." He went to pet the dog. "And my best boy."

"Girl," Jane corrected. "Queenie's a girl." She turned to Eliza. "We need to go."

Eliza looked over at the chess board. They would have to finish the game later. Right after Theo finished the ending to his book! Something to look forward to. "Alright."

Theo stood in the middle of his room looking mournful.

Eliza retrieved her coat and hat from a chair. She glanced over at him and shrugged as if to say, *Sorry*.

He shrugged back as if to say, *Can't be helped*. He dropped back onto his bed.

She gave him a little smile. "Meet me at Gambit this evening to finish our game."

Sitting on the edge of his bed, he yawned. "Fine. But don't say I didn't warn you." By the light of dawn, with his hair sticking out in every direction, the adorable dormouse had become an adorable hedgehog.

"See you later, then." She took Queenie's leash and followed Jane out.

"See you later, mate," he called after her in a sleepy voice. "And, good to meet you, sister Jane."

The taxi home was a test of her patience. Jane gave her the silent treatment. She was in a man's flat. Big deal. She was an adult. They were playing chess. It wasn't like they were canoodling. Not exactly. Not like Emily and Leo in the novel. At least Queenie didn't judge her. The dog licked her hands and wagged her tail.

When they reached their flat, Jane finally broke the silence. "I couldn't say anything in the car, but we've got to talk." Jane got that familiar determined look on her face.

"What about?" Eliza didn't like the tone of Jane's voice.

"I'll put on some coffee." She flashed a weak smile. "You can make the toast and clear your scraps of paper off the table. Then we'll talk."

Usually, no matter how unforgiving the rest of the world could be, Jane's smile was always heartening. This morning, it was making her nervous. Still, Eliza did as instructed. She gathered up her notes off the table and then laid out the plates while Jane put the kettle on to boil. "What's so important you came out at six in the morning to find me?" Queenie trotted over and sat next to the table. Eliza patted her head and whispered, "You're on my side, aren't you, girl."

Jane cleared her throat. "You're not going to like this." She stood by the stove, fussing with the coffee pot. "I didn't go out to find you. I went to find Mr. Theodore Torrent Sharp." She pursed her lips. "When I found you at his flat... well, I decided to talk to you first."

"What? Theo?" Eliza dropped into a chair. "Why? What's going on?"

"We have reason to believe your friend *Theo* is the one receiving state secrets." Jane lit the burner and then turned back to Eliza. "And then delivering them via mystery readings for the BBC."

"Theo? I don't believe it. Not possible," Eliza stuttered. "He wouldn't."

"In his latest broadcast," Jane said, fetching two cups from the cupboard, "he used the code name for a top-secret location of our code-breaking facility." She delivered the cups to the table.

Eliza got up and paced the length of the room. "Stay," she said to Queenie, pointing to a spot on the floor. "Sit." Queenie sat as still as a statue. "Good girl." She went to the counter and stood in front of the breadbox. "It's got to be just a coincidence."

"My boss doesn't believe in coincidences." Jane raised her eyebrows.

"I'm telling you. It has to be." She retrieved the half-loaf of bread and roughly sawed off two thick slices. "Crap!" Her finger was bleeding. She sucked at it.

"My boss expects me to find out." Jane lifted the percolator from the stove, went to the table, and poured coffee into their cups.

"And you want me to spy on him?" Eliza shook her head. The thought of Theo being a traitor was ridiculous. He was a mystery writer not an espionage agent.

"Afraid so." Jane sighed. "You're already embedded in the club... not to mention his—"

"Alright. Alright." Eliza held up her hand. "Just let me do this my way." She exhaled. "And in my own time."

"As long as your way gets to the truth before Christmas." Jane gestured toward the steaming coffee. "Better drink it while it's hot."

Eliza wrapped a towel around her bleeding finger and then put the bread in the oven. She didn't like spying on her friends, especially since she had so few of them. And Theo. Well, Theo was more like... like... like an older brother. She'd known him for years. There was absolutely no way he would pass on state secrets. She was sure of it. She took a seat next to Jane and wrapped her hands around the warm cup. "No. I don't believe it."

"How well do you know him?" Jane asked. "Really know him?" She took a sip and peered at Eliza from over the lip of her cup.

Eliza twisted a lock of hair around her finger. It was true. What did she really know about him? "I hadn't seen him for a decade when I ran into him at Gambit a couple months ago." She didn't know anything about his childhood, or his parents, or where he grew up. All she knew was he was smart, a good chess player, his parents were rich enough to send him to Eton and then Oxford, *and* she liked spending time with him. "But my gut tells me..." Her lips twitched and she didn't finish the sentence.

"I'm sorry to put you in this position. I wouldn't if I had a better option." Jane reached over and took her hand. "Tell me about Theo... your young man." Her tone softened. "What does your gut tell you? And what about your heart?"

"He's not *my* young man." Eliza paused. "He calls me cruel. Says I torture him. And then he pushes me away when I..." She stopped herself.

"When you?" Jane cocked her head.

"Nothing," she said into her coffee cup.

"When you what?" Jane's mouth turned up into a knowing smile. "You fancy him."

"I do not." Eliza's cheeks warmed. "We're friends, that's all. Chess buddies," she lied. Well, not exactly a lie. They were friends. They were chess buddies. But was Jane right? Did she fancy him?

"Then why are you blushing?" Jane's eyes danced.

Eliza's hands went to her face. "I'm not blushing." Another lie.

"You may be able to fool everyone else." Jane grinned. "But you can't fool me." She tapped the table with a finger. "Look, consider this an opportunity to get to know him better." She opened her palms. "If your gut is right, then there's nothing to lose." She sighed. "And if you're wrong, then we'll have our man." She tilted her head. "And since you don't fancy him—"

"Crap!" The smell of burnt toast sent Eliza dashing to the oven. She opened the oven door, waved her hand in front of it to diffuse the smoke, and then used a tea towel to grab the bread. She dropped it onto a plate. "So much for breakfast." Still using the towel, she held the edge of one of the burnt pieces and scraped off the black with a knife. Once she'd scraped off most of the burnt bits, she sat the plate of toast on the table and then fetched the marmalade and butter.

The marmalade reminded her of Mrs. Christie drinking cream. *It's from a cow, you know.* From now on, she'd have to keep a close watch on Agatha Christie and Theo... and the rest of the Detection Club members. Jane was relying on her and she wouldn't let her sister down. But what if it meant exposing Theo? *Exposing Theo.* Her cheeks warmed. She thought of the night in Harrogate. Theo in his smalls, looking *very* attractive. Not at all like a brother.

"A penny for your thoughts." Jane smiled.

Eliza shook her head. "I'll do it." She tightened her lips. "I'll spy on Theo and the Detection Club."

"Thank you." Jane reached out and patted her hand. "I owe you one."

In silence, they continued to munch their toast and sip their coffee. Maybe Jane was right. It was a good excuse to get closer to Theo. But not too close. She didn't want to get burned. Not after the last time she got close to an attractive man.

"I know there is something on your mind." Jane stood up and started to clear the table. "If you really don't want to—"

"No. I'll do it." Eliza's tone was firm. "I can do it."

Jane nodded. "Yes, you can." She went to the hutch and opened the top drawer. "I have something for you." She pulled out a fine leather notebook. "A peace offering. Maybe you can use this instead of scraps of paper and receipts."

Eliza took the notebook and weighed it in her hands. The leather was smooth and cool. "Are you trying to make a writer out of me?"

"I know better than that." Jane chuckled. "But maybe a neater and more efficient detective."

"There is a system to my bits of paper," Eliza said with mock indignation.

"I'm sure there is." Jane shook her head. "But our flat looks like a ticker-tape parade blew through, throwing confetti every-where." She grinned.

"I guess you're right." Smiling, she opened the notebook. "Thank you."

"You'd best write up your report on the Detection Club while it's all fresh in your mind." Jane went to the sink and turned on the tap. "Don't worry about the dishes. I'll do them. You get to work."

"Right, boss."

New notebook in hand, Eliza curled up in front of the fire-place with a second cup of coffee and Queenie at her feet. She wrote everything she'd witnessed while embedded with the Detection Club:

Dorothy Sayers's quick wit and even quicker temper and her mysterious trip to Cowley; Eliza fully intended to find out what was in Cowley and why Dorothy was keeping it a secret.

Anthony Berkeley Cox's charm and philandering. Nothing so mysterious about a womanizer, unfortunately.

Gilbert Chesterton's absent-mindedness and good disposition. Behind the jolly façade, Eliza suspected a complicated mind.

Maud Wilkerson's flamboyance and loyalty to her friends.

Agatha Christie's elegance, sharp mind, and goodheartedness. She wouldn't be harboring state secrets, would she?

And Theodore Sharp's... Theo. All she could think of was that lock of hair falling over his forehead and his last move in their game... and the scent of lime and cedarwood... and that kiss. She shuddered and then wrote:

*Theodore Sharp is insightful, focused, and trustworthy.*

She underlined the word. If it weren't for Jane's suspicions, she just might let her guard down. Her gut told her to trust him. Her heart, on the other hand, wasn't so sure.

"I hope Theo's novel has a happy ending." She reached down and scratched Queenie's head. Now, if only life imitated art. *If it's worth wanting, it's worth working for.* She smiled to herself and fetched the dog's leash.

"Queenie, sit." The beagle sat to attention while Eliza attached the leash to her collar. "Come on, Queenie." She gave the leash a little tug. "Theo's waiting for us at the Gambit."

\* \* \*

## MORE FROM KELLY OLIVER

Another book from Kelly Oliver, *Poison in Piccadilly*, is available to order now here:

# AUTHOR'S NOTE

The Detection Club was a supper club for mystery writers started by Anthony Berkeley Cox with informal dinners at his house, which eventually by 1930 became codified into more formal club suppers at the Café Royal in London and other venues. The founding members of the club included Dorothy Sayers, who acted as the first club secretary, Gilbert Chesterton, who was the first president, along with Catholic priest and writer, Ronald Knox, Agatha Christie, and many others.

Dorothy Sayers was instrumental in developing the club initiation rituals, complete with Eric the skull (later discovered to be Erica the skull). Initiates had to swear to abide by the rules of the club, most especially "playing fair" with the reader. Ronald Knox famously developed his Ten Commandments for mystery fiction, which also included playing fair. In the novel, the fictional Neville Lively is inspired by Ronald Knox. Reportedly, after the publication of Agatha Christie's novel *The Murder of Roger Ackroyd* (published in June 1926 by William Collins, and previously serialized between July and September 1925 in the

*London Evening News*), there was some talk in the group of expelling her for not playing fair.

This novel takes liberties with these "facts" and weaves them into a fictional story that imagines a convergence of Agatha Christie's famous eleven-day disappearance in December 1926 and talk of expelling her from the Detection Club, which probably came later. After her car was discovered near Newlands Corner, Mrs. Christie was eventually found at a spa in Harrogate, apparently suffering from confusion about how she got there. Some of the details of her disappearance appear in my novel, but in a condensed version and with added fictional flourishes related to my story. No one knows for sure why she left her house on the evening of 3 December 1926 and was missing for eleven days. Although her husband Archie Christie had asked her for a divorce and went on to marry his secretary, Nancy Neele.

Edith Price founded the Gambit Chess Rooms and was a champion chess player in her own right. Although mystery authors such as Dorothy Sayers and Sir Arthur Conan Doyle enjoyed playing chess, and the game shows up in some of the writings, using the strategies of chess to solve mysteries is perhaps a missing piece of the detective writer's puzzle.

# ACKNOWLEDGEMENTS

Thanks to the staff of the Marion E. Wade Center at Wheaton College, Illinois, for helping me navigate the Dorothy Sayers and Gilbert Chesterton archives. Reading Sayers's private letters was especially enlightening.

Thanks to Team Boldwood. I'm fortunate to have such a wonderful and talented group of professionals supporting my writing.

Thanks to my writer's group for critiquing the first chapter. And special thanks to Benigno Trigo, who is always willing to read and comment and discuss all things murder mystery as we take our daily walks together.

# ABOUT THE AUTHOR

**Kelly Oliver** is the award-winning, bestselling author of three mysteries series: The Jessica James Mysteries, The Pet Detective Mysteries, and the historical cozies The Fiona Figg Mysteries, set in WWI. She is also the Distinguished Professor of Philosophy at Vanderbilt University and lives in Nashville, Tennessee.

Sign up to Kelly Oliver's mailing list here for news, competitions and updates on future books.

Visit Kelly's website: www.kellyoliverbooks.com

Follow Kelly on social media:

𝕏 x.com/KellyOliverBook
f facebook.com/kellyoliverauthor
◎ instagram.com/kellyoliverbooks
♪ tiktok.com/@kellyoliverbooks
BB bookbub.com/authors/kelly-oliver

# ALSO BY KELLY OLIVER

**A Fiona Figg & Kitty Lane Mystery Series**

Mystery in Manhattan

Covert in Cairo

Mayhem in the Mountains

Arsenic at Ascot

Murder in Moscow

Poison in Piccadilly

**A Detection Club Mystery**

The Case of the Christie Conspiracy

# Poison
## & Pens

POISON & PENS IS THE HOME OF
COZY MYSTERIES SO POUR YOURSELF
A CUP OF TEA & GET SLEUTHING!

DISCOVER PAGE-TURNING NOVELS FROM
YOUR FAVOURITE AUTHORS &
MEET NEW FRIENDS

JOIN OUR
FACEBOOK GROUP

BIT.LYPOISONANDPENSFB

SIGN UP TO OUR
NEWSLETTER

BIT.LY/POISONANDPENSNEWS

# Boldwⲟⲟd

Boldwood Books is an award-winning fiction publishing company seeking out the best stories from around the world.

**Find out more at www.boldwoodbooks.com**

Join our reader community for brilliant books, competitions and offers!

Follow us
@BoldwoodBooks
@TheBoldBookClub

Sign up to our weekly
deals newsletter

https://bit.ly/BoldwoodBNewsletter